SCARLET
Disaster

By Colette Rhodes

"No woman gets an orgasm from shining the kitchen floor."

-Betty Friedan

Prologue

This is like a dream. I was staying in a *gorgeous* hotel in *gorgeous* New York, courtesy of a *gorgeous* guy.

Frank:

What are you wearing, Scarlet?

I mean, he was a paying client and he was calling me a fake name, but for the first time in years, I felt hopeful that there was potential. That maybe I'd met someone I could build something *real* with.

Pulling my red hair into a high bun so it wouldn't appear in the shot, I stripped off my fitted sweater and took a selfie that showcased my boobs in my fitted camisole, lips parted like I was about to orgasm. I tweaked the colors a little and sent it off to Frank, not really expecting a reply. I wasn't his *real* girlfriend, just his paid one. For now.

I pulled my knit sweater back on and let my hair down, ready to tug my beanie on before I left the hotel. I was flying home to Alaska later today, and Frank hadn't exactly asked me to stay or anything, which was... well, less than ideal. But he was a wealthy, successful investor—or something like that—and I doubted he'd be able to make decisions like asking me to move here permanently on a whim. Or proposing that this move from a paid arrangement to something... vanilla. A regular relationship. A *real* relationship.

Would he even do that? Maybe I had to be the one to bring that up?

Last month, Frank had requested that I stop camming as part of our arrangement, which I was happy to agree to. I'd been camming for five years and I was ready for a change anyway, plus he was paying me enough to justify it. Surely that was a sign that he wanted more from this?

I should bring it up. I was going to bring it up.

Once I was safely back in Fairbanks.

I did a final sweep of the room and finished packing my suitcase, lovingly laying the new La Perla lingerie Frank had given me on the top and zipping it up. Hopefully someone at the airport would open it up. That would give me some entertainment for the long-as-hell flight home.

Job done and getting fidgety that Frank hadn't bothered replying, I dropped into the armchair by the window and checked my social media apps, scrolling through the comments on my latest post. I'd tastefully showcased some of my new lingerie in a mirror selfie—a pale blue set that matched my blue contact lenses—with an oversized knit cardigan and the blonde wig I wore as 'Scarlet' both artfully arranged to keep the pic social-media safe. The high-end hotel room was in the background, and there were a bunch of comments about me living like a queen with crown emojis that made me smile.

Praise from online strangers was an addiction I had no desire to kick, even if it was all a show. It was *Scarlet* they were complimenting—a filtered, edited, fake version of Lou, complete with blonde wig and blue contact lenses.

Maybe I could stay in New York, living my best inauthentic life forever? My good friend and ex-roommate, Ria, was staying with her family in Queens, and while she had a few extra houseguests at the moment, I doubted she'd turn me away if I asked to stay with her for a couple of days.

Get it together, I scolded internally, shaking my head. My savings were pretty healthy, they weren't *spontaneously move to New York* healthy. I owned a home in Fairbanks that I'd have to deal with before anything more permanent could happen with Frank.

If that's what he wanted.

Ugh, maybe I *should* go back to camming. I was a pro at figuring out what got someone's motor running, but when emotions were involved, I was on totally foreign ground.

There was a knock at the door and I slipped my phone into the pocket of my jeans, crossing the room to check who it was through the peephole. An elegant woman stood in the hall, dressed in expensive-looking beige slacks, a white blouse, and low heels. Her dark hair was threaded with silver and was neatly pulled back into a chic bun. She looked a lot older than me, but she'd had some subtle work done on her face that made her age hard to place.

I pulled the door open a little, angling myself slightly behind it.

"Can I help you?"

"*Scarlet*, right?" she asked, in a voice that implied she *definitely* knew that wasn't my real name.

"And you are?" I replied, as politely as possible.

5

"Elena Ashford."

My breath caught in my throat. Ashford was Frank's last name. It... it was probably a coincidence. Right?

"I'm Frank Ashford's wife."

That lying sack of shit. That lying *married* sack of shit.

Chapter 1
Christmas Eve

"So how come you wanted to come with me today?" Ria asked as we picked our way down the snow-covered sidewalk towards the tattoo studio. "I'm not complaining, but you sounded pretty eager considering you're just going to be sitting there, probably bored."

"I won't be bored," I told her confidently, clutching my hot chocolate that was already feeling more like tepid chocolate, but it was December in Alaska so I didn't know what I'd expected. This is why I usually stayed in my house until April. "I've never seen anyone get a tattoo before and I want to watch. I've wanted to get something for the longest time."

"Oh yeah?" Ria asked, waiting for me to elaborate. We'd been roommates for a while, but I'd always been cagey about my career, not wanting her to judge me. I should have known she wouldn't. Ria had been very cool and open-minded about life, even before she got into a relationship with three men at the same time. Now she lived out in the woods with all her lovers like a freaking goddess.

I just wanted to find one man to love me for me, and she'd managed to find *three*. They were hot as fuck too, but I'd rather chew off my own arm than move out to the woods, so I wasn't that jealous.

"I couldn't get a tattoo while I was camming—I didn't want anything identifiable, you know?—but now I'm not..." I trailed off, the subject still a bit of a sore spot. I mean, I felt good about my decision for the most part, but it had been my life since I was 20 and adjusting to a new reality was taking me longer than I thought.

"You're not?"

"Originally, I put the camming on hold because of Frank." *Fucking Frank.* "It didn't work out with him, and I haven't been in the mood to get sexy on camera since then."

It was irritating as fuck that he'd been the one who'd asked me to stop, because it felt like he was dictating my decisions even though I'd been ready to stop camming anyway. I was ready to *explore*. To see the world in real life, not on the internet.

Frank had started off as a regular cam client, and I should have left it there. He'd suggested a more "girlfriend experience" type package with *very* generous compensation, and in a moment of weakness—or maybe loneliness—I agreed. The sexy stuff was still there, but there had been video calls talking about each other's days, messages and pics throughout the day, some sexy, but not always. He'd assured me it was exclusive.

There was a reason I'd never indulged in anything like that before, and it's because I knew I wouldn't be able to maintain my professionalism if I actually liked the person. I'm not even sure I *did* like Frank, but the attention had been addictive after so long being on my own. Even during my doomed starter marriage straight out of high school, I'd never had anyone focus on me like that.

I could see now that I'd gotten too attached to Frank, too wrapped up in the fantasy of it all, which should have been an obvious risk since I've always been a romantic at heart. When he flew me to New York for a whirlwind trip of sex and pampering, it had seemed too good to be true.

I'm sure his wife would agree.

"I'm sorry, Lou," Ria said, wrapping one arm around my shoulders and giving me a squeeze. "Was he an asshole? Do we need to go toilet paper a skyscraper in NYC?"

Every girl needed a friend like Ria.

She did her best to perk me up as we approached the tiny tattoo studio, only identifiable by the *Mountain Ink* sign above a nondescript black door. Nothing ominous about that.

"Don't suppose your many, many lovers could introduce me to their friends?" I teased, trying to play along with her efforts to bolster me even though I was still feeling pretty surly about life in general, and *immensely* grinchy about all the Christmas shit everywhere.

Ria snorted, tossing out her coffee cup before pushing against the door to the studio. "Bold of you to think they have friends. Though, we're sort of meeting one today, I guess..."

Considering her boyfriends lived out in the middle of the fucking woods like actual mountain men, that checked out. They were hardly the type to head down to the bar on a Friday night for a few drinks with the boys.

I briefly registered the clean, minimalist space all done in monochromatic colors with an exposed wood floor, but then my attention became fully engulfed by the god-like specimen of masculinity standing up to greet us.

He was so *tall*. I was a pretty petite woman anyway, but he must be at least 6-foot-five, with lean muscles visible through his fitted black t-shirt and dark jeans. His shirt scooped just low enough to see a hint of ink on his chest, and it covered almost every inch of his arms, all done in black that stood out against his pale skin. He had pitch black hair that was longer on the top and pushed to the side, and the most incredible eyes I had ever seen. They were green, but not the sort of dull olive green that I had. His eyes were like shiny emeralds.

Where the fuck had this guy come from? They did not make them like this around these parts. They did not make them like this on *Earth*.

My libido, which had been lying dormant for the past few weeks with a wounded ego, slowly stuttered back to life, revving up like an old lawnmower that needed a few pulls to get going.

"Nate, this is my friend, Lou. She came along to observe, I hope that's okay. She's working her way up to getting some ink of her own," Ria said, her voice sounding far away. I wasn't used to flirting with men in real life, without *Scarlet* as a cover, and I suddenly felt like an awkward teenager again.

Why hadn't I dressed better for this? My options were pretty limited for winter anyway, but I'd chosen my bright white parka and fluro pink beanie and matching gloves to brighten my mood and now I was regretting not picking something more sophisticated to go with my black fleece-lined leggings and black snow boots. I had a full face of makeup on out of habit, but without the wig and the contacts, I felt kind of... *plain*.

"I certainly hope you'll come to me for your first tattoo," Nate said in a low voice, his unusually bright green eyes trained on me. I nodded mutely. I'd probably agree to anything he asked me at that moment. Ria could close her eyes. I could be quiet.

This was going to be a very long couple of hours.

* * *

I had three New Year's resolutions for this year: sell my house, start my world adventure, and have sex with a penis that was attached to a real man, not suctioned to whatever hard surface I had handy.

Oh, and overhaul my career and get a tattoo.

I didn't think that was asking for too much. I'd spent Christmas Day and the subsequent week in my house alone, figuring out what my next steps would be, and these were the goals I'd decided on. The house needed some work, and the travel couldn't happen until it sold, but a real-life penis shouldn't be hard to find, right?

I could do this. Normal people used dating apps all the time.

Lou, 25.

Totally nailed that part. Now to come up with a funny, flirty bio that summed up my personality in 500 characters or less.

Hi. I'm an ex-camgirl who has barely had sex with actual humans in my life, and I'm going to be leaving town soon forever, so this is strictly a temporary I-need-penis arrangement. K thx bye.

Too forward?

Too forward.

These winter nights are long and cold, I'm looking for someone to keep me cozy. Fiery redhead. Yoga fanatic. Fairbanks → anywhere and everywhere.

That sounded pretty flirty. And 'yoga fanatic' was a solid code for 'flexible enough to get my feet behind my ears'.

My thumb hovered over the 'save' button as I chewed nervously on my lip, trying to talk myself into doing it. The pictures I'd chosen were cute—a combination of selfies and posed, but not too posed, photos Ria had taken of me in New York before I'd had my heart and pride crushed, but they looked weird to me. I had practically lived my life on camera for years, but it was never *me*. It was blonde bombshell 'Scarlet', not regular redheaded Lou.

I didn't know how to be myself—on camera or off.

I tapped my screen agitatedly with my cherry-colored nails for a few moments before closing the app without saving. This was stupid. I was planning on leaving Fairbanks as soon as I could get the house fixed up and sold anyway. If I wanted a one-night stand, I could just go to a bar like a regular person. No awkward sexting required.

My phone buzzed in my hands and I glanced down, rolling my eyes to find yet another message from Frank. He was persistent, I had to give him that. It had been a couple of months since I'd gotten back from New York, and he was still messaging me.

Frank:

I'd like to talk to you, Scarlet.

Oh, would he now? The fucking asshole. I should just block him, I don't know why I didn't. Okay, maybe I did. I'd gotten used to his attention in the weeks we'd been "together" and I was lonely. So even though I never replied, I didn't block his number either. Or send back the cash he kept transferring me.

Before Frank, I'd been content with solo cam work. Some live shows, sexy content creation, plus a few regulars I did private shows with who had become like friends to me over the years. Nothing... *girlfriendy*. God, a teeny bit of attention and now I was panting after more like an eager puppy. I was embarrassed for myself.

I threw my phone down on the couch and let myself into my bedroom to get ready for the day. Five years of camming had given me a strict morning routine that I didn't think I'd ever be able to break. Always get ready in the morning—makeup on, hair ready to hide under a wig, sexy outfit laid out, ready to go. Some clients wanted to talk early in the day, and I never wanted to be unprepared. Besides, even when I wasn't actively talking to someone, I still had to create content.

Content, content, content. Content is king.

While I closed my camgirl profiles, I was maintaining *Scarlet* on mainstream social media platforms. They were clean anyway, nothing on there would get my account deleted, and I had half a million followers, a lot of whom had been there since the beginning. And in a weird way, they were my friends. I'd worried them enough by stopping my live shows, the least I could do was post a few cute pics to let everyone know I was alive.

Besides, those half a million followers had been a source of revenue in the past, but they were going to be how I paid my bills going forward.

I sat down at the vanity and carefully applied my makeup, making my cheekbones look sharper, my lips fuller, and my eyes appear wider. *Cute,* I decided, looking at my reflection. *Photo time.*

I pulled my hair up just enough to tuck into the wig cap for a quick pic. The blonde wig felt like it weighed a hundred pounds as I pulled it on and fussed with it in the mirror to get it straight and make the sweepy bangs fall nicely. It used to feel like slipping into a sexier second skin, but now it sort of felt like manacles that I voluntarily shackled on each day.

The ring light in front of an oatmeal-colored sheet I'd hung from the ceiling to take pictures in front of, and I hooked up my phone and tugged down my chunky knitted sweater on one side to mostly hide my pale pink panties. Standing in frame, I looked down to hide the fact that I wasn't wearing my contacts and laughed like my bent knee was the funniest thing I'd ever seen, using the clicker hooked up to my phone that was discreetly tucked up my sleeve to take a few different pictures, adjusting my poses slightly until I was satisfied I had a good range to choose from.

Another day in the office.

Pulling the phone off the tripod, I flipped through until I found one I liked before running it through a couple of different editing apps to make my skin glowier and my thighs smoother. Every single time I posted a picture, I swore I wasn't going to edit it, but I always ended up doing it anyway. Because everyone else was doing it, right? I couldn't be the only one who *wasn't*.

I quickly typed up a generic caption about sweater weather before I hit post, knowing I needed to come up with some longer video content later, but not in the mood to do it just then.

I had more exciting things to focus on today.

Satisfied, I put the wig back on the mannequin and fussed with my natural red hair, fluffing it out until it looked presentable again. Today was a big day, after all. Today was the start of something new. I'd spent the last few weeks in limbo, but I was officially ready to put the past behind me, and getting a tattoo was one of the ways I was doing that.

Step one: Tattoo. Step two: Do all the things I'd only dreamed of when I'd been bouncing around from house-to-house with my shitty mom or crashing on my grandparents' couch. Or when I'd been in a loveless marriage I had no business being in, or when I'd been going through the motions in the years since, spending more time as Scarlet than Lou. Or worse, when I'd been staying in a lavish hotel in New York, mistaking lust for love.

Step three: Be happy.

* * *

You've got this.

I took a deep breath of the freezing cold air before letting myself into Mountain Ink, taking in the small but bright space, the gallery of framed artwork dominating the back wall.

I'd felt a lot braver about this when I was just chilling alone in my house.

I'd wanted a tattoo for *years*, but I'd always been paranoid about putting anything on my body that would make me identifiable under the wig. In the beginning, I'd been worried that my ex-husband or his friends would see me on those sites and I'd have to deal with their judgment, and after a while, it had just been easier to pretend I was a whole different person.

No more pretending. Or at least, like, a lot less pretending. Baby steps.

"Lou," Nate greeted me, standing up from the small desk in the corner he'd been working at.

Oh my god, it should actually be illegal to look like him. He was like the sexy bad boy vampire in every TV show—artfully messy black hair, piercing green eyes, and the world's sharpest jawline. And that *ink*. It covered almost every visible inch of him, peeking out over the top of his black henley and all the way down those roped forearms.

So fucking hot.

"Hi," I said lamely as I pulled off my winter layers, wondering where all my sexual confidence had gone. I was not a shy woman, but this guy turned me into mush. Or maybe Lou was actually a shy woman, and I could only be sexy when I was channeling Scarlet.

"How are you feeling?" he asked, his smooth low voice doing things to me that usually required the assistance of battery-operated devices.

"A little nervous, but not too bad," I replied. Honestly, I was probably more nervous about acting cool in front of Nate for a few hours than I was about getting something permanently inked into my skin. I already knew he was good—Ria's tattoo was awesome, and he'd sent me a bunch of pictures of his work over the past few days when we'd been finalizing the design.

"Good. Nothing to be nervous about."

He cleared his throat, and I could have sworn he was checking me out for a moment. I didn't think I was *ugly*—I took care of my body and skin since my appearance was central to my income, and I used henna dye to make my naturally reddish brown hair a glossy shade of crimson—but Nate was fine as hell and could probably have any woman he wanted. I couldn't help but think I would look a lot more attractive if I was in costume.

"Here, I have the final design for you to look at," Nate said, shaking his head slightly and handing me a sketch. We'd been going back and forth messaging over the past couple of weeks to make sure it was exactly what I wanted, and I couldn't have asked for anything better.

"It's perfect," I breathed, staring at the drawing in awe. It was a phoenix, shooting up out of flames like a rocket. It was a rebirth, but it wasn't the slow, unfurling kind. It was rapid and dramatic, like I wanted my own new adventure to be.

"And you still want it on your hip and thigh?" Nate asked, his voice dropping an octave as his eyes ran down the length of my leggings.

Well, now. Maybe Lou did have it in her to seduce a man.

"Uh yes, my hip and down my thigh," I breathed, remembering that questions usually required answers. God, I had zero chill around this guy. "I hope this will be okay," I added, plucking at the long tunic top I was wearing over my leggings. "For modesty."

Nate's answering grin was a little wicked as he nodded, and something flipped low in my stomach at his expression. "Sure. Get yourself comfortable and lie down on the table."

He turned his back and I found myself disappointed that he wasn't going to watch me strip. Boo for professionalism. I pulled off my boots, socks, and leggings, before pulling the socks back on. It was warm in here, but not *that* warm. It was a fucking miracle I'd left my house in this weather, honestly.

Never again. Next Christmas, I'd be lying on a beach somewhere, tanning my ass in a thong, sipping mojitos, reminiscing about how good it felt to set my snow boots on fire.

I'd picked my skimpiest thong for today, figuring I wouldn't want material rubbing on the tattoo, and anything more substantial would only get in the way, though I was semi questioning how wise that choice was now. I was already feeling a little frisky just from being in the same *room* as Nate. Who knew what kind of state I'd be in after he had his hands all over me for a couple of hours? I'd just keep my thighs clenched. Like, all the way clenched.

I climbed on the table and lay on my back, pulling the top between my legs but high over my hip to keep the skin there exposed, twisting slightly so my legs lay to one side and Nate could see his canvas.

There was so much ass out. So much. People had paid good money to see my ass over the years, so I decided to roll with it. Maybe Nate was an ass man.

He sucked in a tiny breath as he turned around, and I decided he was at least a little bit of an ass man.

"I'm, uh, just going to prep your skin then apply the transfer, okay?"

His head was tipped forward to examine my leg, but he lifted his eyes to look at my face and my breath caught a little bit. He was objectively attractive, but it was more than that. Like he had an aura about him or something, something a little bit superhuman, that made it almost impossible to look away.

I nodded mutely in response to whatever he'd said, zero idea of what I'd agreed to.

Nate's movements were quick and efficient as he encouraged me to lie on my side facing away from him. I forced myself to examine the drawings on the wall instead of obsessing over what the 6-foot-something fallen angel behind me was doing as he applied the transfer to my hip and thigh, his hands heating up my flesh even through the gloves.

As much as I wanted to go full hussy and throw myself at him, I had another session planned for tomorrow to finish the outline and it would be mighty uncomfortable to sit through that if I embarrassed myself now. Full hussy would have to wait.

"Alright, take a look and make sure you're happy with it," Nate rumbled. I swore my skin missed the feel of his hands the second he removed them.

Touch-starved. I was just touch-starved.

Happy with the stencil, I settled myself in for a long couple of hours, picking up my phone as a distraction before putting it down again. Surprisingly, the pain wasn't nearly as bad as I'd imagined it would be, and I took a few pics of my lower body for my channel, annoyed I hadn't worn the wig to film reaction shots of my face.

I rolled onto my back at Nate's urging, which gave me a much better view of him. Dangerous, on all levels. The expression he wore while he was concentrating had temptation written all over it, brows slightly furrowed, eyes narrowed, looking all focused and professional.

Logically, I knew that was a good thing because he had a needle in my skin, but I also desperately wanted to unravel him and find out what got him going. I'd literally made it my job to find out what got people hot.

I was going to blame my urges on that.

"So, is Lou short for anything?" Nate asked casually after a silence that had gone well beyond awkward. It wasn't *'can I spread you out and eat your pussy until you scream?'*, the question I'd been hoping for, but small talk was good too.

I huffed a quiet laugh, careful to keep my leg still. "Louisiana."

It really could not suit me less. *Louisiana* sounded like an innocent, country girl who made sweet tea for her sorority sisters.

"I wasn't expecting Louisiana," Nate admitted. His head was bent low over my thigh so I couldn't really see his face, but it sort of looked like he was smiling.

"I went through drug withdrawals as a newborn, which tells you a lot about my mama and her decision-making skills," I replied wryly. She was a real peach of a woman, which was why I hadn't seen her in years.

Nate looked up, no trace of a smile on his face. In fact, he looked like he was ready to go to war on my behalf, and something in my chest fluttered at his reaction. Probably a mixture of being attention starved and never really having anyone in my corner.

"What about your dad?" he asked.

"Never met him," I said easily. I doubted my mom had spent more than three minutes with the root cause of my daddy issues either. "My grandparents helped out a lot. I would live with them for a bit, then go back to my mom when she got her shit together. It didn't last long—she'd meet a man and everything would all fall apart again."

"You sound so calm about it," Nate observed, brow furrowed. I was more confused about why I was laying myself bare for a guy I'd just met, honestly. Something about him made me want to open up, which was not a sensation I had... ever.

Maybe it was a therapy vibe of just chilling in this chair with one other person in the room.

"I've had time to come to terms with it," I said lightly, wincing as Nate began on my hip bone. "My grandparents died when I was in high school. Mom stuck around until graduation. I think she's in Arizona now."

"You don't keep in touch?" he asked, tilting his head to examine his work. Did he like what he was working with? It had been years since I'd felt even remotely self-conscious about my body, but I was second guessing myself now.

"Hard no," I told him. "I'm a firm believer in cutting toxicity out of your life, DNA be damned."

"I can get behind that."

"What about you?" I asked. "Any overly personal stories you'd like to share with a stranger?"

That was flirty, right? Totally flirty. Wig-free, no contact lenses in, no fake name, flirting like a goddamn pro. Nailed it.

"My family is pretty ordinary, just big. I'm the youngest of eight."

"Eight?!" I squeaked. "That's a lot of people."

My brain would shut down living with that many people. Just reject my surroundings and go into hermit mode. I used to get overwhelmed just staying with my grandparents. With my mom, she was mostly out doing... whatever it was she would do. My grandparents had been home all the time, and it had been an adjustment living with other people in the house.

"In fairness, we didn't all live at home at the same time. The eldest two had already moved out by the time I was born," Nate said, leaning in close. Could he smell me? His nose twitched like he could smell something. I hadn't put my coconut lotion on my leg because of the tattoo, but it was lathered on the rest of my body. "My oldest brother, Chase, lives not far from here. I spent a lot of time with him growing up. In recent years, I've been traveling mostly."

"Where?" I asked instantly, cringing internally at how eager I sounded. *Be cool, Lou.* I've wanted to travel my whole life, but instead I'd gotten married straight out of high school because I hadn't quite broken free of my loser mother yet. She'd told me it was a good idea to marry my high school sweetheart, and I believed her.

In hindsight, she'd been planning on leaving the state the second she was able, and marrying me off was her way of easing her guilt about abandoning me.

"All over," Nate chuckled. It was a deep, raspy sound that set off another round of butterflies in my gut. "I started traveling around the States, then South America, then Europe, but I hopped around a lot. I got back from Greece a couple of months ago."

"And you came back *here*?" I replied incredulously. Not that Alaska wasn't beautiful in its own way, but give me sun drenched beaches over snow covered mountains any day.

"My family is here," Nate said with a grimace. "They think I should settle down in the area. They're probably right."

Hello. Settle right down with me, big guy. Let me come to your rescue.

No, that wasn't strictly what I wanted. Boyfriend-slash-potential-husband? Sure. But I didn't want to live in this town for the rest of my life and pop out a bunch of babies. The very idea made my uterus shrivel up in terror.

"Anyway, I guess we'll see what happens," Nate continued. "I've tried to make a go of it here before and it didn't work. I ended up backpacking through Peru two months later."

Obviously Nate was definitely not boyfriend material, but that worked out pretty well in my favor.

I'd just casually suggest mutually beneficial, no strings attached sex tomorrow when the tattoo was finished. Despite the big game I talked—and walked—on camera, I'd only been with my ex-husband and that asshole Frank in real life, and I really could use some decent in-person sex to prove to me that the whole concept wasn't a write-off.

Nate looked like he'd do better than decent. Nate was probably packing the Womb Ruiner 5000 under those dark jeans, and knew exactly how to use it.

Besides, if I managed to snag a little one-on-one time with Nate, then I wouldn't have to do the whole pick-up-a-guy-at-the-bar thing that I'd been low-key panicking about.

"I'm going traveling in a couple of months," I told him, trying to seem a lot cooler and worldlier than I was.

"Oh yeah? Where to?" Nate asked, immediately perking up. He definitely didn't sound like someone who was one hundred percent settled, the travel bug wasn't completely out of his system.

"Everywhere," I replied decisively. If Frank had given me anything, it was the desire to explore. He'd taken me to a fancy sushi restaurant in Manhattan, and now I was determined to eat fresh sushi in Japan. We'd eaten incredible pasta one night at a rooftop restaurant, and I wanted to eat pasta under the stars in Italy. I wanted to drink sangria in Spain, and scuba dive the Great Barrier Reef. I *was* going to do all of those things.

"Everywhere is a great place to start," Nate replied with a slow, sinful smile that made my toes curl a little.

"Not too ambitious?" I teased. Ria had looked at me like I was bonkers.

"No such thing," Nate said, shaking his head. "When I first left Alaska, I thought I'd roadtrip for a while and that'd be it."

He smiled a little wistfully, and I wondered what a young Nate had been like. Not that he was old now, but he definitely had a few years on me.

"The more I saw, the more I wanted to see. The more new people I met, the more I wanted to meet. It's an addictive feeling," he sighed, leaning forward as he began working on an intricate part of the design. I glanced down the line of my body, noting that my skin had instantly broken out in goosebumps when he'd moved in closer. My body had not got the memo that we were trying to be discreet.

"Where was your favorite place you traveled to?" I asked, my voice breathier than before despite my silent reminders to myself.

Nate hummed as he considered the question. "Depends on my mood. There are a few places where I ended up staying longer than I intended because I hadn't got enough of them. On my last trip to Europe it was Toledo, Spain and Rothenburg, Germany. In Asia, I ended up staying around Ubud in Bali for a few months when I'd only planned to be there a week. In the States, it was Charleston."

I mentally added all of those places to my ever-growing list of destinations, planning on adding them to my travel Pinterest board later.

"*Bali*," I sighed dreamily. "Maybe I'll go there first. I want to go somewhere hot. Like, really fucking hot. Like wear bikinis all day and throw out my pants kind of hot."

Was I deliberately putting the idea of me with no pants in his head to test the waters? Yes. Yes, I was. A vain part of me needed to know if Lou was an even remotely attractive prospect on my own—no wig, no contacts, no performance. Just me.

Nate grunted in acknowledgment, angling himself slightly away in a move that was absolutely meant to end the conversation, and I had to accept that maybe Lou *didn't* have it in her to seduce a man after all. Or at least not a man like Nate.

The realization stung more than I thought it would.

NATE

Chapter 2

If Lou could see the things in my head that I wanted to do to her, she'd call the cops.

Damn it. Why'd she have to mention a bikini? I'd *just* been getting my dick under control after seeing her half naked body laid out in my space, and now I was back at square one. Her skin was a perfect fucking canvas, and that breathy laugh she had was like a siren song for my dick. Plus her *scent*. It had been sugary sweet melted chocolate when she'd walked in, mixed with the artificial coconut scent of her lotion, but now it was tart with the hint of her arousal and my dick was *here for it*.

She seemed so sweet, so innocent, but with an unexpected hint of sexual confidence.

Not enough for me to act on the attraction between us though. Maybe she was confident with humans her own age, but she was probably a decade younger than me and even if I had myself under control, I'd be too rough for a sweetheart like her. Any shifter would be, and yet I was more tempted than I'd ever been in my life.

I'd been with humans before, but none of them had ever threatened my control the way Lou did. Never made me want to wrap them in cotton wool and fuck their brains out all at once. They were never as sweet and innocent as Lou. I didn't have anything against a casual fling with a human, but I had to be one hundred percent in control of my mind, body, and beast, and I absolutely wasn't.

I was a professional! A goddamn professional. I'd seen plenty of attractive bodies in my time, more naked than Lou was now, and yet this petite woman was entirely unraveling my self-control.

She's too young for you.

She's a human.

You'd fucking decimate her.

Don't ask more questions. Don't get to know her.

Her skin was so soft though. Her legs were lithe and toned, and the graceful curve of her hip was the perfect space for the phoenix bursting into flight.

That's what I needed to think about. The way the art would look on her body, and *not* how flexible she was. Despite the moments where she seemed to slip on a sultry mask, there was still a vulnerability in her olive-green eyes that gave me pause.

I'd just have to remind myself every time I picked up the scent of her arousal that she was probably imagining some gentle, third-date missionary sex, and I was not the guy for that.

If I got her in bed with me, I would terrify her.

I knew I'd made the conversation awkward with my abrupt silence, and I felt like an asshole, but it was probably for the best. Not only did she interest *me* in a way that very few people did, my cougar had been captivated by her since she'd come into the studio with Ria. Probably because she smelled so good.

Lou opened her mouth to say something, but I needed to nip this in the bud now before I did something idiotic.

"Why don't you put on your headphones?" I suggested gruffly. "We'll be here awhile."

"Oh, er, okay. Yeah, that makes sense," she replied, her voice a little higher pitched than before as she reached hesitantly for her headphones, refusing to look at me.

Well done, Nate. Idiot. You didn't have to make her feel bad.

I glanced at her out of the corner of my eye as she pulled herself together like she could read my thoughts. The disappointment was wiped away like it was never there, even the softness around her mouth vanished, leaving a harder expression in its place.

The moment she focused her attention on her screen, I had to swallow the impulse to demand her eyes again. To demand that open, honest look on her face again.

For fuck's sake, I was losing my mind. When she'd first requested doing the sessions two days in a row, I'd tried to talk her out of it. Now I was grateful.

Just one more day of this exquisite torture, and I'd never see her again.

She was gone. After the longest couple of hours of my life, Lou was all bandaged up and on her way, shooting me an indecipherable look after I'd basically panicked and ushered her out the door. It was a total asshole move and *terrible* customer service, but I'd been *this close* to telling her I could smell how much she wanted me and that would have probably earned me a well-deserved slap.

There was something about Lou that got me all mixed up. If I'd opened my mouth and entertained the idea of spending more time with her, I wasn't sure if I'd have asked her to dinner or demanded she take her winter clothes back off and let me eat her instead. Both were bad ideas, but the former was *unsettling*. Maybe all my mom's lectures about finding a nice woman and starting a family were embedding themselves into my subconscious.

The sweet, tart scent of Lou's arousal lingered in the studio as I cleaned up my equipment as efficiently as possible, forcing myself to concentrate. Fuck, I should get out the strong-smelling chemical cleaners, but I wasn't sure it would matter at this point. Her intoxicating scent had soaked into my skin, my lungs, and every inch of this room the longer I left it, torturing me.

I'd never had a response like this to human pheromones before. Biology encouraged me to pursue shifters, even though my personality wasn't suited to a shifter mate.

Focus, I berated myself. I had plans tonight. Go back to my depressing rental house. Burn some steak and potatoes. Stream a movie. Convince myself that I was happy here. They weren't good plans, but they were plans.

I glanced at my phone that was sitting on the desk in the corner, on silent all day, noticing I'd missed six calls from my mother. I was sure that if anyone else found that, they'd be panicking that there'd been some kind of family emergency and calling back right away, but not me. If my dad or my brother Chase called me, I'd believe it was an emergency. With my mom, she was just bad with technology and didn't understand that I couldn't answer the phone whenever she felt like talking to me.

I hit 'redial', balancing the phone between my ear and my shoulder as I cleared up my desk. A conversation with Mom was exactly what I needed when I wasn't feeling happy and settled in Fairbanks. Not because it made me *feel* happy, but because she guilted me into feeling like I *should* feel happy.

"Why don't you ever answer?" Mom sighed the moment she picked up the phone. *"I miss you, and you're always running off and abandoning me, and then you come home and you can't even answer your phone."*

"Mom, I can't talk on the phone while I'm with a client," I explained patiently. For the millionth time.

"When are you coming to visit, Nate?" she replied, ignoring me. It came from a place of love—she was excited to have me closer to home, like the rest of my siblings—but the coddling tone never failed to make me feel like a child again. Fortunately, my parents lived close to Denali State Park, as did most of my siblings, which was a couple of hours' drive from the house I was renting here.

I loved them, but I didn't need to see them every single day.

"I'm going to visit Chase this weekend," I told her. "Lacey's making brisket."

Mom humphed. Chase was my oldest brother and Lacey was his mate. She was also mated to Rodrigo, Sergio, and Casen, and they lived not far out of Fairbanks in the woods. Chase was the only one of my siblings who *didn't* have a monogamous mating, and Mom definitely had some *thoughts* about it, no matter what she tried to convince us otherwise.

She also hated that Lacey was a better cook than her, but she'd never admit to that either.

"You're always visiting Chase. It's lovely that you're so close with him, but your father and I aren't getting any younger..."

Mom took a deep breath like she was settling in for a long speech, and my brain almost instantly tuned out, traveling back to Greece in my mind to avoid the guilt-trip my mom was trying to take me on.

Back to the last day I'd spent in Paros before returning to Athens and then flying back to Alaska, I'd spent hours swimming in the warm Aegean Sea, before eating loukoumades on the beach, memorizing the feel of the sun on my bare skin before I returned home.

I hadn't even gotten to visit Naxos, which had been the next destination on my list. I'd given in to my mother's demands and returned like the dutiful son I was, determined that *this time*, it would stick. This time, I'd be content. I tapped my fingers impatiently on the desk, fighting the urge to check for flights.

This is what my family referred to as my "itchy feet". That moment where I was just twitching with energy, ready to get back out into the world and explore.

It really didn't matter how thoroughly I guilt tripped myself, I was happiest when I was exploring. I resented that sensible voice in the back of my mind that constantly reminded me that I was 35 and should find myself a nice mate, settle down, and have a litter of kids.

I didn't want to settle.

"—I didn't visit my parents as much as I should have when I was your age, and I've regretted it every day since—"

God, it was fucking cold here, and I liked my job, but the business side of it was so goddamn boring it made my head throb, and my rental was a soulless shit hole that I had no desire to return to each night.

"—and one day, hopefully, you'll have a family of your own, and then you'll want to spend more time with us, but it won't be so easy to travel with little ones—"

Today hadn't been so bad though. Not with Lou's half-naked body spread out over my table, the sweet scent of her pussy filling the studio. The clouds that seemed to hang over me constantly in the moment had briefly cleared with Lou's vibrant presence in the studio. It was a stupid, dangerous line of thought.

"Mom, can I call you back? I just need to finish up in the studio, then get some dinner."

"I bet you're not eating properly. You never take care of yourself. Okay, I love you. Call me later. Bye."

I shook my head to myself as I tucked my phone away. She really did mean well. I was the youngest of eight kids, but now even the youngest grandkids were getting older and more independent, and Mom was feeling a little lost. She hadn't given up hope that I'd give her more grandbabies, no matter how many times I'd gently told her that it probably wouldn't happen.

If I wasn't on the receiving end of her machinations, I could almost admire that level of stubbornness.

The bell above the door jingled, and I turned around to tell whoever it was that the studio was closed for the day, but surprise froze me in place.

"Honey, I'm home," Brooks sang, striding into my studio like he owned the place, just like he did with every room he walked into, shoving his floppy reddish brown hair out of his unnerving ice blue eyes. They'd probably been traveling for days, but Brooks always made sure he looked pretty. He was vain like that.

"What the fuck?" I asked as Gabriel trailed behind him, all dark and brooding in comparison with his gray eyes, olive skin, black hair and stubble, looking vaguely amused at our friend's dramatics. "I thought you two were in Santiago."

"We missed you too much to stay away," Brooks said solemnly, except Brooks was never really solemn, he just liked to pretend sometimes to fuck with us.

"Shut up," I replied, punching him lightly in the gut. Brooks and Gabriel were the only shifters I'd ever met who had the same nomadic tendencies I did, and we'd been friends since we met in Mexico in our early twenties. "Seriously, what are you doing here?"

"We're a pack," Gabriel said simply, his Brazilian accent still thick after over a decade of traveling the globe.

"No, we're not," Brooks and I replied in tandem. We had this fucking argument every time we were together. We may be like-minded, but we weren't a *pack*. Packs had territory and structure and an Alpha. We were just... buddies.

Gabriel scoffed, pulling his black beanie down over his dark curly hair. The stubble on his jaw was almost thick enough to constitute a beard, and there were dark shadows under his eyes. None of us could ever sleep on a plane, the noise was uncomfortably loud for our sensitive ears. "*Ai*, you aren't going to pretend you haven't missed us, are you? Don't insult our intelligence, Nate."

I glared at him without any real heat in it. I *did* miss them. I always did when we weren't traveling together. Brooks and Gabriel were more like brothers to me than most of my biological siblings were.

We still weren't a pack though. We weren't even the same kinds of shifters. As big cats, Gabriel and I had a few traits in common, but Brooks was a fucking *wolf*. We quite literally fought like cats and dogs half the time.

"Damn," Brooks whistled suddenly, sniffing the air. "What have you been up to?"

"Working," I clipped, my cougar rising in warning.

"Well, she was obviously a fan of your work," Brooks laughed before inhaling again. "She smells *amazing*."

"Stop sniffing my clients," I groused. I wasn't *jealous* per se, just... irritated.

"It's not like I'm getting up in her grill and inhaling, she's not even *here*," Brooks pointed out with a grin. "Which is unfortunate, because I would *love* to meet the woman who smells like this. How big is Fairbanks anyway? Maybe I'll run into her."

"She won't smell like this around you," I shot back with more confidence than I felt. Out of the three of us, Brooks was by far the most popular with women. Probably because he looked like he should be in a boy band with his artfully messy hair that he was constantly flicking out of his eyes before he delivered The Smoulder.

It was disappointing how few women laughed in his face when he did it.

"Nate," Brooks gasped with mock offense. "Are you feeling okay, man? Is your memory getting a little fuzzy? All this cold air going to your head?"

"I'm already eager for you to leave," I sighed, trying not to smile.

"Liar," Gabriel laughed. "I bet you rented a house big enough for all of us, hoping we'd show up."

Damn it. I had rented a three-bedroom house just for me, which had seemed excessive even to myself at the time. Gabriel grinned like he was reading my mind.

"Give me the keys and the directions, *irmão*. We'll go make ourselves comfortable while you are hard at work."

"Bastards," I muttered affectionately before digging out my keys and pulling the house one off the ring, rattling off directions. "Can you even drive in the snow?" I asked dubiously, trying to remember if we'd ever traveled somewhere this cold together and coming up short.

"I'm from Colorado," Brooks shot back, looking offended even though he hadn't spent any time in Colorado since he was a teenager.

"And yet, I'm the one driving," Gabriel replied, clapping Brooks on the back. "We'll see you soon, yes?"

"I won't be long," I assured them as they left, finishing up in the studio, feeling that cloud around me dissipate a little more.

✳ ✳ ✳

By the time I got back—with cheesesteaks, fries, and cheese curds—Brooks and Gabriel had already set themselves up in the two spare rooms at the house and got the fire going. I hated to admit how much homier the place felt with those two assholes in it. I was supposed to be adjusting to life on my own.

"I come bearing food," I announced, kicking the door shut behind me and letting myself into the miniscule living room. It had felt snug when it was just me, but all three of us were big guys, and now it was uncomfortably cramped.

"That smells so good," Brooks groaned, following me into the kitchen. There was a small dining table pushed against the wall, and we pulled it into the center of the kitchen so we could comfortably sit around it. "We've alternated between airline food and airport food for two days."

"Beer?" Gabriel asked, pressing his back against the wall and inching his way around to the fridge.

"Of course," I chuckled. There was fuck all else to do at night. "Have you guys slept?"

"Not yet," Gabriel replied, getting three bottles out of the fridge. "We'll probably crash right after we eat."

"So," Brooks said, helping himself to food. "When can we leave?"

"Don't be a dick," Gabriel snorted, giving him a reproving look. "Perhaps it's a little colder here than we're used to, but winter in Alaska is going to be a huge hit, you know that."

Brooks took a huge bite of his cheesesteak, making a disgruntled noise of agreement. He was a photographer and Gabriel was a travel writer—the two of them collaborated on projects all the time while I fucked around, doing my own thing. I knew as well as Gabriel did that once Brooks got out there with his camera, he'd fall at least a little in love with the landscape. He always did.

"So, a few weeks?" Brooks asked hopefully, after swallowing loudly.

"I'm not leaving. I opened a studio," I pointed out unnecessarily.

"For the winter," Brooks replied, like it was obvious.

"For*ever*."

"No," he said simply, shoving some fries in his mouth.

"No?" I repeated. "What do you mean, *no*?"

"He means *no*, we are not staying here forever," Gabriel replied, wrinkling his nose as Brooks attempted to speak around a mouthful of fries. "You are miserable here, *irmão*. We've seen you for all of fifteen minutes and we can tell you are miserable."

"I'm not miserable," I shot back, a little defensively. "The studio got off to a stronger start than I thought it would—especially considering the time of year—and I've been spending time with my brother..."

"And you're miserable," Brooks said with a grin. "But fine, fine. You're not ready to accept the inevitable yet. We'll play along."

"Eat your fucking cheesesteak," I grumbled, annoyed that they were both looking at me like they were just humoring me. Dickheads.

So, the idea of spending *the rest of my life* in Fairbanks felt like a vice around my ribcage, breaking bones and squeezing the air out of my lungs. That was probably normal in the beginning. I just had to push through the initial terror to get to the good bits, until I wanted to stay and I'd settle in and be happy.

But Brooks and Gabriel would eventually leave. They'd find an exciting new place to explore and drop everything to go, and I'd be left behind, wondering if I'd made the right choice. And that vice around my ribs tightened a little further.

Chapter 3

I flowed smoothly from half-plank to an awkward cobra pose before rising to a modified downward-facing dog, my movements unconscious, though the sting of my new tattoo made my practice a little less fluid than I would like. Usually I tried to be really present for my morning yoga routine. It was my daily ritual to center myself, clear my mind, and show gratitude to the body that had paid my bills for the past few years.

Life used to be so straightforward. Wake up. Yoga. Make myself presentable. Combination of content creation, live shows, and client sessions. Online shopping. Meal prep.

Getting a tattoo was easy, but a pretty superficial life change on reflection. I loved the ink on my hip that Nate had done, and I was pumped to get the rest of it today, but it wasn't like my life had substantially improved because of it. Plus, my confidence had taken a hit when Nate iced me out yesterday, but I was choosing to take it as a sign to focus on more concrete, more intimidating moves.

Like preparing the house for sale. The walls in the living room were teal on two sides, and a garish yellow on the other two. The wood floors weren't too bad, but the light fixtures were relics of the 1980s, and the kitchen was super dated. I'd sell it as is, but I was relying on the money from the sale to fund my travels in case the social media stuff didn't work out.

Besides, lying in bed and watching renovation shows was my number one self-care technique. How hard could painting be? I'd watched enough house flipping shows to understand the gist of what I had to do.

God, I was missing Ria today. She would absolutely endorse my HGTV-inspired plans. I'd had a few roommates over the years, but she was the best one I ever had, and I missed our morning ritual of me doing yoga on the floor while she sat on the couch, clinging to her coffee like it held all the answers to life itself, looking at me like I was an alien before she dragged herself out of the door to the diner where she'd worked before she moved to the woods, resting bitch face firmly in place.

I stepped one foot between my hands and moved into a standing warrior pose, the pain from my tattoo preventing my movements from being as thoughtful and intentional as I liked them to be.

My phone flashed on the coffee table, but I ignored it. Frank had sent a few messages last night with a slightly different tone to the ones he'd been sending since I got back from New York. More conversational, like the messages we *used* to exchange before everything happened. Like I'd just... ignore everything that happened and somehow forget what it was like when that beautiful, elegant woman knocked on my hotel room door, with a completely blank look on her face.

"Hello. My name is Elena Ashford. I'm Frank's wife."

I hadn't felt shame like I'd felt in that moment since I was a kid and my mom showed up two hours late and high as a kite to a parent teacher conference. My seventh grade teacher, Ms. Ellis, had bought me a cheeseburger for dinner and I'd eaten so fast I felt sick.

The worst part about Elena Ashford showing up was that nothing about me had been a surprise to her. She had politely held out a non-disclosure form for me to sign like it was totally routine. Like she had a stack of NDAs printed out in the office of her penthouse apartment, ready to drop on women half her age who were banging her husband. I hadn't signed it. I grabbed my rolling case and ran, jumping in the first cab I could find, messaging Frank for the last time to tell him he was a liar and to leave me alone.

Everything about it was mortifying.

I'd *asked* Frank beforehand, I'd asked him! When he suggested the whole 'girlfriend experience' idea, I'd asked if he was single and he'd assured me he was. Stupid! Stupid, stupid, stupid.

Even if he hadn't been married, this was probably the way it would have always turned out. I'd gotten caught up in the romantic notion of a man whisking me away to New York, not realizing that what Frank had been after was a toy, not a girlfriend.

The sex had been good though. And he'd been packing some *great* equipment. Or maybe I'd just been holed up in my basement with my toys for too long. Frank's had been the first real life penis I'd seen since my divorce, which was a little humiliating even in my own head. God, that was what, six years ago? *Come on, Lou.* You are in the prime of your life. Go get that D!

Nate's penis would definitely be better than Frank's had been, if he was willing to let me borrow it for a couple of hours, which didn't seem super likely. Last night I'd had dreams so filthy—most of which involved Nate pinning my ankles up by my ears and fucking destroying me—that I'd had a solo session with my Bad Dragon dildo that had been sitting in the cam room in the basement, left unused since before going to New York.

It was the biggest toy I had, and I felt like Nate was packing some serious equipment under those distressed black jeans. Too bad he hadn't seemed interested.

Concentrate, I chastised internally, stretching my arms above my head and leaning backwards as much as I could before the stinging tattoo became unbearable. It was probably going to hurt like *hell* tonight when the whole outline was done. I'd never been a particularly patient person, and once I got an idea in my head, I was like a dog with a bone.

Curious about cam work? Immediately set up an account and start doing it.

Guy suggests an all expenses paid trip to New York to fuck him for a few days? Book a ticket.

Vaguely consider getting a tattoo? Get a giant tattoo finished in two days.

This was very on-brand decision making for me.

My phone buzzed again and with a frustrated groan, I gave up on yoga and stomped into my bedroom to get ready, grabbing the device on my way.

Frank:

I have a lot of meetings today, very frustrating.

Frank:

What are you wearing, Scarlet?

40

Frank:

I'd like to video call you tonight.

I gaped at the screen, stunned at the audacity of this man to message me like nothing had changed. Did he think I'd just... be fine with everything that went down and ignore the elephant in the room? Was that his goal? I knew a lot of men didn't like confrontation, but this was a whole different level of denial.

Refusing to let Frank get in my head, I sat down at my vanity to put on the sexiest makeup I could get away with for the middle of the day, absolutely for Nate's benefit. It'd be too weird to show up in the wig now, but I was going to channel Scarlet as much as I could and see if I could seduce my tattoo artist. If it didn't work, then I'd download that stupid dating app again, because damn it I was going to fuck a real-life man. A real-life man with a real-life penis and more importantly, a real-life tongue.

I mean, I had substitute dicks in almost every material they came in—silicone, glass, stainless steel—but I was pretty sure that none of the clit stimulator toys *really* felt the same as oral sex.

Not that I would know, I'd never had it. But I'd heard things. I knew what I was missing out on.

Logically, I understood the answer to all my problems wouldn't be a dude feasting on me like I was his last meal, but it couldn't hurt. Right?

I *deserved* this.

The bell above the door rang as I let myself into the studio. Nate was already looking at me like he'd sensed me coming, his gaze inscrutable. Hopefully we weren't in for a repeat of the awkward put-your-headphones-on moment from yesterday. That had definitely shaken my confidence for this whole seduction plan, but I'd put my metaphorical Scarlet knickers on and was ready to give it another shot.

"Hi," I said airily, pulling off my layers inside the doorway. "How are you?"

I was as cool as the snow outside. Totally chill.

"Fine," Nate replied carefully. Every time he'd gotten remotely close to flirty yesterday, he seemed to catch himself. It looked like he'd used the past 24 hours to strengthen his resolve. "How are you, Lou?"

Damn him and his hypnotizing voice.

"Great," I said, a little too brightly. He glanced away as I pulled off my boots and socks, before removing my leggings. I'd chosen another mini dress today. For ease of access.

"Whenever you're ready," Nate grunted, gesturing at the table. My phone dinged from my jacket pocket and I fished it out to check the message.

Frank:

We are not done, Louisiana.

A shiver of fear ran through me. I'd only ever been Scarlet to Frank. From when he'd found me through the cam site to when we'd done the whole girlfriend experience thing, I'd been 'Scarlet' the whole time. When he'd asked me to come to New York, I'd insisted on booking my own flights and accommodation, and he'd just sent me the money.

He shouldn't know my real name. My hands shook a little as that thought ran around my brain on a loop. I didn't use my real name on *anything*. I'd never told him. Never.

Frank was rich though. A wealthy hedge fund type, who had plenty of money to spare. He certainly had the resources to do some digging into my background if he wanted to. That thought was... well, a little terrifying.

God, the sooner I sold my house and got the hell out of Fairbanks, the better. For a whole lot of reasons.

I hit the block button so fast, I almost dropped my phone. My need for attention only went so far. Big nope from me.

"You okay?" Nate asked, concern evident in his tone. God, what was it about him? I'd heard thousands of guys' voices over the years through my computer speakers, but no one's affected me like his did.

"Fine," I managed to reply with an unconvincing smile. I silenced my phone and shoved it on the small table next to the chair in case Nate insisted on the ignoring-each-other route again.

His hands spanned my waist, lifting me onto the chair like I weighed nothing. The movement was so brief, I half wondered if I'd imagined it, yet I could still feel the heat from where he'd touched me sinking into my skin through my dress.

Knowing that I was probably blushing, I quickly laid down on my side, not bothering to push my hair back when it partially fell over my face. I hitched my dress up like last time, tucking it in between my legs, but I could feel the fabric brushing a little more substantially over my butt this time.

When Nate returned with the equipment, he hummed a noise that could have almost been disappointment. Definitely an ass man.

"So, how was the rest of your day yesterday?" I asked. Oh my god, I sounded like his mom or something. Why was I so bad at this?

"Unexpected," Nate replied thoughtfully. "Yours?"

"Very expected," I said drily, looking back at him over my shoulder. "Boring and expected."

The corner of Nate's mouth tipped up as he met my eyes, and I swallowed down a breathy sigh. For a brief moment, Nate's eyelids lowered, his head tilted just a little to the side, his lips *ever so slightly* parted... It was a look that was pure seduction. *That* was what I wanted. The man who looked like he was imagining what my lips tasted like and if I was a screamer when I came. My gut tightened with lust, and I felt my shoulders roll back a little, my head held a little higher, because he was having that reaction to me. Just me. Just *Lou*.

But it was gone as quickly as it came, so fast I wondered if I'd imagined it. Gone was the guy who looked one smooth line away from getting laid at all times, and back was the attractive yet distant professional.

"So," I said, clearing my throat. "Tell me all about Greece."

Nate smiled—not the sultry smirk—but it was obviously the right thing to say, because he was more than happy to talk about it. As he worked, he told me about the islands he visited, how he'd almost been run over while bike riding in Athens, and the life-changing food he'd eaten every night. Occasionally he'd fall silent to concentrate, but then he'd pick up where he left off, and I was more than happy to listen, imagining the idyllic places Nate was describing.

I was going to do that. I was going to chase summer around the globe, and drink ouzo on the beach under the stars, and *live* every day of my life rather than forever counting down to the next thing, waiting for little pieces of happiness to float past that I could grab onto.

A negative voice in the back of my mind reminded me that I would be funding all of this by maintaining and monetizing my Scarlet profiles, and that I wasn't *really* living my best authentic life when I was pretending to be someone else.

That negative voice could go shove it.

The session passed quickly, and mostly the pain was pretty bearable, but one particular section made me suck in a startled breath, and I forced myself to focus on my breathing, yoga-style, until Nate had finished.

"Good girl," he murmured in his low, delicious voice. "You're doing so good, Lou."

I could have sworn angels descended from on high, singing in chorus. My head was so hot, I was sure my face was as red as my hair, and I fought the urge to fan myself.

Good girl. Good girl. Good girl.

The smooth, approving way Nate had delivered those two words was going to live rent-free in my head for the rest of my life.

Nate's nostrils flared for a moment and I could have sworn I heard a rumbling noise, but I'd probably imagined it in my lust-addled haze.

I wanted to hear him say *good girl* while he stroked my hair and I choked on his dick. I was a simple girl. I wanted simple things. Was a praise-filled blowjob really too much to ask for?

"Keep breathing," Nate rasped as I winced again, forcing myself to focus on keeping my leg still instead of thinking about blowjobs.

"Hurts," I grunted, scrunching up my face.

"I know," Nate said in a soothing voice. "You're doing so good. Not long now."

I couldn't have chosen a teeny little daisy tattoo or something that could have been done in one session in a nice comfy spot, could I? Oh no. I had to go for the big fuck-off phoenix that dominated my entire hip and required two sessions with the hottest guy I'd ever seen and was failing to seduce.

Operation Seduction looked like a bust. Either he wasn't interested in me, or he *was*, but wanted to keep the lines of professionalism firmly in place. I could work with option two. After today's session, we would no longer be artist and client, and there would be zero barriers to working out this sexual tension on each other's bodies. *If* he was also feeling the sexual tension. If. Why couldn't I tell?!

Understanding people's desires was my bread and butter. Though that was a lot easier when they deliberately sought me out. Or sought *Scarlet* out, which was seriously making me doubt my fuckability without the wig and fake persona.

I wanted this, *him*, as myself. I wanted to seduce him, and fuck him, and hear him say my name.

Both because I was into Nate, and because I had to prove to myself that I could exist outside of the persona I'd been hiding behind.

"Nearly done, Lou," Nate reassured me, his cool professional mask back in place.

What would Scarlet do?

The phoenix looked fucking epic. Nate wiped away the excess ink, and I admired the smooth, flawless lines of the bird, the way it followed the curve of my body perfectly. It was all done in thin lines with no shading at my request, and I was already dreaming of all the other cool things I could get tattooed on my body in the same minimalist style.

"It's amazing," I told Nate as he carefully bandaged it, shooting me an apologetic look as he covered up my pretty with saran wrap again. Boo. Hopefully it healed quickly so I could properly admire it some more.

"How are you feeling?" Nate asked, removing his hands from my leg a little slower than necessary. Was that a sign? I needed a guidebook.

Operation Seduction. Part one: Flirt.

Scarlet style.

"My leg is kind of cramping," I replied, looking up at him through my lashes and wincing as I flexed my toes. "I don't suppose you could rub it for me?" I asked, my lower lip sticking out just the absolute faintest amount because I was for sure too old to get away with a full blown pout.

An emotion flickered in Nate's eyes too quickly for me to identify, and then his gloves were off, his hands wrapping around my calves, strong fingers gently digging into my too-tight muscles.

Yes fucking please.

My head tipped back, an embarrassingly breathy noise escaping my throat at how good it felt to have his skin on mine. Maybe I was more than a little touch-starved. For a few moments he worked in silence before he cleared his throat and my lusty haze cleared a little.

"Let's get you moving around," he said gruffly. "Get the blood flowing."

Let's not! Let's do more of the rubbing stuff!

Fortunately—or maybe unfortunately—Nate was guiding me up gently, his hands sliding around my back to pull me upright before I could vocalize that thought.

"Not too painful?" he asked, nodding at the bandaged tattoo on my hip.

"Hm, I'm not sure," I replied, dropping my voice to a seductive purr that was usually a hit with my viewers. I licked my lower lip subconsciously, my legs parting a little of their own accord as I sat on the edge of the bench. "You might have to carry me."

Nate's expression was heated, but there was definite hesitation in his eyes. Damn it, what did a girl have to do? Strip naked right here in the studio? I mean, I wasn't opposed to it, but I'd really prefer some clearer signals before I got my vagina out.

"You should go home," Nate rasped, dragging his hand down my exposed leg. Despite his words, he gripped my ankle lightly for a moment, and I imagined him dragging me down my bed, flipping me onto my stomach, and climbing over my back.

He had such big hands. I could almost imagine what it would feel like with one of them pinning me to the bed, his palm pushing down on the center of my back as he pressed that big monster cock he was definitely packing into me from behind.

"Go home?" I repeated breathily, watching the movement of his hand, still half lost in the fantasy I'd concocted.

"We can't do this."

"Why not?" His words penetrated the fog of lust, and my words came out a little more petulantly than I'd intended, but I was frustrated. And horny. "Do you have a girlfriend?"

"What?" Nate asked in surprise. "No, definitely not."

He sounded sort of appalled at the concept, which was somehow reassuring and disappointing all at once.

Nate leaned forward, trailing his knuckle down my cheek and scanning my features like he was memorizing them. I was more acutely aware than ever at the lack of a blonde wig on my head and the absence of my bright blue contacts and dramatic makeup.

I felt exposed.

"I'm not right for you," he told me softly. *Apologetically.* That was not going to work for me.

"I'm not expecting a ring," I snapped, batting away his soothing hand and cutting him an irritated glare. "At best I was hoping you'd have a talented tongue and a generous disposition."

This fucking guy, letting me down easy like like I was trying to *date* him or something.

"I'm too much for you," he attempted again. "You're so sweet, Lou."

Should I tell him that I literally fucked myself to orgasm with a dragon dildo last night, imagining him in bed?

I mean, where was the line? What constituted normal flirting? Was the dragon dildo too much information to drop straight off the bat?

"Bold assumption," I replied instead, doing my best to look down my nose at him despite him towering over me. "If anything, I'm too much for *you* to handle."

His eyebrows shot up in surprise, an excited grin flashing across his face before he could catch himself. *I see you, Nate. I'll show you I'm not the delicate little flower you seem to think I am.*

"Is that so?" he drawled, still trying to hide his amusement. But it was the kind of indulgent amusement adults felt towards particularly theatrical children, and that was not exactly the vibe I was going for.

"That is so. You really think *you're* too much for *me*?" I asked coolly, tipping my chin up. Scarlet would eat this guy *alive*.

"I know I am," he replied matter-of-factly. "Besides, don't even try to pretend that your leg isn't hurting."

Okay, that much was true, I could admit. I wasn't exactly on form for all the things I wanted to do to Nate with my stinging thigh.

"Tomorrow, then," I challenged.

"It'll still be hurting then." Nate shook his head slightly, still smiling to himself like he found my tenacity cute. He lifted me off the chair, making sure I was steady on my feet before reluctantly stepping away, his fingers flexing at his sides. I swayed a little like I was going to follow him, which would have been *really* embarrassing.

I wasn't going to *throw* myself at him.

I was going to make him throw himself at me.

Nate busied himself tidying up his equipment, reciting the same aftercare instructions he'd given me yesterday as I gingerly tugged my loose trousers up my legs and began the tedious process of putting all my layers back on. He was making a concerted effort not to look me in the eye, and that just wasn't going to work for me.

It would be one thing if he'd said he wasn't interested. I'd have given up and walked out of here with my head... well, probably hung in shame, to be honest. But still. I could take no for an answer. I wasn't accepting this 'I'm too much for sweet, innocent little you' garbage though.

It was offensive, honestly. To me and my vagina. My vagina was offended.

I tugged my sky blue beanie on my head and strutted up to Nate with as much sass as I could muster with a limp. He may have had a point on the sore leg front because now that I was moving around, fucking *ouch*. I stepped into his personal space, my head only coming up to his chest which slightly ruined the powerful, confident image I was attempting to project.

"Give me your phone," I demanded, holding out my hand expectantly.

"Persistent little minx, aren't you?" Nate murmured, his lips twitching. He did reach for the phone on the desk though, quickly unlocking it before handing it over for me to put my number in.

Operation Seduction. Part two: Show Idiot Man What He's Missing.

"I'll be in touch when my leg heals," I announced, sending a message to my phone so I had his number and handing his phone back.

"Lou—" Nate sighed as I turned to walk away.

"One phone call," I insisted, turning back to face him and holding up a finger, walking backwards to the door. "Just one. If you still think you're too much for little old me to handle, you'll never hear from me again."

Despite all of his objections, he didn't look thrilled with the prospect of never hearing from me again either, though I didn't know what he expected. Clearly, neither of us were looking for a relationship.

"One phone call," he agreed slowly. "This is the strangest rejection ever."

"You are not rejecting me," I informed him with a smirk. "We are negotiating terms. Until then, Nate."

I spun on my heel, red hair flying out behind me, and let myself out of the studio.

GABRIEL

Chapter 4

"I have a suggestion," Brooks announced, sitting on the sagging beige couch with his feet outstretched, flicking through images on his camera. "Let's find a less shitty house to stay in."

"No one is making you stay here," Nate sniped as he all but paced back and forth in front of the television, glancing at his phone for the millionth time this week before shoving it back in his pocket. I had no idea what his problem was lately, but he'd been a miserable bastard these past few days. More miserable than usual, and nothing dragged Nate's mood down more than when he came home to Alaska and pretended like he was happy to settle down here for the rest of his life.

"You need coffee, *irmão*," I teased, bumping him with my shoulder as I squeezed past him to get into the tiny kitchen. Both Nate and Brooks trailed after me like lost puppies at the mention of caffeine, even though there was barely enough space for two of us in the kitchen, let alone three. It was a good thing that none of us were particularly enthusiastic cooks.

Well, perhaps not a good thing. Many of the restaurants here closed in the winter months because it was too quiet, and we were rapidly getting sick of our takeout options.

"Obviously no one is *making* us," Brooks said exasperatedly, sitting down at the dining table with his eyes still trained on his camera. "I just don't understand why we're needlessly suffering."

I understood why Brooks wanted to find somewhere else. There were three bedrooms in the cabin-style home, but they were barely big enough to contain a double bed each, considering the whole place was only 900 square feet. The living room was just big enough to house a three-seater couch, small coffee table, fireplace, and a wall-mounted TV. We couldn't get through the kitchen door unless the dining table was pushed up against the wall.

Perhaps if we weren't all such large men, it wouldn't have been an issue, but we were big shifters and immensely uncomfortable in these cramped quarters.

Between the cramped quarters and the weather, I was beginning to question Nate's sanity, and we'd only been here a week. The amount of snow that fell here was truly appalling, and I felt like the sun had retired from the sky, there were so few hours of daylight.

Just a few weeks ago, we had all been in Greece, relaxing in the sun all day. We'd spent months traveling through the country together before Nate had gone off on his own at the end and Brooks and I headed to Thessaloniki to collaborate on a train cemetery article for a travel magazine.

Being here was... definitely different.

"Why don't you guys find somewhere bigger to rent?" Nate asked, bumping into me as he looked for the creamer for Brooks' coffee while I added the grounds to the machine and switched it on. "You don't have to stay here."

"Well we're hardly going to stay separately from you," Brooks pointed out as though it was obvious, despite vocally denying we were a pack at every given opportunity.

I loved Brooks and Nate. They were my best friends, and I was closer to them than I was to my own brother, who still lived in Brazil. But they were idiots who constantly claimed to be loners, even though the three of us *were* a pack, albeit a strange, nomadic one.

"Then tough luck, I've rented this place for the whole winter," Nate groused.

"Why not longer?" I challenged, leaning back against the counter as the machine percolated. "If you're so happy to stay here forever, that is. Isn't the plan to meet a nice shifter woman, put a mating mark on her neck and a baby in her belly?"

"No," Nate shot back, shoving his hand through his hair. "Well, I don't think so. Fuck, I don't know. That's what my parents want, but the whole concept makes me want to jump on the next plane out of here and never look back."

"Amen to that, brother," Brooks murmured before pointing his camera at Nate and taking a few shots that we both ignored. Brooks had been documenting our lives on film for a decade now, we barely noticed it most of the time. Why he wanted pictures of Nate looking like he was about to burst a blood vessel from stress, I had no idea.

"Then let's go," I replied with a shrug. "Wrap things up here and book a flight."

Nate glowered at me, but I wasn't about to support plans that so clearly made him miserable, even if he wanted me to. He was my packmate, and I wanted him to be happy. And with me and Brooks, where he belonged.

"Where are you guys heading to after this?" he asked as though he wouldn't be coming with us.

"Somewhere warm," Brooks said immediately, and I nodded my head in agreement. If I never saw snow again in my life, it would be too soon. "Though this wintery escape has made for some great images. If I ever get around to editing them, I think they'll sell well."

"Yeah?" Nate asked with a small smile. "Have you got your aurora shots yet?"

"Not yet," I replied for Brooks, preparing the coffees and sliding Brooks' across the table to him before downing half of mine in one go, barely noticing the heat and grimacing slightly at the flavor. I had never developed a taste for American-style drip coffee. "One of the sites we work with wants to do a sponsored piece, they're trying to find the right partner for it. Something adventure-based."

Brooks and I didn't always collaborate on projects, but there were a few publications who were always willing to buy my articles as well as his photos since they made for a more cohesive narrative together.

Nate nodded thoughtfully. "You should probably get some decent gear if you're going out exploring. Proper boots at least—even the hardware store around the corner sells them."

"Don't make me buy snow stuff, I'm not hanging around," Brooks objected, sipping his drink before focusing on his camera again, flipping his chestnut hair out of his eyes. "I escaped the snow as soon as I could, and I have no desire to recreate anything from my childhood."

I snorted. "Well, I will be investing in suitable footwear. And Nate and I are the same size, so I can always give them to him when I leave and he stays here *forever*, like he's repeatedly told us he's going to do."

"Yup," Nate agreed, dejectedly staring into his coffee cup. "That's a great idea."

Ai, Nate was truly his own worst enemy. I admired his dedication to doing what he *believed* was the right thing, even when what he believed was so obviously wrong.

"Ótimo. I'll go get boots now. I can't stand looking at these four walls anymore. Anyone want to come with me?" I asked, finishing my drink and rinsing out my cup.

"Nope," Brooks said, popping the 'p'. "I'm going to edit these and avoid the snow."

"Then it's going to be a long couple of months for you, *irmão*," I laughed. "Especially if you hate this house. Nate, you coming with me?"

Before he could answer, his phone buzzed and he pulled it out of his pocket so fast I was surprised he didn't rip his jeans. He'd been glued to it the entire week, even though the only people who ever seemed to contact him were his eldest brother and his mother, both inviting him for dinner.

"I'll take that as a no," I chuckled as Nate frowned at the screen, so absorbed in whatever he was looking at he didn't even seem to realize I was talking.

"Girl trouble," Brooks observed sagely, holding up his camera and examining Nate through the viewfinder. "Or at least I hope it is, because if Nate's life here really is this boring, I'm going to start crying on his behalf."

✳ ✳ ✳

If Nate and Brooks just admitted we were a pack and had been for at least the past ten years, all of our lives would be so much easier, I grumbled internally as I trudged through the snow to the store, slipping in my impractical shoes. The bottom of my jeans were soaked and heavy, and my cable knit sweaters weren't cutting it, even with my additional shifter body heat. Having cold wet socks had made my mood plummet. None of us even wanted to be here! Not even Nate. It was ludicrous to suffer this way.

For a decade, we'd argued about our pack status. We were unified on nearly every other issue, but on this one, we never seemed to agree. They were both so narrow minded when it came to this sort of thing—to them a pack had to have fixed territory, a leader and a hierarchy, and none of us were interested in that kind of life. Brooks, because he was traumatized by the pack he'd grown up in. Nate, because he had a wandering spirit and constantly craved alone time after his chaotic childhood. Me, just because I liked my job and seeing the world.

The mixed community of shifters I'd grown up in—in the Pantanal— had been good. Supportive. Loosely structured, but not overly hierarchical. I left because I preferred to explore, but I had no desire to be alone all the time. A pack was about its people, not its property.

Brooks didn't want to be alone either, or he wouldn't come with me all the time. Nate was more stubborn, but we always ended up reuniting in the end. My friends were good people with short-sighted visions of our future, but that was okay. We were all equals, but I would guide our pack through their denial.

I let myself into the hardware store, welcoming the blast of hot air. As soon as I got back, I was going to work on convincing Nate and Brooks that we should go back to the Phillipines for a few months so I could fucking defrost. Perhaps we could spend some time in Puerto Princesa— the underground river there had been on my 'to-see list' for years, and it would definitely give me some great content.

Nate would probably insist he was fine here, then join us in six weeks or so, pretending he hadn't tried to move permanently back to Fairbanks *again*.

The store was small, a family-owned place and mostly empty, but I could hear two voices in the aisle next to mine, and the sweet huskiness of the woman's voice immediately caught my attention.

There were a million chemical smells in the store that were offensive to my senses, but the sweet tempting scent of melted chocolate was vaguely present under all of them. I thought there was something familiar about it, but I couldn't place what. Perhaps I was overthinking it and there was just chocolate in here somewhere.

"Little Lou, all grown up," a man whistled, packing an impressive amount of lechery into one sentence.

"EJ," the woman replied warily. "How have you been?"

Her cautious tone called to my protective instincts, and I moved to the end of the aisle where I had a clear line of sight over their conversation, pretending to examine paint brushes. I didn't want to jump in and risk making the poor woman even more uncomfortable, but there was no one else in the store and I couldn't help but keep an eye on the situation.

I'd like to blame it solely on my animal, but perhaps I was a little curious about the owner of that delightfully husky voice. The melted chocolate scent grew stronger the closer I got, and I began to suspect it belonged to her.

I was probably no better than this "EJ", hovering here like this.

"Oh, you know, same old," he said, waving his hand absently. *Move*, I growled silently, irritated that his wide frame and oily dark hair was blocking my view of her. "You've really taken care of yourself, you know. Damn. Lots of women just give up after high school. It's a real shame."

The guy sighed heavily and I grew even more still as I strained my ears, hoping I'd hear the sound of her palm cracking across his face. She could use me as an alibi, I wouldn't mind.

"Yeah, it's a real pity," she deadpanned. "What's your excuse?" There was an awkward pause before she added, "Kidding, kidding. *Obviously*."

She most certainly was not kidding. I smiled to myself. I appreciated a snarky woman. After all, Oscar Wilde didn't just say "sarcasm was the lowest form of wit." He also called it "the highest form of intelligence."

"Ha, yeah," EJ replied awkwardly. "Funny. Don't I get a hug? How have you been?"

What a creepy, revolting man. Should I intervene? My jaguar growled in my head, flicking his tail in irritation. I thought he'd rush to get away from this place with the chemical smells and the fluorescent lighting, but even my animal side wanted to be sure this woman was okay.

"Sorry," she replied drily before I'd made up my mind. "I have this, um, disease that's transmissible via hugs. I'd hate to give it to you."

He immediately took half a step back, and I saw a flash of pale skin and dark red hair before the man's body obscured her again.

"Ha, yeah. Wouldn't want that... um, anyway, where have you been, Lou? I assumed you left town, it's been so long."

"I've been here." She—*Lou*—didn't bother elaborating, and I smiled to myself again at the cool politeness in her tone. "I need to paint my living room, I don't suppose you could help me find the right stuff for the job?"

I took a few steps out into the main aisle, intending to find what I'd come here for. Despite the guy's original creepiness, he wasn't trying to touch her now and his tone was conversational. If I didn't leave them to it, I was basically eavesdropping.

I dragged my feet though, the sound of their voices easily carrying in the empty store.

"It'd be my pleasure to help you, Lou. You, uh, got someone helping you with the job? I'd be more than happy to come and give you a hand. Little thing like you shouldn't be tackling that on your own," he said in what he probably thought was a charming voice.

"I'm sure I'll manage," Lou replied airily.

I paused in my awkward shuffle away, grabbing a bottle of something and pretending to examine it as I shamelessly listened in. The dating scene was more dire than I thought if this man's version of a pickup line was implying she was a helpless woman who couldn't wield a paint brush. If he wasn't being such a creep, I'd be embarrassed for him.

"Really, I insist. I'll sort you out with whatever you need, then I'll bring it around to your place. I'm off this weekend, I can help you then. You can always come back to mine while your house airs out. I have a spare room, actually. You could stay a few days..."

I was moving before I even realized I was doing it, striding down the aisle and stepping silently around the blustering man, finally giving me an unobstructed view of the beautiful redheaded woman. She was a tiny thing, perhaps as tall as my chest, all bundled up in brightly colored winter clothes.

Her expression morphed from thinly veiled irritation to surprise as she took me in, full lips parting slightly, olive eyes widening, the hitch in her breath only audible to my sensitive ears.

Beautiful.

"There you are, querida," I said, recovering from my momentary shock and flashing her what I hoped was a reassuring smile. "Find everything you need?"

"Just trying to pick the exact right shade of off-white," she replied breathily, playing along with my lie. She sidled closer to me, just close enough that our jackets brushed. It was hardly a dramatic display of intimacy, but it was enough to make EJ take a step back. How grim that my presence had been more of a deterrent than Lou's own words.

"Well, I'm sure this *gentleman* will be happy to assist us," I told her, not breaking eye contact.

Her eyes were an earthy shade of greenish brown that reminded me of the wetlands where I'd grown up, and her hair was a vibrant dark red, standing out against her pale skin. She was beautiful, but also *interesting* to look at. Brooks would love to photograph her.

"Of course," EJ said, sounding dejected. Good.

It seemed as though Lou was forcing herself to focus as he described the different brands and their suitability in a monotone voice, pointing out all the things to consider when painting in winter, before settling on an off-white color that EJ agreed to go mix at the counter, leaving us alone in the deserted aisle.

What had I come here for again? Something to do with hiking. Rope?

"Thank you," Lou murmured once EJ was out of earshot.

"My pleasure," I replied, before frowning. "Well, not really. In an ideal world, men would take a hint and beautiful damsels would never be in distress."

"Mm, that should have been cheesy, but your accent could make anything sound sexy," Lou laughed, a glorious raspy sound, while I preened silently to myself. "And yes, that would be an ideal world," she agreed.

"My name is Gabriel," I said, holding out my hand.

"Lou," she replied, slipping her much smaller, softer hand into mine. Despite the heating in the store, her hands were still ice cold, and I barely resisted the urge to wrap her in my arms just to warm her up a little. "Nice to meet you. What brings you to Fairbanks?"

"Ah, I am staying for the winter with a friend of mine," I told her with a fond smile, thinking of the either bored or sullen roommates I'd left back at the house. "I have visited him here before, but never this time of year. It's snowier than I expected."

Her lips twitched, olive eyes sparkling with amusement. "Oh? You didn't expect winter in Alaska to be so *snowy*?"

"Foolish of me, I know," I laughed. "I usually spend my time in milder climates. Are you from here?" I asked, still chuckling. She smiled back at me almost shyly, and I grew even more curious at the mixture of biting sarcasm and sudden vulnerability.

"I am. Lived here my whole life."

"You don't sound thrilled about that," I noted, thinking of Nate. They'd get along well, these two. He'd like her scent too.

"I keep meeting people who've seen the world lately, and I'm a little jealous. I'm going to travel though," she said with a soft genuine smile that transformed her entire face. There was a far-off look in her eyes like she was already thinking of all the places she wanted to go. "But I need to get my house ready to sell," she added, gesturing at the paint samples.

"Well, I certainly have time to kill if you need a hand, but I can also take no for an answer, unlike our friend over there," I replied, mouth kicking up one side.

"I guess I could always give you my number..." Lou trailed off coyly, before looking a little surprised at herself for suggesting it. She was an enigma, this one. Confident one moment, shy the next.

"I'd like that," I replied, pulling out my phone. "I firmly believe you can handle painting all on your own, but I am happy to help if you'd like me to. If not, there's always dinner..."

I would only be here a couple of months at the most, but a winter fling with a beautiful woman certainly held appeal. Of course, I would be very honest with her that I was leaving, and if she wasn't interested, that was fine. We'd have a fun dinner. No pressure.

I was certain I'd need a break from Nate and Brooks' company soon anyway. That house was too small for all three of us to be spending so much time there.

Lou was definitely both Nate and Brooks' type too, and I wondered how they'd feel if I started spending time with her. Lou would probably meet them and start dating one of them over me, given the choice. Nate had the brooding bad boy thing going on, and Brooks just had to smile and a phalanx of women appeared, throwing their panties at him. Perhaps I wouldn't mention this little encounter to them so I could selfishly keep her to myself.

"I like dinner," Lou said, accepting my phone and quickly typing in her number. She kept her head bowed, and I wondered if she was trying to hide her cheeks, which had flushed as red as her gorgeous hair. Honestly, I wouldn't be surprised if she'd given me the wrong number.

"I better go pay," she told me, handing my phone back. As Lou leaned in to give me my phone back, I caught another wave of her scent, and that nagging feeling that I'd picked up before came back with a vengeance.

"I'll come with you. It might look a little strange if I didn't," I added with a wink.

"Very true. Come on, fake... friend? Fake boyfriend? Let's go rub salt in EJ's wound," Lou replied with a saucy grin, her confidence suddenly back as she led me towards the counter.

I shot her my most seductive smile—not ashamed to be pulling out all the tricks to make an impression on this beautiful woman—before trailing after her, completely forgetting what I'd even come into this store for anyway.

Chapter 5

Well, my day had gotten a lot more interesting than expected.

Pervy EJ and Sexy Gabriel finished loading the paint and supplies I'd chosen into the trunk of my old Yukon while I stood on the sidewalk and supervised, so thoroughly bundled up in my winter layers that only my eyes were visible.

Eyes that I was struggling to take off Gabriel, which was a bit inconvenient since I was planning on making a move on Nate tonight. My tattoo had stopped hurting, so he couldn't use that as an excuse, and I had mentally prepared myself to get back into Scarlet Mode after taking a long break from her. Not just a few social media pics. *Proper* Scarlet Mode.

I'd messaged Nate this morning after yoga and a chia seed bowl, requesting that he video call me at 8pm, which he'd reluctantly agreed to, then decided to head to the hardware store so I didn't spend the entire day at home obsessing about it.

I had *not* expected a little flirtation with one of the hottest guys I'd ever seen.

Gabriel had a tan that gave me serious envy, dark curly hair, a square jawline covered in dark stubble, and *exquisite* eyes. They were a unique shade of dark, cloudy gray and so incredibly kind that I could have gotten lost in them. I didn't think I'd ever seen anyone who was so intimidatingly attractive and yet obviously gentle all at once.

Nate was gorgeous, obviously, but in a kind of bad boy, emotionally unavailable way. Gabriel's slate gray cable knit sweater was definitely made of boyfriend material, and that made him a lot more dangerous.

I couldn't believe I'd given him my number. He'd suggested dinner. *Dinner!* Was that code for casual sex? It had been a while since I'd dated, but dinner seemed more like a get-to-know-each-other activity than a rip-your-clothes-off activity. Hopefully Gabriel hadn't got any *girlfriendy* ideas just because he'd helped me deter the overly persistent EJ.

Why had I given him my number? Oh my god. I flirted one time and turned into a shameless hussy, giving my number out to any good looking guy who looked my way.

Relax, Lou. It's not like I *had* to have dinner with him. I hadn't made any promises. Operation Seduction was still in full effect.

EJ stormed back inside the store the moment my vehicle was loaded up, sulking like a toddler who didn't get his way, and I rolled my eyes at his back as he disappeared into the store. I hadn't seen him since my divorce, and I could have sworn my stomach dropped all the way onto the cement floor when I realized he was the only one working there. He'd been good friends with my ex-husband, and honestly, I'd expected some sort of hostility—bro code and all—but apparently EJ's creepiness outweighed any loyalty he had to Jake.

Ugh. I couldn't believe he'd asked me for a hug. Or asked my *tits* for a hug rather, since he'd apparently forgotten where my face was even though I was wearing all my enormous winter layers and looked like a marshmallow. I already regretted not slapping him in the face, but I'd had my hand shoved in my purse, clasping my pepper spray. Just in case.

"Thank you for your help," I told Sexy Gabriel as he sidled up next to me, all warm smiles and gray eyes I could drown in. So fucking pretty.

"You don't have to thank me," Gabriel said with a dismissive shrug, shooting an irritated glare at the door EJ had just gone through. I appreciated how affronted he was on my behalf by EJ's... flirting? It was possibly meant to be flirting.

"Aren't you freezing?" I asked, brushing at the sleeve of his woolen jumper with my gloved hand.

"A little," he shrugged. "I run hot, but this weather is uncomfortable even for me."

"Um, yeah," I replied like it was obvious, hoping he could see my judgy eyebrows because the rest of my face was covered. "It's like three degrees. You'd better get inside before you get frostbite."

He smiled again, all slow and languid, apparently not as worried as I was about him losing his toes. *Those eyes.* I did not know I could get hot for eyes, but my lower extremities were a-fluttering. Or maybe eyes *were* my thing, and it had just been awhile since I'd gotten to appreciate the impact of real-life eye contact. The kind so intense, you wondered who'd break it first or whether you could just hang in that moment forever without it being awkward.

His eyes were almost striking enough for me not to notice how freaking *tall* he was, or that he was stacked with muscles under that fitted cable knit sweater. Almost.

"Right you are, querida. It was a pleasure to meet you."

I didn't know if it was the accent or just his voice, but his words were almost a purr. My belly dipped traitorously as he leaned in to kiss my cheek. Apparently my body didn't care that I had a scheduled flirtation booked for later today.

"Nice to meet you too," I managed to get out, not a drop of my Scarlet confidence in sight.

"I'll be in touch," Gabriel added, patting his phone in his pocket before strolling down the snow-covered sidewalk in his ridiculously impractical sneakers.

I shook my head slightly to clear it, half wondering if I'd daydreamed that whole interaction. Life was a lot less complicated when I didn't leave my basement.

I attempted to concentrate on the snowy road while I made the short drive back to my house rather than the two pretty guys that had captured my attention recently. There must have been something in the water in Fairbanks then or something. Then again, the mountain men that lived outside of town were attractive as hell too, just super reclusive and insular. There was a whole community out there, but their kids didn't even come into town for school. It was kind of weird.

Ria's boyfriends were like that. They occasionally came into town to sell their wares, but I'd never come across them until she somehow ended up in a relationship with all three of them. They also had that kind of animal magnetism that Nate and Gabriel had in spades.

Maybe it was all the fresh air out there in the woods?

My phone buzzed, and I stupidly wondered if it was Gabriel messaging me already, even though he was probably still driving back to wherever it was he was staying.

Hopefully he'd leave me a voice message so I could hear him speak again in that sexy South American accent. Just the *thought* of that in my ear whispering filthy things while I panted underneath him made my belly flip.

I bet he'd look me in the eye the entire time. He was clearly a confident guy and he'd looked at me with the unwavering calm of a man who knew exactly who he was and what he wanted out of life.

Even sexy AF Nate didn't look like that. He had a lingering uncertainty about him that he wasn't quite able to hide. I was no psychologist, but I'd encountered plenty of people in my line of work who didn't feel comfortable in their own skin. It was why a lot of them had sought me out—my confidence turned them on, even if it was all an act.

Get your head in the game. No more Gabriel. You are supposed to be seducing Nate tonight.

Though if Operation Seduction didn't work out with Mr. You-Can't-Handle-Me... it was always good to have options. Gabriel may end up being Operation Redeem Myself After The Failed Seduction.

Why not Operation Seduction Part Two? The Scarlet-shaped devil on my shoulder asked. It wasn't like I was going to date either of them, I was leaving town in a couple of months anyway. Sleeping with them both wouldn't be *that* weird, so long as I was upfront about it being a casual thing, right? I would just have to give myself a stern talk about not getting attached, because Gabriel was a guy I could *easily* see myself getting attached to.

God, I was so out of my depth here. In my entire life, I'd only had real life sex with my husband—who I'd lost my virginity to in the cab of his pickup truck in senior year—and Frank the Liar. I mean, zero regrets, I knew how to get myself off and I didn't need a man, but now I was feeling a little lost on the politics of dating and/or casual sex.

Correction, one regret. Frank the Liar was a definite regret.

I parked my Yukon in the garage, grabbing my phone from the center console to check my messages.

Not a sexy message from Gabriel.

My eyes widened as I looked at the deposit that had just come through. $10,000. Crap on a cracker, that was a lot of zeroes for zero work.

'A monthly allowance, if you move to New York.'

I mean, I'd been telling myself I couldn't be bought, but that was a lot of money. I was torn between disgust that Frank thought this would actually work, and disgust at myself for feeling even a little bit tempted by his offer. While I'd earned a lot from camming, being Frank's on-call *whatever* was surely a lot less work than constantly creating new content and doing shows.

No. Bad Lou. Eyes on the horizon. You don't need this shit in your life.

I'd been letting Frank's smaller payments pile up in my account because fuck it, if he was going to send me guilt money, that was his problem. But I didn't want to keep this one. I didn't want to accept anything else from him now. It felt too much like I was agreeing to something I didn't want to agree to.

Frank hadn't even wanted me until after I was gone. He didn't want *me*, period. He wanted a pet.

I quickly sent the funds back and shoved my phone away, turning my attention to bringing the cans of paint to the living room so they wouldn't freeze, and sweating slightly from exertion by the end of it.

I managed to push all the furniture away from the walls into the center of the room and covered it all with a drop cloth before flopping down on the couch to recover, pulling out my phone automatically.

Perhaps a day would come where I didn't feel like I was missing a limb whenever my phone wasn't in my hand, but today was not that day.

My most recent photo was from this morning. I'd reluctantly pulled on my skimpiest red bikini and taken a bunch of quick pics because even with the heating on, it was *not* bikini weather. It had been sent to me by a smaller brand, and I only made money when people purchased via my affiliate links, so winter or not, I had to hustle.

I scrolled mindlessly through the comments, blocking a few people because there were always a few mouthy assholes in my comment section who made my skin crawl, but most people were nice. There were lots of fire emojis because I *was* fire. In the heavily curated photos I posted at least.

@ComputerWombat:

Why don't you do shows anymore? No one gives a fuck about this ad shit you're doing.

A bunch of people had liked it, and even though there were supportive replies saying I had a right to move on and pursue new things, the complaint stuck in my mind.

I was bound to lose followers while I transitioned from less sex-specific content to more sex-positive empowering content, with a dash of travel pics and behind-the-scenes snaps sprinkled in, but what if I lost so many that this whole idea wasn't even worth pursuing?

I wanted to banish that little insecure voice in the back of my head down to the depths of hell where it belonged, but I hadn't quite managed it yet. The little voice that piped up at the most opportune moments to question if Lou was worth knowing, or if I should change my name to Scarlet, bleach my hair, and roleplay my own life.

Suddenly not liking the device in my hand very much, I locked my phone and tossed to the end of the couch, staring at the cans of paint on the floor and drop cloths throughout the room. If anything, seeing the place like this made the job feel even more daunting, but I was determined I could do it. I was prepared.

I'd watched about eighty hours of home decorating shows over the past week when my healing ink had bothered me, and came to the conclusion that maybe I couldn't go full Chip-and-Joanna on my kitchen, but painting the main rooms this week and possibly adding a backsplash in the kitchen were probably manageable.

Then I'd add some new lights to make the place look fancier, chuck in some houseplants to make it all look pretty for the listing, call the realtor, pray to the Property Brothers gods that it sold for above the asking price within twenty-four hours, then book a flight out of here.

On Pinterest, painting a room seemed so simple. Buy off-white paint, wear cute overalls, bop along to a great playlist while I got the job done. In reality, once I'd gotten into the hardware store, there were at least forty shades of off-white paint, all available in different finishes, and because I'd decided to do it in winter, I had a whole bunch of weather considerations to take into account as well so I didn't pass out from all the fumes.

Basically, I needed to spend less time thinking about internet trolls and juggling dicks, and more time thinking about proper ventilation.

Until eight o'clock tonight, anyway.

At eight o'clock tonight, all bets were off.

I sat at the vanity in my bedroom, staring at my reflection in the mirror like I was looking at a completely different person. I sort of was. Scarlet wasn't Lou. It was more than just wearing a wig, contacts, makeup, and losing the brightly-colored yoga pants that made up my regular wardrobe. Scarlet was a state of mind for me. *That was where I'd gone wrong with Nate,* I'd decided after mulling over our last interaction roughly a million times over the past week.

In the beginning, I'd flirted with Nate as Lou, just like I had with Gabriel this morning. Lou was coy. Lou liked to bat her eyelashes and be pursued, from memory. I'd liked that when Jake had done it at least, but that was back in high school. He'd stuck notes in my locker until I'd agreed to go to Sonic with him on a Friday night and we'd split a chocolate shake and some tots.

Scarlet, for the most part, was sexually confident, overtly seductive, and totally in control.

Scarlet had any man or woman she wanted wrapped around her finger. She read their desires and molded herself into whatever they wanted her to be.

Everyone wanted a piece of Scarlet.

Obviously, plain old Lou didn't hold the same appeal, that much had become clear from my interactions with Nate. Maybe I didn't need the wig, but if I'd channeled some of that brazen confidence, he wouldn't have been all *'oh, but you're so sweet, I couldn't possibly fuck you!'*

I'd show him just how *not* sweet I could be. I had a point to prove. I'd get out the dragon dildo if I had to.

I dressed in a simple dark silver slip, the cool silver sliding easily over the itchy as *fuck* tattoo that I'd already doused in lotion, and forewent the bra and panties.

The tattoo looked... not great, but I had done a lot of Googling and apparently it was normal for my skin to be shedding like a goddamn snake. It wasn't the sexiest accessory, but I was hoping it wouldn't be a dealbreaker for Nate since he was the one who'd put it there in the first place.

I pulled the matching robe over the top of my slip, put in my unnaturally aqua blue contact lenses, and took extra care with my smoky eye and red lips. The lipstick kind of clashed with my natural hair, but it matched my champagne-colored wig perfectly.

Sultry, old Hollywood glam, that was Scarlet's look. It was over the top and unattainable, which had been a big part of Scarlet's appeal with viewers. How Scarlet acted depended on who she was talking to.

For a moment, I stared at my reflection in the mirror with Scarlet's face and my regular red hair. This look almost seemed the most fitting— one foot out the door into the real world, but still wearing my camgirl armor.

It was probably a little ironic that in order to prove to Nate I could *handle* him, I was putting on an entirely different identity. It did undercut my messaging slightly. Whatever.

Sighing at my own stupidity, I braided my hair into two plaits and wrapped them around the crown of my head, pinning them into place before pulling my wig cap on. The wavy, pale blonde wig was in pride of place on my dresser as always, and I pulled it off the mannequin head, running my fingers gently through it before stretching it over my head.

I fussed with the blunt wispy bangs until I was happy with them, took a few selfies so I could show off the outfit and tag the brand later, then grabbed my laptop off my bed to head down to the basement.

Out of habit, I'd been going down to the cam room in the basement each week, tidying it up and keeping everything in order.

It felt like a drug I had to wean myself off. Camming was what bought me this house, and the basement room was my sexual sanctuary.

I ran my hand over the white fitted sheet on the double bed, and flicked on my three point lighting system that illuminated the bed perfectly on camera. I'd strung fairy lights along the back wall—for ambience, rather than lighting—and turned those on too. There were soft cushions along the headboard, and that combined with the fairy lights made the space feel cozy and romantic.

Well, except for the wooden shelf above the bed, just visible in shot with my collection of sex toys. That was slightly less soft and romantic looking.

I hooked my laptop up and turned it on, ready to take Nate's call through that so I could use my HD webcam, already in position. I was no amateur—I had the perfect setup to give the perfect show, and the more I thought about it, the more I wondered why I had walked away from this.

Oh yeah, to build a regular life and have real sex outside of the internet. Because that was going so well so far.

A rare rush of nerves sent a shiver down my spine as I fussed with the belt on my robe and fluffed out the ends of my wig again, waiting for the call to come in. Nate oozed untamed sexuality. He was worldly, cool, and well-traveled. He'd probably fucked half of Fairbanks' most eligible in the few months that he'd been back.

It had been *years* since I'd doubted my sexual appeal, but I suddenly felt like I was turning the camera on for the first time again, awkwardly pouting at the camera in a cheap lace negligee and costume party wig I'd worn in the beginning. Would he even be interested in this? God, he might laugh in my face.

I'd sell the house as is and leave town tomorrow if that happened.

Get it together. You are Scarlet. Scarlet made thousands of dollars a month doing this for years. Nate is no different from any other guy.

Except that didn't feel strictly true.

Maybe because I'd actually met him and talked to him about myself and my life. I'd listened to him talk about his travels and seen the way those memories made his eyes light up, unlike when he talked about moving home. I couldn't exactly pretend he was any random stranger when I'd given him my childhood sob story.

Eight pm on the dot, my phone rang.

Okay. Okay, that was a good sign.

I mean, he'd agreed to call me, but I'd still been worrying he might back out. I guess curiosity got the better of him.

Now he just had to not laugh in my face, and we'd be golden.

The butterflies in my stomach leaped to life as I hit 'accept', and Nate's obscenely handsome face filled the screen. He was sitting forward slightly, white wireless earbuds in his ears. The room he was in was dimly lit, but I could see his black hair sticking out at messy angles, like he'd been running his fingers through it.

Maybe he was a little nervous too? I imagined him sitting on the end of his bed, watching the clock tick down until eight o'clock, waiting to hit 'call', and then got distracted wondering what his room looked like. What his *bed* looked like. What he looked like on his bed.

Did he sleep naked?

This was an important scientific question that I needed an answer to.

Right. Concentrate. No more thinking about Nate's naked body rubbing against his sheets.

I had a show to put on.

NATE

Chapter 6

"Lou?" I asked uncertainly as the call connected. Maybe I'd got the wrong number? The blonde-haired, blue-eyed, heavily made up woman on screen had Lou's face, but looked nothing like her at the same time. She didn't even hold herself like Lou did.

It was a little unsettling.

"Yes and no," she replied coyly. Even her voice wasn't quite *right*. Not quite her. "In this room, I go by Scarlet." She flicked at the long blonde wig to illustrate her point.

I squinted at the screen to try to figure out what I was looking at. She was sitting on a bed, but there was just a fitted sheet and some cushions, no other bedding. Behind her was a shelf with some... unusually shaped items I couldn't quite make out.

And then there was Lou. Scarlet. Wearing some silky little robe, loosely belted to show a matching slip underneath. She didn't look like the fresh faced innocent young woman who'd been in my studio last week. *Was she that innocent though?* I asked myself. She hadn't seemed all that innocent when her pert little butt had been hanging out of her micro dress, and the scent of her arousal was so potent I could still feel it in my lungs a week later.

"Okay... tell me about Scarlet," I rasped, trying to put together the pieces of the puzzle in front of me before my dick could drain all the blood from my brain.

I wasn't working fast enough, to be honest.

Lou smiled back at me, but it wasn't like the sweet, flirtatious smiles she'd given me in the studio. This one was a little more seductive, a little more predatory, and a lot less genuine.

Much like the wig and the contact lenses, I didn't like it.

"Well, Scarlet," Lou drawled, leaning towards the camera to give me a view of her cleavage. "Scarlet can be whoever you want her to be. Scarlet can be coy." Lou pulled the robe tightly around her body and crossed her lean legs, looking at the camera through lowered lashes.

"Or she can be bold." With practiced fingers, Lou unbelted the robe, discarding it on the side of the bed, then spread her legs wide, pushing them out at the knee. I got the briefest glance at the prettiest pussy I'd ever seen before she closed them again, winking confidently at me.

She crawled up the bed, the slip doing little to cover her luscious ass before returning to the center of the frame with a selection of objects.

"Scarlet can enjoy pain," Lou began, teasing her nipples over the top of the slip with clamps connected by a silver chain, and glancing up at the screen, clearly trying to gauge my reaction. "Or she can be totally naive." The clamps were set aside, and Lou massaged her breasts hesitantly, as if she was touching them for the first time.

Fucking hell.

My dick didn't get the memo that this was a performance, even as my brain—blaring warning signals like crazy—did. My dick was fine with all of this, even if it wasn't... real. Even if the things I'd liked most about Lou, the things that made her such a fucking temptation in the hours I spent with her, were hidden underneath this sexy facade. Her naturally dry tone of voice, her wide-eyed curiosity about the world beyond Fairbanks, her guarded flirtations, her gorgeous hair...

"So, what'll it be?" Lou asked in her slowed down, overtly sultry tone. "I can be a domme too," she added as an afterthought. "You didn't seem like a submissive guy, though."

"I'm not," I replied, my voice coming out like a raspy grunt. "What does Lou like?"

She shot a dubious look at the camera, like she couldn't understand why I was even asking, and the warning bells in my head grew more insistent.

"Lou's not here," she replied eventually, amping up the sensual purr in her voice as she danced her fingers lightly up and down her inner thighs, avoiding the probably itchy tattoo. "You can call me Scarlet, and I'll call you whatever you like. Master? Sir? Daddy?"

"Just Nate is fine," I replied eventually. I wanted to hear my name on her lips, nothing else.

"Well, Nate, since you don't seem like the kind of guy who regularly talks to camgirls, why don't you sit back and enjoy the show?" Lou suggested, rising onto her knees with her legs spread and teasing the hem of her slip before running her hands up her stomach and cupping her breasts, holding them up like a fucking offering. She leaned forward, glancing down and licking her lips like she could see my cock slipping between her tits and was swiping precum from the tip.

I knew it was rehearsed. It was clear she'd done this before, and knew the exact angles to maximize the impact of her movements, but my dick didn't mind that at all. It pressed painfully against my zipper, and I adjusted it as discreetly as I could, though apparently not discreetly enough.

"Don't be shy," Lou said with a wink. "Feel free to enjoy yourself. You're always welcome to give me a show too."

Then she slowly pulled the slip off, revealing the absolutely goddamn nothing she had on underneath.

I almost groaned at the sight of her rosy nipples, toned waist, curved hips... the phoenix looked *magnificent* climbing up her thigh, even though it was obviously in the itchy peeling phase, though Lou was doing a great job of ignoring any discomfort as her dainty hand moved between her legs, her middle finger dragging slowly up her slit. Her other hand circled her nipple, plucking at it gently as she gave the clamps next to her a contemplative look before returning her gaze to the camera.

"You don't seem like someone who'd be a fan of accessories," she said decisively. "You seem like the kind of guy who wants to show off exactly what he can do with the equipment he's already packing."

"Damn fucking right," I gritted out, sounding just this side of feral. The TV was on and I hoped that Brooks and Gabriel were absorbed enough in what they were watching to not pay any attention to me in this tiny house with its paper thin walls.

Lou pushed her middle finger into her pussy, her head tipping back, teeth sinking into her lower lip like she'd never felt anything more fulfilling than her slim finger inside her.

I fought back the urge to growl at her. This was performative. I could give her real pleasure. I could make her come from just my teeth on her nipples if I had the chance. Fill her up properly until she felt a stretch that bordered on pain, but was all pleasure. Lou dragged her finger up to circle her clit, hips rolling slowly, and I swore my dick turned to granite in my pants. I semi wondered if I'd ever be able to get it back to normal after this. I might not ever get it down unless I buried it in Lou's pussy.

Don't do it. This is a bad idea. You're not in control.

"Hmm, what am I in the mood for tonight?" Lou pondered breathily, tilting her head to the side, finger still slowly circling her clit. I wanted to trace each movement with my tongue. The scent of her arousal was embedded in my lungs a week later, and I wanted to fucking *taste* it.

"What are you in the mood for?" I asked, my voice thick. My teeth scraped my lower lip, wishing it was Lou's soft skin instead, and my breathing was so fucking heavy I wouldn't be surprised if the guys came in to make sure I wasn't having a goddamn heart attack.

"Well, I'm definitely in the mood to be filled up. *Stretched.*" Fuck. That was exactly what I wanted to do to her. "I guess I'll have to see if I can find a toy that works as a substitute for your cock. What do you say, Nate? Give me a little peek so I know what I'm trying to match?" she asked coyly, pausing to reach for something on the shelf behind her and presenting a thick glass dildo to the camera.

I was on my feet before she even finished moving, the animalistic part of my brain fully in charge. No, that wasn't true. Maybe I wanted to blame my actions on primal urges, but I knew exactly what I was doing.

I just wanted her. I wanted Lou like I'd never wanted anyone.

"You'll have my cock or nothing," I growled, glaring at the dildo like I could light it on fire with my eyes through the phone screen. "What's your address?"

Stupid.

Stupid. Stupid. Stupid.

There was a flash of something across Lou's face, an emotion I wasn't fast enough to identify, before she smiled victoriously and rattled off the address.

Perfect. She lived not far from here, in a fairly isolated spot that I could get to mostly through the trees. There was no time to go through the human motions. Fuck that. I needed to bury myself balls deep in her before I lost my goddamn mind, feel her come around my cock, then flip her over and spank her ass raw for putting on this tempting show when I was trying to stay away from her for her own good.

"Don't come," I warned her, my tone brooking no room for argument. "You can play with that pretty pussy all you like, but that orgasm belongs to me. Understand?"

"Yes, Nate," Lou replied breathily, a hitch in her voice as she sat back on her heels.

I disconnected the call, chucking my phone on the bed and rushing out of my room in just the long-sleeve t-shirt and jeans I'd been relaxing in like the hounds of hell were on my ass.

"Where are you off to, *irmão*?" Gabriel asked, glancing up at me in surprise from his spot on the couch.

"I'll explain later," I grunted, already peeling off my shirt as I ran out of the door.

It was pitch black out and I could run by the trees next to the highway to get to Lou's house from the place I was renting near town. I usually wouldn't take risks like this, but I couldn't seem to help myself. She tested my control on every level, which was exactly why I should be staying away.

But I wouldn't.

I stripped out of my clothes, bringing my jeans and t-shirt with me as I walked naked into my backyard, and let the shift take me. I used the familiar pain of breaking bones and stretching muscles to ground me, reminding me that I had to be at least a little cautious. *Don't get caught.*

My cougar stretched, grabbing the clothes in his teeth. He and I were in perfect agreement on this. We had to get to Lou. My cougar didn't seem to care that Lou was a human. He'd been captivated by her last week when she was in the studio, and he was even more entranced now.

That level of interest should have been the only warning sign I needed to slow down, but I didn't. I sprinted through the trees, kicking up snow in my wake, just aware enough of my surroundings to avoid trouble.

I skidded to a stop in the trees outside of Lou's home, shifting back and shoving on my clothes as quickly as I could. Fuck, I should have worn shoes. No shoes in the snow was going to be a dead giveaway that something wasn't quite right.

It was a reasonably sized place, dimly lit and painted a surprising shade of pink, with no neighbors in immediate sight. I was glad for that as I strode to her front door half dressed, but the idea of her living alone out here was alarming.

What if something happened? That obviously wasn't her first time performing on camera. What if someone stalked her?

Humans were injured so easily.

I knocked on the front door impatiently, suddenly anxious about Lou's safety. I needed to see her with my own eyes. Smell her delicious chocolatey scent. Feel her skin under mine.

I heard her jogging through the house, and was gratified that she at least looked through the side window before pulling the door open, dressed only in the silvery robe and that wig I hated so much. Not to mention the contact lenses. Covering up her beautiful olive eyes was a fucking travesty.

"That was fast," Lou breathed, cheeks flushed, with the scent of arousal permeating the air. "Like, really fast. Do you live around here?"

She stepped back to let me inside, and I should have answered her questions, but fuck. The smell of her. I *needed* to feel her, taste her, make her come.

I closed the door behind me and had her against it in the next second, my hips pinning her in place. My hands slid over the silky fabric of her robe, the luscious feel of her curves calling to me as Lou's pupils dilated, her breath coming in short pants.

"You're right, we can talk later," she breathed, hands ghosting over the fabric over my shirt. "Follow me."

Barely holding it together, I stepped back enough for her to pass me, every inch of my body yearning to touch her again. This petite little human had entirely unraveled me.

Lou hesitated in the short hallway for a moment before pulling open a side door that opened to a staircase. I followed her down to the basement, hunching so I didn't bang my head on the low ceiling. There was a single door at the bottom of the staircase, and I knew what I'd find before Lou even opened it.

The white bed with no blankets, a few cushions in the corner, sex toys decorating the walls, and an elaborate computer setup on a desk at the end of the room.

"You can watch me unplug it all," Lou said hurriedly, tugging the cables out of the wall. "I'm not filming this."

At this point, I wouldn't care if she was, only that this wasn't her bedroom and she'd said she was Scarlet in this room.

The second she got the laptop plug free of the wall, I was on her. Lou squeaked as I tossed her onto the mattress, her barely belted robe falling open as easily as her legs.

How could I ever think there was anything shy and fragile about the naked woman underneath me, writhing unconsciously, trying to get closer?

I leaned down and captured her lips with mine, swiping my tongue into her willing mouth instantly. My dick throbbed at the sweet taste of her. It was heady and rich, like her scent. A decadent melted chocolate mixed with the scent of her coconut lotion.

I had to see if she tasted as sweet everywhere.

Lou mewled impatiently as I pulled away from her lips, ripping my t-shirt over my head with one hand before securing my mouth around one hardened nipple.

"Oh my god, Nate," she breathed, head tipped back. There was nothing performative about this. No coy looks or flirty lip bites, no conscious angling of her body for maximum impact. This was the Lou I wanted to see—a woman totally lost to her desire, short of breath, squirming for more, arousal glistening on her thighs. Fucking *beautiful*.

"Take off the wig," I demanded before moving my mouth down her body, sucking marks on her skin. I *needed* to mark her. Needed to claim her for my own.

She froze at my directive, and I scraped my teeth over her skin, bringing her attention back to me.

"Are you sure?" she asked hesitantly. I glanced up the line of her body, seeing her hands resting at the front of the wig, ready to pull it off.

"Very," I mumbled against her skin before leaving another love bite on her hip. I was vaguely aware of her fiddling with it as my mouth moved slowly towards the apex of her thighs, licking and teasing as I went.

Make it good. Make sure she remembers you.

I pushed her legs apart, bending one at the knee to give me better access as I settled between them.

"Oh, are you going to—" she began, before I licked a long, slow path up to her clit and she seemed to forget how to speak.

I started off slowly, every movement intentional, cataloguing Lou's reactions. The way her thighs twitched under my hands, or the moany little sighs she made when something felt good. Then I was picking up my pace, flicking my tongue over her clit as I pushed a finger into her soaked pussy, feeling it tighten around me almost instantly.

"More," she demanded, almost whining. "Oh my god, is this what oral sex feels like? Are you just extra good at this?"

I *was* good, but it helped that it was Lou. I never wanted to take my mouth off her pussy.

"Is this what oral sex feels like?"

Had she really asked me that? I needed to explore that question more. After. She just tasted too fucking good for me to stop.

I added a second finger, curling them upwards until she went off like a rocket, back arching high off the bed as her walls clenched around me. Lou was almost sobbing as I continued my movements, dragging a second orgasm from her body before the first could end.

Make her remember you.

She tasted so fucking good, but I wanted her next orgasm on my dick. *Needed* it. My control was rapidly slipping away from me, and I wasn't confident I was going to last as long as I usually would.

What was it about her that unraveled me like this?

"Nate," Lou breathed, grasping wildly at my hair, encouraging me upwards. "I need you, I need you..."

Yeah, you fucking do.

I could usually spend *hours* on foreplay. I loved satisfying my partner, and I had no problem waiting for my own release. But if I didn't feel Lou's wet heat wrapped around me within the next five seconds, I was pretty sure I would die.

I didn't even think about it. I shoved my pants off so fast I was surprised they didn't rip, hitched Lou's leg over the crook of my arm and thrust into her with one hard stroke, burying myself balls deep in her tight, soaked pussy. Pleasure was already building at the base of my spine, so I closed my eyes for a moment, taking a deep breath in to center myself.

Bad move. The scent of Lou's arousal in this small enclosed space was heavy and intoxicating. I knew I'd be able to recall the exact aroma of her desire for the rest of my fucking life.

"You feel incredible," I gritted out, opening my eyes and focusing on the beautiful woman underneath me. Two red braids fanned out on either side of her head, such an improvement over the blonde wig she'd discarded. It would be even better if she wasn't wearing the blue contact lenses and the sparkly makeup, but I doubted I'd be able to stop long enough to convince her to remove them.

Her eyes widened slightly, and I remembered the way she'd broken out in goosebumps when I'd told her what a good girl she was last week getting her tattoo.

Something to explore.

"Please move," Lou breathed, bucking up against me. "It feels so good. So, so good. *Move.*"

I wasn't about to deny the lady what she wanted.

I braced my forearm next to her head before pulling all the way out and driving forward again, watching Lou's reaction. The harder I snapped my hips, the more she seemed to lose herself, her nails clawing at my chest and shoulders, anywhere she could reach.

That's it, baby. Mark me.

"Good girl," I purred, testing my theory. "You like feeling my cock stretch this tight, pretty pussy? Of course you do."

Lou whined slightly, her inner walls clenching around me as her nails dug harder into my skin. *Eu-fucking-reka.* Lou got off on praise, and I was going to goddamn praise her.

I leaned down to capture her lips again, biting her bottom lip before soothing the sting with my tongue, before moving my lips down her jaw and to her neck. I inhaled deeply, running my nose up the column of Lou's throat, and she tipped her head back eagerly, giving me better access. *Human*, I vaguely reminded myself. She didn't know what a gesture of trust and submission this was. I knew. I had to be the one in control.

Yet my cougar was growling impatiently, my instincts encouraging me to claim her. *Mark her throat. Bite.*

No, that was a very dangerous train of thought.

"Be good and flip over for me," I instructed, pulling out and encouraging Lou onto her front. She didn't protest at all, just pushed herself up onto her knees and looked at me over her shoulder.

Mark her.

Fuck! I forced myself to stay still just long enough to pull both elastics out of her hair, grateful that Lou immediately followed my lead and loosened her braids, even though she had no idea why I was doing it.

I needed to hide all of that delicious unmarked neck that was on display.

Her dark red hair fell around her face and Lou looked back at me with an expression that was anything but coy. It was *hungry*. Unable to wait a second longer, I grabbed her hip, forcing myself to remember that she was human and I had to be gentle, before driving into her again. This had to be a one-time thing. *Had to be.* But I wasn't entirely sure how I was ever going to leave this behind, because sex had *never* felt like this before. This was like... our fucking souls touching or something. Something way more poetic than I was able to come up with while Lou's pussy was strangling my cock, and my balls were on the verge of imploding.

She pulled her hair over one shoulder and instinctively, I found my body curving over her back again, drawn to her throat like a magnet. I was careful to keep my weight off her by planting my hand next to her head, but her skin was like a siren's call to me. I had to have my mouth on it. *My teeth*. I wrapped a hand gently around her neck, encouraging her head back so I could capture her lips again, distracting myself, and Lou whimpered as each thrust hit even deeper than before.

She felt so petite underneath me, but everything about her radiated strength. I felt driven to protect Lou, while at the same time feeling like she didn't need my protection at all. She was a fearsome little warrior who could absolutely hold her own.

"I'm going to come again," Lou sobbed. "It's too much, oh my god."

"Shh, you're doing so well. Just relax for me, beautiful," I growled in her ear, my own movements growing more erratic with my impending release. "Let go for me, Lou. I've got you."

If I had my way, I'd never let her go.

Chapter 7

I'd definitely had more orgasms in my life than the average 25-year-old woman. Multiple orgasms a day in fact, though they were almost exclusively for someone else's viewing pleasure. I knew my body inside and out, I knew my tell-tale signs, and what I needed to push me over the edge.

This... this was nothing like what I expected.

I *needed* Nate's encouragement to push me over the edge because for the first time in my life, I was apprehensive. It was *too* much, *too* intense, *too* everything. I wasn't sure I would be able to recover from the kind of pleasure Nate was offering.

I didn't feel like I was about to be consumed by a crashing wave of pleasure. I felt like I was about to be unraveled from the inside, and I wasn't entirely confident I'd be able to put myself back together again.

This was just meant to be sex, I remembered hazily. *Just some real life dick to get me back on the horse.*

"My good girl," Nate murmured. "You're taking my cock so well. You're so fucking beautiful, I could watch my dick sliding into this tight wet pussy every goddamn day."

My noises had become steadily more incomprehensible, and now I was just sobbing, his words traveling through my body like little arrows honed in on my clit.

I had never experienced anything like this before. Not with Jake or Frank, and definitely not with any of my clients—most of whom preferred to talk to me in ways that women in their real lives wouldn't tolerate. With them, it was just background noise, meaningless words that I let drift in one ear and out the other.

Each filthy compliment from Nate burrowed into my brain and took up permanent residence there.

"Be good and come for me. One more time, beautiful. I want to feel you squeezing me when I come inside this pretty pussy."

My head tipped back, my spine arching of its own accord as I threw myself into oblivion, trusting that he'd catch me at the other end. Nate's mouth closed over the juncture of my shoulder and neck, the lightest scrape of sharp teeth on my skin setting off that deep primal urge I couldn't seem to control. I didn't want to control it.

"Bite me," I moaned, pushing back against him as best I could, pleasure consuming me like a ravenous beast that would eat me alive.

Nate made a strangled noise against my skin, his teeth pressing in harder just as I felt his release filling me, his hips grinding against my ass like he couldn't get close enough. In that moment, nothing mattered more to me than his teeth sinking into my flesh. I craved it, *ached* for it in the depths of my soul. I needed his strength, his dominance, his... *something*. Something important.

"Bite me!" I demanded, vaguely aware of how hysterical I sounded. Why wasn't he biting me yet? Didn't he know I needed this?

There was a slight sting as his teeth—definitely sharper than I expected them to be—pushed harder against my skin and I gasped, twitching away from the source of pain reflexively even as relief flooded me that he was giving me what I wanted.

But that slight movement broke whatever spell Nate seemed to be under. He pulled his teeth and his cock free with alarming speed, practically throwing himself off the bed, stumbling back against the wall. Blinking at the sudden loss of him, I rolled over slowly, sitting up with my legs pressed together, my fingers tracing the small mark his teeth had left on my neck.

It was only an indentation, not even deep enough to break skin, but I could have sworn it *tingled*. Or maybe in my weird sex high haze I was just imagining things, but it felt oddly significant.

Now there was some distance between us—an awkward amount of distance, actually, considering what we'd just done—the weird urgent *craving* to have Nate's teeth in my flesh wore off like the delicious effects of my orgasm. Boom, vibes gone. Just like that.

Even though his weird reaction had thoroughly killed the mood, I still found the small grooves in my skin kind of sexy. Clearly we were feeling differently on that front, because Nate was staring at them like he'd just discovered 666 tattooed on my skull.

Way to make a woman feel special.

"Are you okay?" I asked cautiously, tucking my legs underneath me, suddenly acutely aware of my nakedness and the fact that he was plastered back against the wall with wild eyes, looking like he'd seen a ghost.

This... wasn't exactly how I'd seen this part going.

"Nate?" I tried again. His breathing was shallow, like he was *trying* not to breathe too deeply, and for a bizarre moment, his green eyes looked almost like they were glowing in the dim light. I blinked twice, questioning my own eyesight, and when I refocused on him, his eyes appeared normal. Strange.

"I'm sorry if I made you uncomfortable," I said hesitantly. I could feel our shared release sticking between my thighs, and my face heated at the realization we hadn't used protection. I had an IUD, but I didn't *know* this guy. We hadn't even had a cursory conversation about his STD record. What was I thinking? From the moment he'd phoned me, we'd both been in some kind of sexual trance.

"You're apologizing?" Nate replied incredulously, huffing a horrified laugh. "You're apologizing to me."

"I got carried away and asked you to bite me, it clearly made you uncomfortable," I replied, a little snark coming into my voice at the distance he'd put between us. I knew this was just a one-night thing, but I guess I'd assumed I'd get a little cuddle or something after we'd done the deed.

Obviously, I'd been expecting too much.

"You didn't know what you were asking for!" Nate said, his voice thick with frustration as he ran his hands through his hair. "I shouldn't have let it get that far. I could have..."

What was happening here? I guess biting hard enough to break flesh was a little on the freaky kink side, and probably something we should have talked about first. Like the condom thing.

"Um, okay. Well, no harm, no foul, right? It's fine. I'm fine," I told him, attempting to smooth over this awkward encounter. "Are you fine?"

Nate made a distressed noise in the back of his throat, and I felt a twinge of sympathy for him because whatever he was worried about, it was definitely upsetting him. He was acting like he'd assaulted me or something, which didn't sit right with me. I'd been on board with everything that we'd done.

I opened my mouth to tell him that, but he spoke first.

"I can't trust myself around you," Nate said hoarsely, shaking his head slowly, snatching up his clothes and edging towards the door. "You test my control, I knew that. I shouldn't have let this happen. Fuck, I almost took away your choice. I could never... I would never forgive myself. I'm so sorry, Lou. So fucking sorry."

I barely caught the tail end of his apology as he scrambled up the stairs like there was a fire on his ass, the front door slamming shut with a bang that made me jump.

Had I only heard half of a conversation? It felt like I was missing a key piece of information. And as much as I was insulted and lowkey furious at being run out on, something had obviously spooked him. Nate hadn't looked like a cocky fuckboy walking away from a one-night stand. He'd looked... kind of terrified, to be honest.

Maybe if I actually understood what he'd been so upset about, we could have sat down and had a rational conversation and come to some kind of understanding, but he hadn't even given me the chance.

Did any of those hypotheticals matter when I was sitting here on a bed alone, naked, with Nate's cum still dripping down my thighs? No, not really.

I looked up at the ceiling, blinking away the hot rush of tears that threatened to fall. My throat was painfully tight, and I blew out a shuddering breath as I tried to get myself under control. I was stupid. He'd only come here for Scarlet anyway. It had been Scarlet who'd cracked his resolve. Scarlet who'd seduced him.

Scarlet didn't give a fuck about post-sex cuddles. That was the energy I needed to be channeling right now, because being Lou just wasn't cutting it.

Lou wanted to cry. Lou wanted to take the hottest shower imaginable and burn away the evidence from tonight. Actually, that idea had its merits. I didn't want to cry over this guy, but burning my skin off my body sounded like a completely reasonable response to a one night stand gone embarrassingly wrong.

Why had I been all worked up about finding a real penis to have sex with? Real penises came attached to real men, and real men were *the fucking worst.*

I angrily wiped away a few stray tears that had escaped my idiotic leaking eyes with the heel of my hand. *Enough.* Enough pining. I felt sticky, and gross, and a little ashamed, and I needed to wash away the evidence.

My fingers brushed the small indents at the base of my neck where his teeth had pressed against me. I felt strangely bereft at the idea of losing it, which was a fucking *bizarre* train of thought. Maybe Nate was right to freak out about the biting stuff.

I dashed up the stairs naked, never so grateful to live alone as I was at that moment, heading straight for the bathroom, blasting the shower as hot as it could go. As soon as I was clean, I was going to put on my comfiest pjs, get fucked up on boxed wine, and watch all five hours of the BBC's *Pride and Prejudice*. And maybe order myself a new dragon dildo to cheer myself up. Or one of the spiky demon ones, but in fun glittery pastel colors. Stupid fucking Nate and his stupid fucking real penis.

I knew my toys weren't going to be a substitute for what I'd just experienced though. It wasn't just that Nate *fucked* like a personal sex god made just for me. It was everything else too. Everything I'd been missing out on—warm flesh against mine, hot breath in my ear, soft lips brushing my skin... even with Frank, I hadn't experienced that. He was good in bed, but the positions he'd chosen hadn't been for intimacy. He'd preferred me spread eagle on the bed with my wrists bound, which had felt great, but not very cuddly. It had been *years* since someone had held me while I fell apart, and with Nate, I'd felt so... safe. Just for a moment. Until he'd *thoroughly* ruined it.

Maybe watching *Pride and Prejudice* wasn't a good idea. All this time, I thought I was a Lizzy. A little too honest, a little disillusioned with life, but maybe one day I'd find my Darcy and we'd fall in love and be aloof together, and everything would turn out okay.

Oh god. I wasn't Lizzy at all. I was *Charlotte*, except I'd rather settle into spinsterhood than settle for a Mr. Collins of my own. I'd already learned that lesson the hard way.

Ugh. Operation Seduction had been a successful failure. Now it was time for Operation Salvage Dignity.

Gabriel:

Good morning, beautiful Lou. Do you have plans today?

I drummed a mindless beat on my phone screen with my thumb nails, chewing on my lower lip as I contemplated a reply. Gabriel had messaged me a couple times over the past few days since *the Nate incident*, and I'd been polite but not flirty in the slightest since deciding men were the devil and all. I felt bad, he probably thought I was insane, suggesting he get my number then being so formal in my messages.

Maybe it was better to just nip any and all flirtations in the bud now. I didn't really *want* to, though. Gabriel had been cool and interesting, and I wanted to get to know him better even if real-life dick was firmly off the table, at least until I'd left Fairbanks.

Me:

Just finishing up some painting, then work stuff. You?

That was fine, right? I-want-to-be-friends vibes? I needed a handbook.

The past few days had passed in a strange blur as I tried to reconcile the way I felt with the way I should be feeling, because they absolutely were not the same. I should feel... fine? I mean, annoyed, sure. Disrespected? Absolutely. I felt like I had the right to be angry at Nate, and I was, but there were also all these other emotions that frankly had no business occupying space in my mind.

So Nate wasn't my soulmate. There was nothing wrong with having wild sex with a few frogs before I fucked my prince, or something like that. So why was I so *emotional* about all of it? I'd been getting rid of clutter, cleaning, and spackling the walls as a distraction, and frankly, they were all dangerous activities to do when my stupid feelings were all over the place. Too mindless. Too much time for *thinking*.

In the end, I'd decided that not all of these crazy feelings were related to Nate in particular. Most of them were, but there was this lingering sadness that I knew was all me and my own fucking issues. I'd been one foot out the door with Scarlet, still using the identity for my social media profiles, but giving up the cam stuff and slowly trying to figure out who I was outside of my online persona. The interlude with Nate had knocked me back a few steps.

Was Lou even worth knowing? Scarlet was an act, but the only success I'd ever achieved in my life, financially at least, had been through her. She was the one who was desirable and confident and interesting. When I'd tried to seduce Nate by just being myself, I felt like a weak copy of Scarlet, even though in theory, I was the original.

Whatever ideas I had about at least ditching the wig for my social media profiles and revealing the real person underneath had died a cold death. I guess the accessories were coming in my suitcase. What a pain.

Gabriel:

I'm finishing up some work too. You sound busy, but I hope we get a chance to catch up soon.

Well, I guess he'd taken the brush off. It didn't feel as comforting as I thought it would.

I dressed in an old pair of tie dye sweatpants and matching hoodie that I'd deemed as my painting clothes, with a ridiculous amount of layers underneath because I had to open the windows while I was painting, even though it was five degrees outside.

Ugh, that train of thought just brought me back to Nate's abrupt exit all over again. It had been even colder when he'd shown up, we'd had seven inches of snow that day, and I couldn't remember him even wearing a coat, let alone shoes. I hadn't seen a vehicle either. He'd just appeared out of thin air on my doorstep.

That was... objectively weird.

My closest neighbors were hidden by trees separating the properties, and while I had no idea who lived in those houses, they were still too far for anyone to walk here in the snow with no shoes on.

I mean, why would anyone *want* to? Maybe I'd dodged a bullet. Maybe Nate was a little... odd.

Not odd enough to be into biting apparently, but that particular desire had taken me off-guard too. In my limited sexual experience, I'd never begged a dude to sink his teeth into me before. I'd never even *fantasized* about it until Nate's monster cock had ruined me.

Now I was fantasizing about it *a lot*. I was ruined. Nate had ruined me. I would never be able to have sex with anyone again. He and his stupidly perfect, thick cock and all his muscles, and his tats, and his ridiculously great fucking face. He'd rolled his hips with such stripper-like precision, I could have sworn *'Pony'* by Ginuwine started playing at some point while he was fucking me into the mattress.

And his *mouth*. God, why had no one ever warned me how dangerously addictive oral sex was? What an introduction. If there was a way I could just have Nate's mouth without all the rest of him, I'd seriously consider it.

His mouth felt pretty great on my neck too.

Maybe I'd developed some kind of vampire fetish? Maybe Nate had a vampire fetish too, and that's why he'd freaked. Or he was a cannibal and worried that he'd lose control if he got a taste of my flesh.

The curious part of my brain that obviously didn't know what was good for myself had a lot of follow up questions about that. Like *a lot*. But tracking down Nate to ask him those questions was an idea that had 'humiliation' written all over it, so I did my best to shove my curiosity down deep and focus on things I could control. Like painting my living room.

I hooked my phone up to the speakers and blasted some *Nine to Five* as I taped over all the baseboards, singing along as I worked. My granny had *loved* this song—or any song by our one true queen, Dolly Parton—and listening to it took me back to standing on a dining chair at the kitchen counter, making biscuits and gravy together and singing at the top of our lungs. My grandparents weren't perfect people—they had addiction issues of their own which had definitely contributed to my mom's—but the weeks I spent living with them were always like a vacation from my real life. A vacation that ended abruptly whenever my mom would show up looking sober enough to drag me back to the trailer.

Shaking off that irritating memory, I set up my ladder and filled up my little paint cup so I could paint the edges of the walls first. I may not have my shit together in a lot of ways, but I was determined to break the cycles I'd grown up in at least.

The repetition of the movement made my shoulder muscles burn, but it was mostly a mindless job which was my nemesis right now. Any time I had a free minute to myself, I started thinking more with my vagina than my brain.

Maybe if I dressed up as Scarlet, went to Nate's studio, and asked *really* nicely, he'd let me get a personal dildo made modeled on his package. One with a suction base for maximum impalation impact. Casting a mold was a pretty straightforward process, and frankly, he owed me.

Edges of the wall done, I switched to the roller and was relieved when the process started moving along much faster. I immediately loved the brighter, cleaner palette on the wall. It modernized the entire space, and hopefully would add some value when the realtor came to assess it. Why hadn't I done this sooner? I could have lived in a house I actually liked the look of instead of selling it to someone else.

Doesn't matter. Soon I'd be gone, and I'd be too busy making new memories to reflect on old regrets.

With that thought in mind, I took a deep breath and forced my aching muscles to work faster.

By the time I was done, the house smelled pretty potent, and I decided to give it a couple of hours to air out. After a long shower which hopefully washed the lingering paint smell off me, I took extra care with my makeup, painting on my armor. Maybe it was stupid, but I felt more like a confident baddie that could take on the world when my eyeliner wings were sharp enough to cut glass, and my face was highlighted and contoured to perfection. Pity about the stupid neck gaiter I had to wear over half my face to stop myself from freezing, but I was in the mood for some food that I didn't have to cook myself and a fancy coffee, so I was dragging my ass to the coffee shop.

I hadn't bumped into Nate around town yet, even though I had been making more of an effort to leave the house instead of just holing up away from the world. It's not that I hadn't contemplated staying home in my pajamas, licking my wounded ego, but I was embarrassed at myself for considering it, honestly. The chemistry had been insane, sure, but I barely *knew* the guy. I was at peak hotness right now, and I was not wasting it on a dude who wasn't interested.

Maybe I should consider Gabriel's invitations, because these boobs needed to see some more goddamn action before they started migrating south.

Then again, maybe I should wait until after I'd left Fairbanks. I did not need to be dealing with another tap-and-gap situation while I was trying to get my shit together to move.

I shoved my laptop into my oversized purse, wrapped myself up in my layers, and exited through the side door to the garage, proud that I was actually going to sit in a comfy chair in a coffee shop and work like a professional. With pants on! In public!

I didn't even need dick. I was a badass.

As I reversed out onto the driveway, I glanced back at the house and noticed a package on the front porch that I definitely hadn't spotted before. Had someone knocked? I didn't think so, but I had been singing *Life is a Highway* at the top of my lungs at one point, so maybe I'd missed it. I closed the garage door, and let myself out of the idling SUV, jogging as best I could over the snow to see what it was. Crap, I really needed to shovel the porch steps. *Later.*

The brown box in front of the door looked pretty unassuming from a distance, but once I got close enough to read the address label, fear made the blood rush so loudly in my ears that I couldn't hear anything else.

Louisiana Taylor.

Nothing else. No addresses—either mine or a return one. This had been hand delivered, and while *theoretically* it could be something innocent, I highly doubted it was. Frank was the only person in recent years who'd called me 'Louisiana' unironically, everyone else in my life knew I preferred 'Lou'.

I hesitated, staring at the stupid thing. There was probably some kind of procedure for handling suspicious packages, but I doubted there was anything ominous in there, right? Frank was trying to woo me, he wasn't going to send me a horse's head or anything.

Besides, I was curious.

I jogged back to the car and dug around for a pen I could use to stab the seals, making a mental note to empty my car of all the crap I seemed to accumulate every time I used it, before heading back to the Box of Doom.

It was probably nothing. I was probably being ridiculous.

My gloves were still in the car and my hands were starting to hurt from the cold, but I moved as quickly as I could in spite of the numbness to get the thing open.

The contents were hidden by a layer of tissue paper, but there was a small printed note on the top that I reluctantly picked up.

Pick out something for our next meeting. Your choice. -F

I scoffed as I crumpled the note up, gently lifting up the paper to find exactly what I suspected I'd find inside. La Perla lingerie. Way to be predictable, Frank.

Disgusted at the "gift" and the intention behind it, I closed the box and brought it with me to my car, shoving it into the passenger's seat.

Someone at Goodwill was about to have their mind blown.

BROOKS

Chapter 8

I was so fucking bored. I was tempted to stir up some trouble, just for something to fucking *do*. I'd already gone around the rental house in my wolf form and rubbed myself all over Gabriel and Nate's beds to annoy their cats. I was up to date on my editing, my clients had the images they'd ordered, and I'd listed the spares for sale. I'd even overhauled my entire website yesterday, just for something to do. I was never this on top of my workload.

Maybe I needed to go to a bar and meet someone. A little winter fling might be the solution to all my problems. Or the cause of more. Either way, at least my life wouldn't be so dull.

At this point, things were so dire that I was contemplating making a video montage of all the pictures I'd taken of Nate looking sad recently, set to *The Sound of Silence* and playing it for him when he got home.

Honestly, I'd be doing him a favor. At least if he hit me or something, he'd be experiencing *some* kind of emotion. He'd basically drifted through life in a trance these past few days. Gabriel was contemplating an intervention.

Hm, maybe I should do the montage. Every intervention needed a montage. I'd start on it when I got back to the house.

Nate was at work, and I decided to head to the studio to pester him there for something to fill my time. It's not like there was nothing to do here, but snow really wasn't my jam. I'd grown up in Colorado and left as soon as I could, avoiding cold climates as much as possible ever since. My wolf was totally in his element, but I was... not. I wanted to go back to photographing lush, vibrant vegetation and tropical birds. All my photos here were so... monochromatic. Snow, snow, and more fucking snow.

I'd been super into photographing urban decay recently, and I had a list of ghost towns that I could be visiting if I wasn't stuck here supporting Nate through his premature midlife crisis. I had some *amazing* shots from Greece that had sold really well. Maybe we could head down to New Mexico next, if Nate wasn't ready to leave US soil. There was plenty to see on Route 66.

I paused outside the door to Mountain Ink, using my enhanced hearing to make sure Nate was alone before I barged in.

"You sound relaxed as usual," I announced as I let myself in, the sound of Nate's angry stomping clear even through the door. Actually, his grumpiness was an improvement over the dead inside vibe he'd been giving off recently.

"What do you want?" Nate grumbled, aggressively cleaning the studio.

"I would love to know what your damage is, for a start," I remarked, leaning back against the door with my arms crossed. "You were pissy when we arrived in town, but you've been downright feral these past few days. Is it so bad having us around?"

"What?" Nate asked in surprise, pausing his manic cleaning. "No, it isn't you guys. I'm glad you came, even with your delusional ideas about me leaving and your dislike of the snow."

'Dislike' was a massive understatement, but I'd let him get away with it.

"So? What's eating you then?" I pressed. "Did you meet a nice cougar shifter to settle down with then get cold feet?" I teased.

Nate shot me a withering look, resuming his wipedown of the tattoo seat. The smell of disinfectant burned my sensitive nose, and I wondered for the millionth time how Nate coped. If it wasn't the chemical smells, there were just so many *people* smells he had to contend with. "Don't even joke about that. My mother sent me *suggestions* last night."

"Yikes," I replied with a grimace. I hadn't spoken to my mother in over a decade, but I could imagine the kind of woman she'd pair me up with. Pure wolf shifter, as high up in the pack hierarchy as possible, and young enough to pop out a bunch of pups. I'd only met Nate's parents once, but I imagined his mom would have the same criteria, except with cougars rather than wolves.

His parents weren't terrible like mine were, but they struck me as pretty old school about that kind of thing.

"Big yikes," he muttered. "It's not like there's an abundance of unmated female cougar shifters my age. The ones she sent me were all either eighteen or nineteen, mostly in California. I felt like a filthy old man just for looking at the fucking list."

"35 isn't old," I laughed. God, I hoped not. I was only a couple of years younger. "But you'd have very different life experiences from an 18-year-old I guess."

Age gap aside, most shifters didn't travel the way we did. He'd have very little in common with an 18-year-old who'd barely left her territory. Alaska didn't have much of a cougar population either, and Nate's mother would expect the girl to move up here and pop out a bunch of babies. It would be... an adjustment, for any young woman, that was for sure.

Nate shuddered like he was imagining an awkward first date and I grinned at him. I didn't think that this was what had actually been bothering him these past few days, but I let it slide. Nate played things pretty close to the chest most of the time, even with me and Gabriel. It bothered me occasionally, even though it shouldn't. We weren't a pack, he didn't owe me shit.

"Moving back here was my compromise with my family," he said, finally putting the gross spray away. "I didn't agree to shit about finding a mate."

Guilt flashed across his face before he could hide it, and I frowned at him, trying to find the words to tell him that he didn't need to feel guilty about not taking a mate. Except I wasn't great with serious chat, and really needed Gabriel for this shit.

"Take a break and come get a coffee with me?" I suggested instead. I'd already tried to drag Gabriel out of the house, but he was working on a blog post for a luxury travel agent website today and refused to be distracted.

"Can't, I have a client coming in soon." Nate's tense posture relaxed slightly, eyes brightening at the prospect of getting to work. "It's a huge cover up piece. I'm looking forward to it."

"I'm glad you've got something to get excited about," I replied with a snort. *Workaholic.* "I guess I'll just go drink coffee on my own and be miserable."

Nate raised a disbelieving eyebrow at me. "You've never met a stranger in your life, I'm sure you'll survive."

"If I don't, clear my internet history," I called over my shoulder as I left the studio. Usually, I *was* pretty good at meeting people, but I'd been in a funk lately. Maybe Nate's misery was catching on.

There were cafes close to the studio, but I opted to drive downtown instead. I had my camera with me as often inspiration struck while I was just out and about. Once I was caffeinated, I'd explore a little more and see what I discovered. Maybe I'd encounter a miracle and find something that wasn't covered in snow.

I parked up in front of The Arctic Brew, which was pretty unassuming looking on the outside, but busy enough to make me think the coffee tasted good at least. I shouldered my satchel and walked briskly from the SUV to the shop, resenting the icy ground every step of the way, but the inside was cozy and smelled delicious, so I supposed it wasn't the worst place to kill an hour stuck in my own company.

I ordered the most indulgent, sugary coffee on the menu and a pastry before looking around for somewhere to sit. There were a couple of comfy armchairs at the back with small round tables in front of them. One of them was occupied by the prettiest redhead I'd ever seen, working idly on a slim rose gold laptop on the table in front of her, head tilted thoughtfully to the side as she looked at something on the screen.

Fuck me, she was stunning. Dainty features, rich red hair, long dark eyelashes. It wasn't just that she was objectively pretty with her styled hair and symmetrical features, she just had this *energy* about her that drew me in. It was like she was *trying* to look cool and aloof, and pulling it off pretty well, but there was this underlying vulnerability that had me intrigued.

I doubted a human would notice it, but my animal side could spot prey a mile away, and this woman was definitely prey trying to be a predator. My wolf was as fascinated as I was.

Everything about her was perfectly coiffed and styled, which made me think she was a high maintenance kind of girl. But I was a high maintenance kind of guy, so that didn't bother me too much. These boyband-level good looks didn't just *happen*.

I wound my way through the tables, drawing a few second looks from the locals because I was an attractive dude, but no second looks from the woman I wanted to pay attention to me.

"Hello."

Was I doing my sexy deep voice? Why, yes. Yes, I was.

She gave me a lingering onceover, eyes definitely heating with approval, before shooting me a tight *I-am-busy* smile and returning to her laptop. There was a familiarity to her delicious chocolatey scent, but I couldn't identify it underneath the smells of the coffee shop and the faint paint fumes that seemed to cling to her skin. My wolf grumbled in irritation at the chemical stench.

"Ouch," I laughed. "I must be losing my touch."

Was it my hair? I hadn't been styling it as much since we'd been here because I was always wearing beanies anyway.

"I highly doubt that," she replied drily, before scrunching her eyes shut for a moment, like she was annoyed with herself for engaging with me.

"Oh good," I said cheerfully, dropping down in the armchair next to hers. "That would be a crime. I'm Brooks, what's your name?"

"Not interested," she replied primly, barely sparing me a glance.

"Fair enough." I held my hands up in surrender. I was intrigued by her, but I could take no for an answer. I mean, I'd probably sulk a little, but that was my problem, not hers. "Sorry, Red. I meant no offense."

She scoffed slightly at the nickname—not my most creative work—but her lips twitched in amusement, so I was taking it as a small win. Little Red Riding Hood and the Big Bad Wolf Shifter. It was kind of poetic.

I thanked the server for my coffee and pastry and pulled out my phone to kill time as I snacked, flipping idly through my social media apps. I followed many people that I'd met during my travels from all over the world, and I could admit I was more than a little jealous when I saw their photos come up on my feed. It wasn't even that they were in warm places, it's that they were out *doing stuff*. I wasn't used to being so idle all the time.

Red made a frustrated noise and I glanced over as her laptop ran out of battery.

"I don't suppose you're hiding a laptop charger under all those muscles?" she sighed, glancing at me.

"Ooh, was that a little bit of flirting I detected, Ms. Not Interested?" I teased.

"I thought my name was Red?" she shot back.

"Hey, you're the one who named yourself 'Not Interested'. I assume 'Not' is your first name, which is why I oh-so-kindly bestowed a cute nickname on you. 'Not' is a pretty strange name, you know."

"And you're a pretty strange guy," she laughed. "My name is Lou, but I'm still not interested."

"Maybe I'm not interested. Maybe I was just saying hello and you assumed I was flirting with you," I said smugly.

"How presumptuous of me," Lou agreed seriously. "I mean, you were eyefucking me from the minute you approached, and one hundred percent used your sexiest fuckboy voice to say hi, but you're right. I shouldn't assume anything."

I grinned at Lou, totally losing my "fuckboy" cool in the face of her snarky attitude.

"Okay, I'll let you in on a little secret. I *was* flirting with you," I told her conspiratorially. Lou gasped dramatically, clutching her chest like she was scandalized.

"You *rogue*," she chastised.

"You talking dirty to me, Red?" I chuckled.

"Nope," she replied instantly, popping the 'p'. "I have sworn off men. No offense, but you're all the devil."

"None taken. Well, a bit taken," I added as an afterthought. "Want me to punch the guy for you?"

"Now who's talking dirty?" Lou asked, fanning her face. "And no. No punching required. However, I have banned myself from real-life penises for the foreseeable future so, you know. Go shoot your shot with one of the *many* admirers you seem to have collected since you walked in the door."

I glanced around, finding a few eyes on me and more than a few on Lou. Pft. She did not have a leg to stand on when it came to calling me out on my *many admirers*.

Wait, *real-life* penises?

"Are you passing through Fairbanks?" Lou continued before I could ask an entirely inappropriate follow-up question about fake penises. Or dead penises? *Real-life* definitely left room for interpretation.

"I'm staying for the winter," I replied, that reminder killing any joy my dick had been mustering.

"Oh? Are you a fan of subzero temperatures or something?" she asked, raising an eyebrow at me.

"How did you know?"

"The hoodie gave it away," Lou replied, the corners of her mouth lifting as she ran her eyes down my outfit. "Hoodie, jeans, beanie, no snow boots, no gloves. It's like you want to catch hypothermia."

Ah, fuck. I probably should make more of an effort to fit in with the human locals. There were plenty of shifters around these parts, but they tended to stick to the woods. Just like my old pack did in Colorado, but I did my best not to think about them or I got all punchy.

"I should probably do some shopping, huh? Maybe you can come with me. Show me how to dress like a local." I waggled my eyebrows and she snorted in amusement.

"I have zero desire to witness you undressing. I get the feeling you have it down to a fine art." *I did.* "Let me guess, you do the whole pull the t-shirt over your head with one hand thing that makes your biceps bulge and shows off your rippling abs to maximum advantage?"

"Wouldn't you?" I teased. "I work with what I've got."

"I get that. Trust me, I know the effect of a good bend-at-the-waist to take my pants off," Lou replied absently, reaching for her coffee while my dick attempted to launch itself out of my jeans. "However, as I said, no more men. Unfortunately, I won't be available to bear witness to your strip show."

"In case you lose control and jump my bones?" I asked hopefully.

"I mean, you're passably good-looking, I guess it's a small risk," Lou said drily, eyes sparkling with mischief. I wasn't used to a woman giving me shit. It was cocky as shit to admit it, but they tended to throw themselves at me because I was pretty, and definitely looked like I was a *good time* rather than a *long time* kind of guy.

This conversation was the best foreplay I'd ever had.

"Okay, okay," I conceded. "What about we just be friends? I'll try on clothes in the dressing room, with the door shut and everything. And if you change your mind and decide you need to fuck the last guy out of your system, I'll politely consider your request like any good friend would."

Lou laughed before she could get her cool girl mask in place, and I grinned at her, already planning all the ways I could get her to make that noise again.

"I guess if you're only here for the winter, then we can be friends. I'm leaving then anyway," she said with a shrug, though I was ninety percent sure she was covertly checking me out under those long lashes.

"Oh yeah? Off to see the world?" I teased, not really expecting her to say yes.

"Definitely," Lou replied with a decisive nod.

"Perfect. We'll be besties by then. We'll survive the winter—best friend cuddling for warmth—then jump on a flight to Phuket and you can sleep with your head on my shoulder the whole way, snoring all cute like—"

"I do not snore," Lou said indignantly.

"—and get adjoining hotel rooms when we get there, then spend a couple of days checking out the tourist attractions and eating street food at Naka Market before we travel to Ko Pha-ngan for the Full Moon Party." I sighed blissfully at the mental image, tipping my head back against the plush armchair.

Obviously Gabriel would be there too, but one thing at a time. I had to convince Lou to be my friend first, then she could be his friend too. That would probably be okay. I guess.

She blinked at me like I was insane.

"Not keen on Thailand?" I asked, grinning at her. "I'm flexible."

"Uh, I'm very keen on Thailand. I'm very keen on everywhere," Lou added, shaking her head slightly. "I'm a little wary of *you* though. Energetic adults make me nervous. If life hasn't beaten you down by this point, you're either a sociopath or on something."

I choked slightly on my drink. "Are you always this optimistic?"

She shot me a sugary sweet smile that didn't reach her eyes. "Only on days ending with 'y'. You sure you still want to be my friend?"

"More sure, if anything," I admitted. "I've been bored out of my fucking mind since I got here, and you, Red, are a breath of fresh air."

Lou chewed on her bottom lip, looking at me like she was assessing the truthfulness of my words, but she wouldn't find any lies here.

"Have you been to Thailand before?" Lou asked, curiosity finally getting the better of her. Hell. Yes. I had an opening, now I just had to demonstrate that I wasn't a totally garbage conversationalist. Easy.

"Twice. Want to get some donuts and look at pictures?"

Lou blinked at me. "I'm trying to eat mindfully."

"Vegan donuts," I agreed, already heading towards the counter, thinking of the photos I was going to show her. My last trip to Thailand had been when the guys and I spent a month in Koh Chang, and I had some amazing beach photos that I was determined to impress Lou with. I wouldn't show her any of Nate or Gabriel, obviously. What if she liked one of them better than me? Fuck taking that risk. I'd just throw in a few shirtless pics of me and see what happened. With my new friend.

For the first time in weeks, I wasn't even the slightest bit bored.

NATE

Chapter 9

Lou grumbled irritably to herself as she shoveled the snow off the front steps that led up to her porch, huffing with exertion.

I shouldn't be here. I really should not be here. This was borderline stalking. Except no one would accuse a cougar of stalking.

They *might* shoot me though. Lou didn't strike me as the type to shoot an animal that was just lurking on the outskirts of her property. Then again, a lot about Lou had surprised me. Almost everything.

I wasn't planning on just hovering in the trees outside her property in my fur. I was going to talk with her. I'd left in a panic the other night, and when I had finally calmed down enough to think clearly, I'd realized how fucking awful the situation would have looked from her perspective. How awful it was. I'd thought of almost nothing else since then.

I'd just *abandoned* her, like she was just some meaningless bed buddy. I was so fucking ashamed, I couldn't even look at myself in the mirror.

I would never disrespect anyone by treating them that way under normal circumstances, but those hadn't been normal circumstances.

I had run because I'd been half a second away from irreversibly mating Lou for life. Life! My teeth had been pressing into her skin and she'd been fucking begging me to bite her. Obviously, she had no clue what that would have led to, but I knew better. Lou had tested my self-control from the moment I met her, and I'd stupidly given in, knowing what the risks would be.

I wasn't a hundred percent sure if a mating bond would have taken without Lou actively accepting it, but the risk had definitely been there.

God, I could have ruined her life.

Running had been the right thing to do at the time, but when I thought about it from Lou's perspective...

She must hate me. I hated myself.

Today, I was in control enough to apologize before avoiding her forever. She was temptation like I'd never encountered before, and I had to steer clear for both of our sakes.

I dropped the bundle of clothes I'd been carrying in my teeth and forced myself to shift back. My cougar snarled in response, not wanting to let me lead, already dangerously enamored with this interesting, vibrant, unexpected woman.

Idiot. Idiot man and idiot cat.

As I finished dressing, I heard a vehicle approach, which was unusual since I'd been here every day since my unceremonious exit, and I'd never seen anyone visit her. Keeping to the treeline, I moved around until I had a better view of her driveway as whoever it was exited the vehicle, and froze as the wind blew towards me and I caught a whiff of her guest's scent on the breeze.

Wolf.

Foreign wolf.

Nothing about the way Lou was holding herself—frozen in place, shovel clutched tightly in one hand—indicated that she was expecting company, and my hackles rose even further.

Don't get possessive. She's not yours.

The man who'd climbed out of the passenger side definitely didn't look like a local in his expensively tailored coat and shiny leather boots. He was older than me, with perfectly styled salt-and-pepper hair, and frown lines on his forehead and around his mouth. Despite his advancing age, there was no doubt in my mind that this was a powerful shifter who was not to be fucked with. My cougar had picked up that much from his scent already.

Why the fuck was a wolf shifter visiting Lou?

There was a wolf pack not far from my brother's place in the woods, and they came into town enough for me to be vaguely familiar with their scents, but I didn't recognize this guy's.

But Lou definitely knew him, judging by the way she'd tensed up.

"Louisiana," he drawled, holding his arms out wide like he was expecting a hug. "Though I must say, I prefer Scarlet. I think we'll proceed with Scarlet, hm?" He tilted his head to the side, examining her. "The red hair, you can keep though."

"How generous of you," Lou snapped, a tiny tremble in her voice betraying the fear she was trying to hide. *Fuck.* There hadn't been a chance for me to ask about Scarlet after I'd run out on her, but I remembered Lou referring to herself as a camgirl. So this guy was... a client? Not one she was very excited to see. "What do you want, Frank?"

Frank...

"You, of course. I thought I'd been quite clear about that, Scarlet. Originally, I was content for you to reside here in Fairbanks until I had suitable accommodation for you, but since you've been difficult about it, I think it is time for you to move to New York now."

Nope.

I strode out of the trees behind Lou, immediately catching the guy's attention, though it took her a little longer to notice. She followed his gaze over her shoulder, eyes widening in surprise when she saw me, before narrowing them in irritation.

I deserved that. Hopefully she'd let me play at knight in shining armor for a few minutes, even though we both knew I was the troll from the dungeon.

"Lou," I rumbled, my cougar close to the surface. "Everything okay?"

I saw the split second when she decided that I was the lesser of two evils. Lou may not have been a shifter, but she could sense that she was caught between two predators, and it was better to ally with one than to stand alone.

She reached for me the moment I was within grasping distance, and I was a greedy son of a bitch because I happily let her tug me closer, wrapping my arms around her waist and keeping her pulled firmly back against my body.

"Oh look, it's my big sexy male conveniently coming to visit me. Everything is fine. This is Frank. He's just leaving," she clipped.

"Leaving?" he chuckled humorlessly. "My friends and I just got here. And New York to Fairbanks is an awfully long flight. I think we'll need some time here in town to recover."

I knew the kinds of wolves who lived in New York, and I very fucking strongly objected to the idea of Lou anywhere near them. Wasn't the New York Alpha called Frank something? Ashford? Shit, shit, shit.

How the fuck had Lou gotten mixed up with this asshole?

"New friend?" Frank asked Lou with an oily smile. I didn't like him looking at her. Or talking to her. Or sharing oxygen with her. My arm tightened around her waist like it had a mind of its own, pulling her around so her front was pressed against my side, my fingers splayed possessively over the curve of her ass.

Back off, motherfucker.

"Yup, got myself a big, bad boyfriend now, so you can take a hike," Lou said drily, patting my chest. "Stop sending me shit while you're at it."

If I held her any tighter, I'd leave fingerprints on her ass. What was he sending her? How long had this been going on?

Frank gave me a cool assessing look, not seeming threatened by me in the least, which made sense because I wasn't a threat to him. My cougar could usually take down a wolf pretty easily, but Frank was an Alpha. He'd be bigger and stronger than most.

"I'm not worried," he said eventually, giving Lou a cold smile. "Since it's clearly not serious."

"How the fuck would you know?" Lou scoffed indignantly.

Because we were unmated. Almost every inch of Lou's skin was covered, but he'd be able to scent that she wasn't mated. This was... a potentially problematic lie for us to run with, but I'd be a real fucking asshole to contradict her.

I owed her this lie. More than that, there was a not insignificant part of me that wished it could be true.

"Just a feeling," Frank replied with a deceptively relaxed half shrug, dark blue eyes scanning the way I was holding her, missing nothing.

"Well, you're wrong. We're very serious," Lou replied primly. "We've picked out rings. We're having a Cinderella-themed wedding in Florida. Nate is going to wear a powder-blue suit with tails and a tophat, I'll wear a giant ball gown and tiara, and arrive by carriage with my seven bridesmaids. Nate is great like that. He gives me everything I want," she continued in a completely deadpan voice. I couldn't decide if she was fucking with Frank, or me. Probably both.

Frank scoffed. "Your pretty lies might work on someone who doesn't know you so well, Scarlet. You're more of a simple sunset wedding on the beach type of girl."

"Is that what you had?" Lou asked sweetly. "With the wife you forgot to mention?"

The jealousy that this asshole knew more about Lou than I did morphed into anger on her behalf. Why didn't he have a mate? Had he not mated his wife?

Frank tutted disapprovingly. "So hung up on all the wrong things, sweet Scarlet. It's a business arrangement, nothing to concern yourself over." His eerie eyes remained on Lou for an uncomfortably long beat before sliding to me. "How fortunate for you that this arrangement didn't go too far."

"Too far?" Lou replied dubiously. "If you mean before he fucks me, I'm afraid you're too late. My vagina has already been ruined for all other men."

It wasn't the time, but my ego swelled in response to her words anyway. As well as something else that I was a little less proud of, considering the circumstances.

Frank's lips curled up in an unpleasant smile, his eyes still on me. "That is not what I meant. Secrets are poison to a relationship, you know."

"Oh, secrets?" Lou gasped, clutching her chest dramatically. "Like a secret *wife*? I could keep going all day. If you ever think I'm going to forget that you are *married*, you're sorely mistaken."

"There are secrets with far greater consequences," Frank replied smoothly. "And when you're ready to hear them, I'd be more than happy to enlighten you. It seems... *wrong*, to keep you in the dark this way."

My heartbeat pounded in my chest, and even though I knew he could hear it, I couldn't get it to slow down. If he told Lou about shifters, I was going to let my cougar have free reign over his goddamn spinal cord. The shifter world was no place for unclaimed humans. If Lou found out about shifters without a mating mark for protection, it would paint a goddamn target on her back. Alphas *killed* humans who accidently found out about shifters near their territory.

"Do you two know each other or something?" Lou asked irritably. She twisted back to look up at me, her eyes narrowed in suspicion.

"No," I replied evenly, my fingers flexing against her puffy jacket. "We've never met. He's just talking shit to get a rise out of you. Don't bother listening to it."

"Mm, you're right. He's already proven himself to be a liar. I'd be pretty naive to listen to anything he had to say at this point," Lou said, agreeing with me with a readiness that made my cougar want to purr, even though I knew it was all an act. There was no way she actually trusted me, even if she was willing to pretend for Frank's benefit.

God, she had absolutely no idea of the kind of danger she was in, and panic made my throat feel tight as I tried to decide whether it was better to stop this lie in its tracks or not. No, it was too late for that. Frank had already seen me hanging around her, there was no guarantee he'd keep his mouth shut about shifters even if I removed myself from the picture.

Staying close and protecting Lou up close was safer than putting distance between us and *hoping* Frank had some sense of honor.

Frank tutted. "Again, you are hung up on all the wrong things, silly Scarlet. However, I'm a generous man, I'll give you some time to come to your senses," he continued. "Pretty scenery around here. It'll make for a nice... *vacation*."

I fought the urge to haul Lou even closer to me, not wanting Frank to gain the satisfaction of seeing he'd rattled me. Or giving him any *more* satisfaction, because my heart was still slamming against my ribs like it was trying to escape my body. Lou was calmer than I was, pinning him with an unimpressed glare as her hand stroked my chest absently. God, maybe she could hear my heartbeat too.

"It's a free country," Lou replied lightly, lifting one shoulder. If I couldn't feel how tense she was, how heavily she leaned into me despite the fact that I was probably her least favorite person on the planet, I wouldn't have even realized Frank was bothering her. It was incredible. "Now if you'll excuse us, you interrupted right when I was about to get my womb wrecked. Bye."

With a combination of brass balls and a total lack of awareness about the level of danger, Lou turned her back on the most powerful predator I'd ever encountered, stepping out of my arms and stomping back towards her little pink house.

Frank returned to his vehicle with a derisive snort, and I didn't miss the fact that he had two other people in the car with him who I was confident were shifters from his pack, probably his seconds.

Fuck, I hated to admit it, but he had good reason to be so arrogant. Nothing about this situation was in Lou's favor, and she didn't even fully understand why.

And I couldn't tell her, I reminded myself as I followed her back into the house. Which was going to make it particularly difficult to keep her safe from a threat she couldn't see, since she already hated me.

Frank was an apex predator who had locked onto Lou as his prey. A fake relationship with me might not be enough to shake him off entirely, not without a mating mark, but it might buy her some time.

Best case scenario—he and his wolf got offended that she'd settled for a less powerful shifter and backed off purely out of irritation. But for that to work, she had to look like she'd chosen me, because he'd see any cracks in the facade as a challenge.

Worst case scenario was that he refused to leave her alone unless she had a mating bite that officially took her off the market.

No, the worst case scenario was that he told her about shifters out of spite and painted a target on her back.

My muscles rippled under my shirt, my cougar fighting for dominance even knowing now was very much *not the fucking time.*

The house reeked of paint fumes and I choked slightly on the overpowering smell before reluctantly shutting and locking the front door behind me. I fully intended to question Lou about Frank the moment I had the front door shut behind us, but Lou just kept going, through the entryway and living room at an impressively brisk pace. There were drop cloths all over the floor, half the walls had been painted, and half empty boxes covered the couch. Lou had been *busy.*

I hurried after her, into the narrow galley kitchen where she marched straight to the back door, unlocking it and holding it open expectantly, finally focusing her attention on me.

Lou looked at me like she hated me. Like if she could incinerate me on the spot, she'd do it without a second thought. My chest felt like it was caving in under the weight of my own shame.

I'd done the right thing, I know I had, but fuck if it didn't hurt like a pickaxe to the heart, knowing I'd put that hatred in her gaze.

"Get out," Lou ordered flatly.

"We need to talk—"

"Thanks for doing me a solid back there, but I have nothing to say to you."

"Then just listen," I implored, the panic making my throat constrict. "That guy, Frank, he isn't exactly what you think he is."

"Thank you, Captain Obvious," Lou drawled, giving me a scathing look. "Hence why I am here, and not with him in New York. Because he's a lying liar who lies. Get out."

"But he's *here* now, Lou. You don't understand how dangerous he is," I growled, feeling frustrated that I couldn't just fucking *tell* her that the big bad wolf had her locked in his sights.

Lou scoffed. "He's a fancy finance guy from New York who can't take no for an answer, not like... the head of the mafia or something."

"How can you be sure of that?" I challenged, because that was probably the closest human analogy for a pack. "Wealthy, secretive, showed up with some goons in tow..."

"You're being ridiculous. You do realize I hate you as well, right?" Lou asked incredulously. "You're not the good guy in this scenario. You're also an asshole, just for different reasons. God, I hate men."

"I came here to apologize—"

"How clear your conscience feels isn't actually my concern," Lou interrupted. "You came here to make yourself feel better. Your apology doesn't mean shit to *me*."

I opened my mouth to argue before slamming it shut, realizing she was right. Of course. I should have known she'd never want to see me again. I'd come here to assuage my guilt.

"I have an IUD, by the way, so you don't need to worry that you got me pregnant. And I'm clean. Fuck, of all the people to spontaneously claim to be in a fake relationship with," she muttered, tipping her head back and staring at the ceiling like it could give her answers. "I should have called Mr. Hot Hardware Store Guy, he'd have been game. Or Coffee Shop Guy. Or just asked to borrow one of Ria's big scary boyfriends. She has spares."

The start of a growl rumbled in my chest before I could stop it, and Lou jumped slightly at the noise, giving me a puzzled look. *Fuck no, that wasn't happening.* Not the hardware store guy, or the coffee shop guy, or the fucking *bears*. Not that any of the Bernard brothers would go for it anyway, they would never disrespect their mate that way, but still.

If Lou needed a fake boyfriend, I was going to be that man for her.

"We can be in a fake relationship without me getting in your face," I said quietly. "Just keep me around, Lou. Can you just... believe that Frank is not a guy to be fucked with?"

Oh my god, I sounded so pathetic, but I had no idea how to explain any of this. Where was Gabriel with his smooth words and enchanting accent when I needed him?

"I'm not as helpless as you seem to think I am, despite the brain aneurysm I must have had out there that made me call you my boyfriend. I can handle Frank," Lou replied, tipping her chin up.

"No, you can't! Lou, this guy... he's not *normal*." I hesitated for a moment, my brain scrambling for a suitable explanation. "Can you just trust me?"

Lou gave me an incredulous look. "No, Nate. I do *not* trust you. Are you high? How can you even ask me that?"

I scrubbed a hand down my face, hating that she made sense. Of course she didn't trust me. But now I really *needed* her to trust me.

"Okay. That's fair," I conceded, trying not to show my very real panic on the outside. Most shifters were territorial as fuck. If I wasn't making my presence known, Frank would probably see it as an invitation to encroach. I couldn't stay here though. I'd only been in the house a few minutes and the smell of paint fumes was making me lightheaded. Besides, I could use the backup that Brooks and Gabriel provided.

"Maybe you could just come stay with me for a few days?" I suggested, trying to hide my wince as I said it.

Lou barked a startled laugh before looking at me like she was checking to see if I was actually serious.

"Ah, no. Definitely not. Did you hear literally any of the words I just said? The part about me hating you and not trusting you, et cetera, et cetera?"

"I did," I replied glumly, not entirely sure how I was going to convince her that this was the best idea when everything she'd said had been completely right. "You can still hate me. I deserve that. But maybe if you stay with me for a few days, Frank will lose interest and leave town. He's a big, fancy New York guy, right? Show him there's nothing here for him."

Show him that you're content to settle for a lesser shifter.

"No thanks," Lou replied breezily. For fuck's sake. I wish I'd bought my cell with me so I could phone a friend for advice. Gabriel was calmer and more empathetic, he'd do a better job of convincing her than I would. Brooks would probably try to seduce her.

Maybe it was a good thing he wasn't here.

"I have roommates," I tried again. "They're good guys. It wouldn't be just you and me, if that's what you're worried about."

Lou laughed bitterly. "Trust me, Nate. There is no part of me that is worried you're going to try to get in my pants again."

What? I mean, I was glad she wasn't worried, but she made it sound like I didn't *want* her, which was fucking ludicrous. I *wanted* her to a borderline unhealthy degree.

"I gotta say, I really don't understand why you're pushing this," Lou continued. "You made your feelings on me pretty clear."

"I shouldn't have left the way I did the other night, and I'm sorry. Trust me, it wasn't you—"

"Don't finish that sentence," Lou warned, olive eyes flashing with irritation and I grimaced. *'It's not you, it's me'* sounded like a cop out, even in my own head.

"I fucked up, okay? And I was just going to come here and say sorry, then leave you alone, but the Frank thing changes that."

"It doesn't change shit," Lou argued, shaking her head.

"You just waved a red flag in front of a bull," I snapped, running my fingers aggressively through my hair. "Stay with me, just for a few days. I swear, this is for your protection, Lou. I won't touch you, it's nothing like that."

My cougar growled in irritation, rising up impatiently. Lou frowned at me, her focus on my eyes, and I hoped like hell they weren't glowing.

129

"Look, sorry I implicated you in this, but you don't have to make it into a huge thing. I don't give a fuck if Frank comes here, I'm not going to perform for his benefit anyway. *Again.*" Lou added irritably under her breath. "You can resume your regularly scheduled brooding, or whatever it is you do." She gestured at the back door with an exaggerated flourish.

My heart pounded in my chest at the finality in her tone, my cougar lunging forward like he'd do a better job at convincing her than I was doing. The effort of holding back the shift made my muscles ripple under my shirt and my temper fray.

"You don't understand!" I practically shouted, fear making my heart pound in my chest. No shifter would leave someone they were interested in alone and unprotected, especially a human.

Lou gave me a cool look that would have made a lesser man cower. "Maybe when you've calmed down and are ready to speak to me without raising your voice, I'll consider listening to your explanation. In the meantime, *out.*" She punctuated the last word with an aggressive point at the door.

I was fucking all of this up, and its not like I had room for error with Lou. I hadn't missed the flicker of nervousness on her face when she'd given me marching orders. I was a lot bigger than her, and stronger than she even realized. I'd be a real asshole to hang around, making her feel unsafe. *More* of an asshole than I already was.

I sighed, annoyed with myself as I stalked past her, pausing on the threshold.

"You're right. It's unforgivable to speak to you in anger. But this conversation isn't over. That guy isn't going anywhere, and he's not going to give up without a fight. Let me keep you safe, Lou."

The brisk cold hit me in full force as I stepped outside and I inhaled deeply, forcing fresh air into my lungs, hoping it would clear my head. Lou already despised me, and each time I opened my goddamn mouth I made it ten times worse. I could have really used some backup, but I didn't have my phone and the idea of leaving Lou here alone was untenable to my cougar. The property only smelled faintly of Frank's lingering scent, but I knew he'd be back.

I briefly considered the merits of throwing Lou over my shoulder and dragging her perky ass to safety, but she'd probably have me arrested.

Maybe I could get a hold of Noah? His mate, Ria, was obviously friends with Lou—they'd come into the studio together when I'd first met her. Ria couldn't shift, but she'd grown up in a shifter family and was mated to three bear shifters. Maybe she could think of a better way to explain the situation to Lou? It would probably sound less... *psychotic* coming from her.

But Ria would probably suggest Lou go and stay with her, which made sense to me but made my cougar furious.

Lou had inadvertently put us both in a difficult position by claiming we were in a relationship, yet I couldn't find it in myself to be mad. Keeping her safe was really the least I could do after I'd put her at so much risk by almost biting her. Even if she hated me the entire time.

I'd just have to make sure I kept my teeth to myself.

"Are you just going to keep pacing in my yard?" Lou called out irritably, standing on the back porch with her arms crossed.

"We weren't finished talking," I replied simply, striding to the bottom of the steps and waiting, giving Lou space. She'd been right to kick me out. Fresh air had made me feel a little calmer.

"It seems we're at an impasse," Lou said lightly, raising an eyebrow at me. "You, for some bizarre reason, think I'm going to come and *stay at your house* just because my ex-sugar daddy is in town to *woo* me back. I would rather pierce my own nipples with a blunt safety pin than go anywhere with you."

Considering I was trained in body piercings and fucking *great* at them, that was extra insulting.

"Even for your own safety?" I asked tiredly. "You can meet my roommates first, if that would make you feel more comfortable—"

"My answer is no, Nate," Lou stated, no room for argument in her tone. "Whatever twisted ideas you have in your head about protecting me need to be put to rest. You don't owe me anything because we fucked one time. I don't need your charity."

She walked back into the house, shutting the screen door, then the back door with a quiet click as I scrubbed my hand over my face, wondering where to even begin in undoing all of those misconceptions. I definitely wasn't doing this as some kind of I-owe-you for the sex.

God, is that really what she thought? Her opinion of me was even lower than I realized. Nothing about what we'd shared had been transactional in my mind. It had been *amazing*.

Fuck.

I jogged back into the cover of the treeline, stripped out of my clothes and shifted. Hopefully Lou wasn't terrified of mountain lions, because she'd just earned herself one as a full time guard.

GABRIEL

Chapter 10

I sighed in irritation as I read through the feedback for the article about a reindeer ranch I'd submitted to a trendy online magazine I'd recently started writing for. *Not sexy enough.* How was I supposed to make reindeers sexy? Sometimes the feedback I got was so ridiculous, I questioned why I was writing for other people at all. Online content had been a different landscape when I had started doing this, and I didn't think I'd done enough to keep up with the changes.

My phone rang and I picked it up from the dining table I was using as a desk, absently glancing at the screen. Brooks was watching TV in the living room, and I expected Nate to call from wherever he was, asking what takeout we wanted for dinner again.

Lou flashed across the screen, and I almost dropped it in surprise. I'd given up on ever hearing from her, to be honest. Her cautious flirtiness at the hardware store had morphed into something one step above indifference over text messages, so I'd backed off.

I definitely wasn't expecting a phone call from her.

"Hello, querida," I said in my smoothest voice, perhaps playing up the accent just a little, because if this was the only chance I had to impress her I was going to pull out all the stops.

"*Gabriel*," Lou replied confidently, an unexpectedly sultry purr in her voice. *"How about that dinner date?"*

"When?" I asked, surprised. I must have earned some good karma for being so patient with these asshole 21-year-old Content Curation Experts telling me to make articles about reindeers and auto museums sexier. Lou's sudden interest in me was obviously my reward for my good deeds.

"Tonight."

"Tonight?" This conversation got more and more surprising. "Of course. I mean, I don't have any plans."

Smooth, Gabriel.

"Perfect, I'll message you the details. See you later, Gabriel." She hung up suddenly and I stared down at my phone, baffled. I wasn't *mad*, but that sultry, forward woman on the phone had seemed so different from the one I'd met at the store.

"Who is *queridaaaaaaaaa*?" Brooks sang from the doorway to the kitchen, grinning obnoxiously at me.

"You're a pain in the ass," I laughed, shooting him a look. "A beautiful woman I met at the hardware store who wants to go out to dinner with me tonight."

"Lucky you," Brooks muttered. "I met a beautiful woman at the coffee shop, but she was all hung up on some dude and not interested in dating."

"Well that's lucky, since you don't date," I pointed out. Sometimes I thought Brooks might *want* to, but his wolf was the most distrustful animal I'd ever come across. All of Brooks' worst memories had been caused by his own pack, the people he should have been able to trust the most.

"I guess so," Brooks said dejectedly. "She was cool, though. We're going to be friends, with my dick on tap should she decide to partake."

"Charming," I replied drily. "Can you feed yourself? I have no idea where Nate is."

"Out sulking in his fur probably. He's been in a weird mood lately," Brooks said, sounding more serious than usual. "His mom wants to set him up with some nice cougar girls, but I don't think that's what his issue is."

I didn't think so either. Nate's mom had been trying to set him up with eligible young women for years, even when he wasn't in the country.

"I'll go look for him later if he doesn't come home," Brooks said decisively. "Take him out for drinks or something and get him out of this funk."

"Sounds good." I stood up, clapping Brooks on the shoulder as I passed him. If I was going out on a date, then I needed to tame my beard from antisocial writer back to sexy stubble. "I'll let you know where I'm going for dinner so you can stay far away from there."

If this was my one chance to impress Lou, I wasn't going to risk my friends coming along and stealing her attention.

Lou chose an uber casual grill place that had a game playing on the flat screen in the background, to my immense surprise. She met me just inside the doorway, looking incredibly chic in tight black leather pants with an oversize black wool jumper and black ankle boots, scrolling through her phone with a bored look on her face. Her red hair looked striking against her dark clothes, and she had fancy dark eye makeup that was nothing like the brighter, natural look she'd been sporting at the hardware store, but no less compelling.

I could stare at Lou all day.

She looked up at my approach, eyes lighting up with recognition and maybe something a little more heated as they ran down my body. I knew it had been a good call not to wear a jacket.

"You look beautiful," I told her, leaning down to kiss her cheeks.

"Ooh, fancy kisses," Lou laughed, air kissing me back. "I hope this place is okay."

"I'm not fussy," I assured her, following as she made a beeline for a booth at the back, further away from the rowdy bar crowd. "But I am guilty of assuming *you* would want something a little fancier."

"I got my fill of fancy restaurants when I was in New York a few weeks ago," she replied with a tight smile as I gestured for her to climb into the crescent-shaped booth first. "Besides, sometimes you just want waffle fries, you know?"

"I do know," I chuckled as I sat down, trying to remember what humans considered an acceptable amount of meat to consume in one sitting as I scanned the menu. One 16oz steak was probably the limit.

"Today has felt like a week," she sighed. "I just want carbs and a beer."

"Rough day?" I asked sympathetically.

"Just some old ghosts not staying in the past where they belong," Lou said with a shrug, though I could see it was bothering her more than she wanted to let on.

"Is that why you called? I must admit, I was surprised to hear from you. Happy and surprised," I amended quickly.

The harried-looking server came over, interrupting our conversation, and we placed our orders—steak for me, an enormous burger and fries for Lou, and beers for both of us.

"So," Lou said with a wince after she left. "Would you totally hate me if I admitted this was a spite date?"

I choked slightly on my saliva like the smooth, debonair man I liked to think I was.

"A spite date?" I repeated, clearing my throat.

"I guess I didn't put that much forethought into it when I called you, but now I'm sitting here with you and you're so nice and I feel like an asshole," Lou sighed. "I'm not really *dating* right now—I'm leaving town at the end of winter."

"Okay," I replied slowly. "As am I. Where does the spite part come in?"

Her leaving didn't need to be a deterrent. It was a convenient bonus if anything.

"This guy sort of messed with my head," Lou continued, flicking her hand absently, like she could swat the annoying memory away. "It wasn't serious or anything, it was just... whatever. Anyway, *then* my asshole ex, sort of, showed up in town today and they basically had a dick measuring contest in my front yard. It's all just been a lot, you know?"

"It sounds like a lot," I replied with a quiet laugh, a little overwhelmed at the amount of information she'd just given me. She was a beautiful, fascinating woman. Of course there were other men competing for her attention. I did have one advantage over them though.

"Why don't we use this *spite date* to restore your faith in men, then?" I suggested. "Let me show you how a non-asshole man behaves on a date."

Lou's lips twitched. "Bold of you to assume there was any faith there in the first place to restore, but okay. Frankly, I should be begging for your forgiveness for asking you out under false pretenses. That was a dick move."

"Nonsense," I shot back, shaking my head. "You asked me to join you for dinner, nothing more than that. I was having a frustrating day at work. Some good food and beautiful company is exactly what I needed."

"What is your line of work?" Lou asked with a small smile, relaxing into her seat. I was glad that the overtly sultry voice she'd used on the phone was gone, but she was a real conundrum, this woman. So unaffected one moment, so bold the next.

"I'm a travel writer," I told her. "I freelance write for a few different publications, mostly online. I have my own blog, but I'm not very good with it."

"Oh, maybe we can exchange ideas then" Lou said, thanking the server as they brought over our beers. "My social media is my main source of revenue right now, but I probably need to do some longer form content too. I'm trying to be an *influencer*," she said dramatically.

"Social media is not my strong suit," I admitted with a grimace. Brooks had been trying to convince me for years that I needed to put more effort into it. He had more luck than I did, but he only posted his own photos, which were incredible.

"Why?" Lou gaped at me. "You should have *millions* of followers. Are you not familiar with the concept of a 'thirst trap'?"

"A what?" I asked, mystified.

"It's like... a sexy pic. Designed to draw all those thirsty people in. And you, Gabriel, are a walking thirst trap," she added, running her eyes over my chest and arms in a very gratifying way. "Get them to come for the shirtless selfies and stay for the travel pics."

"You think so?" I asked, contemplating the idea. It's not that I thought I was a bad looking guy, but I'd never considered getting in front of the camera to hook people into my blog.

"Um, yes," Lou replied like it was obvious. "Post a few photos of your rippling muscles at the beach and you'll have so many followers you won't know what to do with them. Ooh, you need a shot where you're emerging from the ocean, Bond-girl style, pushing those dark curls back, chin tilted down but like, looking up at the camera." She fanned herself dramatically, and I laughed at the picture she'd painted in my mind. That was really more Brooks' style than mine.

"I'll consider it," I chuckled. I wasn't sure I had the charisma to pull that idea off.

"So have you found anything to write about while you've been here?" Lou asked, sounding doubtful.

"Winter in Alaska?" I replied, raising an eyebrow. "That's a bucket list item for a lot of people. I'm not short on content, believe me."

Lou wrinkled her nose. "*Not* spending a winter in Alaska is on my bucket list. I'm hoping this one is my last ever."

In the back of my mind, a lightbulb switched on. If Lou was willing to travel, there was the potential for something *more* than just a winter fling. God, I wanted that. Something *meaningful*. Being a spite date wasn't the best start, but perhaps I could woo her?

She's human, the more logical part of my brain reminded me unhelpfully. However much I was intrigued by her and had been longing for the idea of something more permanent for years, Lou being a human complicated things. We could only ever take things so far until I'd have to tell her what I was, at which point I would have to claim her to keep her safe.

I'd never had the experience personally, but I imagined some women didn't respond well to finding out their partner could shift into an animal.

"So, you know what that means?" Lou continued, leaning forward with her elbows resting on the table, chin on her knuckles.

That I should propose to you?

"What?" I asked before taking a long swig of my beer so I wouldn't say something ridiculous.

"That means I want to hear about every single place you've ever been, starting with the hottest, beachiest places first," she said with a grin.

I opened my mouth, ready to do just that, when I caught a whiff of *both* of my friends' scents. Fuckers.

Nate appeared first, his clothes rumpled like they'd been carried in a cougar's teeth and his face like thunder, and my eyebrows shot up at the hostility in his posture. It wasn't like him to get so angry. Brooks jogged after Nate like he was following him in, dressed normally. He must have gone looking for Nate after all.

"Not going to lie, now I'm taking it personally," Brooks announced, bumping Nate with his shoulder and moving to slide into the booth next to Lou. "I thought you weren't interested in dating? I really must be losing my touch."

The woman from the coffee shop?

Before he could sit next to her, Nate grabbed his shoulder and tugged him backwards, sitting next to Lou instead. She tensed instantly, giving him a scathing look.

"Are you stalking me?" she demanded.

"No," Nate shot back, a little too defensively.

Was *Nate* the asshole guy who'd upset her?

What the hell was going on?

Brooks made a noise of disagreement. "I've been stalking *him*, and he sort of looked like he was stalking you. Don't worry though, Red. Nate is good people. It was probably friendly stalking. Stalking among friends, which we are. Best buddies."

"Let me guess," Lou sighed, massaging her temples. "Gabriel and Brooks are the roommates you were talking about."

"You've all met then," I said, looking between them. *Fuck.* That's why Lou's scent had been so familiar to me. It had lingered in Nate's studio when we first arrived in Fairbanks. A sweeter, more *aroused* version of her scent.

"We've met," Lou clipped, still glaring at a sheepish looking Nate.

"Wait, is *this* the guy who put you off men?" Brooks asked in disbelief, a little slow on the uptake. "Nate, the fuck?"

"It's complicated," he rumbled, still looking at Lou. "Did you listen to any of what I said this afternoon?"

"Nope," Lou replied airily. "All the hatred was ringing in my ears, making it hard for me to hear you."

I choked on my mouthful of beer, coughing awkwardly as Brooks laughed and Nate looked an intriguing combination of irritated and ashamed. Who *was* this woman?

"Lou has a persistent admirer who flew in from New York today," Nate told me through gritted teeth. "He's a bit like Brooks. Has a real *wolfy* grin." Nate raised his eyebrows pointedly at me while Lou gaped at him.

A wolf shifter from New York? Not good. The biggest pack there had a particularly unfriendly reputation. Brooks frowned, looking between us. As a wolf shifter, he couldn't even travel into Manhattan without meeting and getting permission from the Alpha there, which is why Brooks never went. Hopefully Lou's admirer wasn't one of those wolves.

"Um, you were really focused on the wrong things," Lou told Nate, before looking at Brooks. "Your grin isn't *wolfy*."

"Thanks, Red," he chuckled, though his expression was still a little grim.

"Anyway, Lou told her *wolfy* admirer that I was her boyfriend, which makes it a strange choice for her to be on a date with someone who isn't me," Nate continued, looking put out by it.

"Oh, it's because I loathe you," Lou replied matter-of-factly. "It was just a convenient white lie that I regret telling immensely. Gabriel already has a great track record as my fake boyfriend, your services are no longer required, Nate."

"Too late," he grumbled.

"Hold on," Brooks said, raising his hand. "Both these dickheads got to be your fake boyfriend and all I got was a 'not interested'? I really am losing my touch," he sighed, slumping back against the booth.

"You could replace Nate?" Lou offered, looking hopeful.

"That's not an option," Nate gritted out. "He'll be watching us specifically, Lou."

Lou was looking at him like he was insane, and Nate looked a little lost and a *lot* frustrated. My brain scrambled to follow the breadcrumbs of information he was leaving.

New York wolf shifter. Lou's ex. Fake boyfriend. Lou hating Nate for some reason.

Okay, none of that was ideal, but I was definitely missing whatever urgent thing Nate was willing me with his eyes to understand.

"His name is Frank. I believe he is a threat to Lou's safety. I invited her to come and stay with us for a few days in the hopes that he'd give up and leave her alone," Nate explained with more pointed looks, willing us to understand.

Frank... wasn't the Alpha of the big New York pack called Frank? Brooks' eyes widened in alarm, and that was all the unfortunate confirmation I needed. Shit.

"And I told him I'd rather pierce my own nipples with a rusty nail," Lou drawled, taking a swig of her beer.

"Blunt safety pin," Nate corrected.

"That was until you stalked me here. Now you've moved up to the rusty nail level, aka tetanus nips level. Congrats."

A muscle in Nate's jaw ticked, and a grin spread slowly over Brooks' face as his gaze darted between them, like he was watching the most exciting tennis match he'd ever seen.

The server returned with me and Lou's meals, and Brooks cheerfully ordered steaks for him and Nate, settling in to properly ruin my date. I should have been more irritated, but they were my pack and I couldn't stay mad at them. Besides, if Lou had caught the attention of a powerful Alpha, the more of us around to keep her safe, the better.

There was no question in my mind that we would rally around to keep her safe. I didn't particularly think of myself as a hero, but nothing angered me more than shifters who toyed with unsuspecting humans.

"Start eating," Brooks insisted, leaning forward on the table so he could talk to Lou around Nate, who was sitting stiffly in his seat, glowering out at the bar like he expected threats from every corner. I had *a lot* of questions for him. He'd been acting strange almost the entire time we'd been here, and I couldn't help but think this little redhead was the reason why.

"So, Red. I'd love to hear how Nate managed to put you off real-life pensises," Brooks said conversationally, never one to self-filter.

"I'm sure you would love to hear about it," Lou laughed while Nate shot him a baleful look. "But we are never speaking of it again, sorry."

"Boo," Brooks replied sulkily.

"Boo yourself," I grumbled, shooting him an irritated look. "You are ruining the conversation. Before you showed up, I was attempting to prove to Lou that not all men are assholes."

"That isn't going very well, by the way," Lou remarked drily, giving Nate a scathing look. I'd never seen the guy look so uncomfortable. He wasn't really someone who people disliked, which made the tension between them all the more unusual. Nate was chill, polite, and respectful of all women.

How had things gone so wrong here?

Brooks grinned, before launching into a conversation about Monkey Beach on Koh Phi Phi that successfully grabbed Lou's attention. Brooks didn't do well with long periods alone. The words seemed to build up and build up, and whenever he found someone to talk to, he'd launch them all at once. Fortunately, Lou didn't seem to mind chatting with him, and Nate was more than happy to sit silently between them like a sentinel.

The others got their meals, and Brooks and I answered Lou's endless stream of questions about scuba diving in the Philippines for a while, lulling me into a false sense of security that this date was not a total fucking disaster.

And then *they* showed up. Nate picked up the scent first, stiffening even more in his seat as his eyes swiveled towards the door. He looped an arm around Lou's waist and tugged her into his side, and for all of her talk about hating him, she didn't fight it. Perhaps because Brooks and I had fallen silent too, going on high alert as we cataloged the distinctive scent of the three wolf shifters who had just walked in.

Heads turned and eyes followed their movements as two men and one woman strode confidently into the bar like they owned the place. There was no question of who the Alpha was. He walked slightly ahead of the others, and power practically rolled off him, awing the humans he passed. I glanced at Lou out of the corner of my eye, wondering if she'd fallen prey to his magnetism, but she definitely hadn't.

She spared him a dismissive glance before returning her gaze to our table. Pride swelled in me at Lou's inner strength. There were shifters who would struggle not to be sucked into that Alpha's orbit, but she didn't look like she was having any difficulty with it. Maybe she was human, but she had the heart of a shifter, and a predator at that.

Nate leaned down, his lips brushing Lou's ear, making her shiver. "He's following you."

His voice was quiet so as not to carry across the noisy bar where Frank and his pack members had made themselves comfortable, blatantly observing our table as they ordered their drinks. Brooks and I could hear all of Nate's words though, and I suddenly felt a sliver of guilt that Lou didn't realize that.

She lightly cupped Nate's jaw, brushing her lips across his cheek, and I couldn't decide if the sight made me jealous or turned me on. "Coincidence," Lou breathed.

Except it wasn't, because Frank would easily be able to track Lou's melted chocolate scent all around town. Suddenly, I understood Nate's frustration. Lou couldn't comprehend the threat Frank presented without all the information, and we couldn't tell her without putting her at even greater risk.

Nate captured Lou's hand, holding it in place against his cheek, and keeping their mouths hidden from prying eyes. "Let's get dessert."

I couldn't see her face, but I could practically feel the disbelief rolling off her. I understood his logic though. If we left now, it would look like we were running and only inspire Frank to give chase.

Pity that Lou hated Nate and everything he suggested sounded terrible to her.

Before she could object, Brooks had hailed the server and was placing an order for three sundaes, but either she wasn't that mad or she was a good actress, because Lou didn't protest. She was too busy torturing Nate.

Her hand slid up from his jaw into his hair, and she used her grip to angle his head closer towards her, her mouth firmly attached to his exposed neck. I swallowed down my surprise that he was letting her do it, even knowing there was an audience watching every move.

It was no small thing for a shifter to let a lover near their neck. Lou may not have sharp enough canines to do any damage, but Nate was still showing her an extraordinary amount of trust. I leaned forward on the table to speak to Brooks, trying to make it seem like I wasn't obsessively watching every move the other party made, and trying not to focus too much on what Lou and Nate were up to. Except he was dragging her closer, one arm wrapped around her waist, the other hand clamped dominantly on the back of her neck, and the syrupy sweet scent of her arousal was perfuming the air around us.

Maybe she did hate Nate, but she definitely wanted to fuck him too.

"So," Brooks said, his cheerfulness a little more forced than usual. "I ate, like, seven Lunchables today."

I blinked at him, not entirely sure how to respond to that.

"The pizza ones?" Lou asked against Nate's neck, her breathy voice shooting straight to my dick. Some part of me was happy that she hadn't tuned Brooks and I out completely in favor of Nate.

Some part of me wondered if we could share.

I definitely wouldn't be averse to sharing.

"Three pizzas, three mini hot dogs, and one nachos," Brooks replied thoughtfully, listing them off on his fingers.

"It's not fair that you look like that," Lou shot back, her pouty lips now hovering just below Nate's ear. Her thigh was right there, and I desperately wanted to put my hand on it, run my palm up her leather-clad leg, see how she reacted...

Nate gave me a warning look, like he could see—or perhaps scent—the direction my thoughts had taken, and wanted to give me a reminder that all of us were putting on a show.

The two of them continued their borderline inappropriate petting while Brooks kept the conversation deliberately dull in case anyone was eavesdropping. When our desserts arrived, Nate alternated between feeding Lou and himself, and my zipper felt increasingly like barbed wire against my dick.

"You've got chocolate sauce on your lip," Nate murmured, moving to wipe it away with his thumb. There was a soft look in his eyes that I had *never* seen before in the decade plus I'd known him. If he was acting, he was a lot better at it than I would have ever given him credit for.

Lou caught his hand, leaning up for a kiss, and Brooks barely stifled his groan as Nate licked the chocolate from her skin before sucking her lower lip into his mouth.

Brooks gave me a look that very clearly said *'I thought she hated him?'* and I sent him one back that replied *'same?'* because now her tongue was in his mouth and it was difficult to tell.

It was certainly the weirdest date I'd ever been on.

Movement from across the room caught my eye as Frank and his cronies stood. Nate stiffened slightly, but kept his attention solely on Lou, putting his trust in Brooks and I to watch their backs and communicating to Frank that he wasn't afraid of him, even if he probably should have been.

Frank strode up to our table, his two pack members hanging back a few feet. With deliberate slowness, Lou pulled back, still staring into Nate's eyes like he was all she could see, and there was no faking the scent of how much she enjoyed Nate's attention. Frank's nostrils flared slightly, a brittle smile plastered on his face.

"You've always been such a beautiful little actress, Scarlet." He turned and walked away without another word, the other two wolves following in his wake.

Who the fuck was Scarlet?

Chapter 11

"I'd like to go home now," I murmured, impressed that I kept my voice even as my face burned with embarrassment. I didn't even know why I was embarrassed.

I wasn't ashamed of my past, but I liked to control the way I brought it up because it was kind of an awkward topic. Frank had just thrown the name 'Scarlet' out there like that, inviting a whole bunch of uncomfortable questions. What an asshole.

What a day of asshole men and their asshole pushy behavior.

To be fair, I was the one who had stupidly claimed Nate was my boyfriend, he was just taking it way more seriously than I expected him to. I couldn't even be mad that I was all keyed up now, because the impromptu makeout session had been my idea too. I *was* mad that he'd interrupted my spite date, and I had wanted to work him up to give him a taste of what he'd never have again. But in my head, I knew how stupid that was. Nate had run out on *me*. I doubted he was sitting around wishing for a do-over.

However annoyed I was with him, I was *more* mad at Frank. I was trying to play it off like I didn't care, but his presence in Fairbanks had unnerved me, especially since he'd shown up with "friends" who acted more like bodyguards. But I'd been alone with Frank a bunch of times, I'd even let him tie me up in bed, and nothing bad had happened. *Unnerving* me was probably his whole point.

Maybe his persistence was just his twisted way of wooing me? He'd give up and go home when I ignored him. It was probably wishful thinking, but I was going to wishfully think it anyway.

"I'll go pay," Gabriel announced, shaking his head when I attempted to object. I'd been the one to invite him out tonight—out of spite—and then had somehow ended up making out with his friend right in front of him, which was... fucking terrible, actually. Oh my god, I should send him an apology fruit basket or something. Maybe I was the biggest asshole here tonight.

"Come back to my place. Stay with us," Nate pleaded quietly. "You already know the guys. Even better."

"Still no," I replied resolutely, shaking my head. Okay, I'd given him *extremely* mixed messages by sticking my tongue in his mouth. I could own that, but Nate had *followed* me here. Frank and his friends might have too, but them being here could have just been a coincidence. There was nothing coincidental about Nate showing up here tonight. He hadn't even pretended there was! Absolutely shameless.

My gut told me that Nate's stalking was less sinister than Frank's stalking, but my gut was also stupid. I wasn't about to go stay at his house. That was how the girls in the horror films always died.

"Come on, Red," Brooks said, jumping on the bandwagon. "Just until the Wolf of Wall Street leaves town."

I snorted at the apt comparison. "Frank is more persistent than I initially thought, I'll admit that, but I really don't think he's *dangerous* to me," I told them, inching back into the spot Gabriel had vacated to put some much needed space between me and Nate. I was all too aware of how his tongue had felt, and then I started remembering how good it felt in other places. And then I remembered he fucked my brains out and ran away with his tail between his legs. The spot on my neck where he'd almost bitten me felt like it was pulsing with the memory.

"If he wanted to hurt me, he had plenty of opportunities to when I visited him in New York a few weeks ago," I continued. "But he didn't. Frank is just a rich guy, throwing his money around and showing me that he can turn up on my doorstep because he's that fucking fancy, you know? You're making it into a bigger deal than it is."

That was my story, and I was fucking sticking to it. No need to panic. Nothing to make a big deal about. Definitely no temptation to backtrack on all the progress I'd made and fall back into old habits. No siree.

I expected Nate to complain again, but it was Brooks who opened his mouth to argue, a far more serious expression on his face than I was used to seeing from him. I scooted backwards and escaped out of the booth before they could gang up on me, frustrated with this argument.

It was nice they wanted to keep me safe—I guess?—but I knew Frank, and they didn't. He hadn't even asked me to stay in New York, which shouldn't still bug me considering he was a lying psycho, but it pricked at my pride nonetheless. Surely, if he had any nefarious plans, he'd have tried to keep me close by rather than letting me leave the state?

Gabriel materialized at my side after paying, as I rudely made a beeline for the door, grabbing my coat on the way out.

"I'm sorry, this was the worst spite date ever," I said with a grimace.

"I disagree," Gabriel replied kindly, his smooth accent making me a little tingly. "This is the best spite date I've ever been on."

"You're actually calling it a spite date?" Nate deadpanned from behind us. "Rub salt in my wound, why don't you?"

"Savage. I like it," Brooks chuckled. I shot him a smile over my shoulder as we exited the bar to show him I appreciated his moral support, and he grinned back at me. Dangerous. Brooks had a *delightful* smile.

"Let me guess," Nate sighed heavily. "You're going to drive home alone."

"Obviously," I sang, already walking through the parking lot. I was trying to be sassy and put a little swing in my step, because I was a baddie and I didn't need no man, but it was hard as fuck to strut on ice. I slipped, and would have definitely bailed if Gabriel hadn't wrapped an arm around my waist just in time.

He pulled me close to his body, and I pressed my hands against his chest, fisting his sweater while my heart rate returned to normal.

"Are you okay, querida?" Gabriel asked in a low voice, his smile languid and relaxed. His eyes dropped to my lips, which I was guessing were bare of lipstick after Nate's attention. *Yikes, Lou. You just made out with his friend. Relax.*

"Guess I'm just swooning," I teased, smoothing over the creases I'd just put in his sweater before running my hands down to his forearms to steady myself. Mostly to steady myself. Well, a little bit to steady myself and mostly because I was a perv. Those *biceps*. Gabriel was packing some big ol' guns under that classy knitwear.

I forced myself to take a step, glancing discreetly at Nate, expecting to see him looking furious, or at least surprised, but he just looked the same level of tense and agitated as he had ever since Frank had shown up. Well, okay then.

"We're going to follow you home to make sure you get there okay. Is that alright, Red?" Brooks asked, giving me a charming smile. I appreciated that he was polite about shoehorning into my life under the guise of "protection". It made it a lot easier to stomach.

"If I say no, will you not follow me home, or will you just follow from further away?"

"Shh," Brooks replied with a boyish grin. "It's early days. Let's try to keep the mystery alive."

He really was trouble in the best kind of way, which was a dangerous line of thought. *Friends. We're just friends.*

"Well, uh, thanks for the weirdest date ever," I said to all three of them, refusing to make eye contact with Nate after telling him repeatedly that I hated him, then licking him like a fucking popsicle in front of his friends.

"Perhaps we could have a do-over without the extra guests?" Gabriel suggested. I chanced a quick glance at Nate, and found him gaping at Gabriel in disbelief while Brooks laughed. Awkward.

"I'll message you," I assured Gabriel, climbing into my car as fast as I could to escape answering. I wasn't even entirely sure it was a serious question. Surely he wasn't asking me on a date right in front of Nate after everything. "Goodnight!"

Why had I ever left my basement? I could be spending my days orgasming for cash and not dealing with this sudden influx of testosterone disrupting every aspect of my life.

After being out for a few hours, the lingering paint smell seemed a lot more offensive than it had when I'd left the house. I took off my outer layers at the door and stripped out of the rest on the way to my bedroom, relying on the moonlight filtering in from outside to illuminate the space.

With each layer I pulled off, the more Brooks' Thailand plan sounded appealing, even if he was a tad... *full on*. Regardless, I wanted to do yoga on the beach as the sun rose, wearing my tiniest crop top and short shorts, and post pictures of myself on the 'gram. Then I wanted to change into my bikini and jump in the ocean for my daily swim, and occasionally wear a coverup during the day when I absolutely had to.

That was the life I was meant to be living. Though Frank drama and Nate drama aside, tonight was actually fun. I never really got to just... go out with friends, like a normal person in their twenties? Even when Ria had lived here, she was the biggest homebody I'd ever met. We went out once in New York, but in general we were way more likely to order takeout and binge watch a series than go to a bar.

If I ignored the fact that I'd had sex with one of them and that theoretically that had been a date—*with a different guy who was also his friend*—then it had been a fun way to spend an evening.

Still feeling a little keyed up from... well, everything, I changed into my comfiest lime green flannel PJs, shoved my hair up in a messy bun, and took off my makeup before curling up in bed with my laptop to watch old episodes of *Friends* until I couldn't keep my eyes open any longer.

Ugh, how could I not have realized Brooks and Gabriel were Nate's roommates? All three of them were almost inhumanly beautiful. Naturally, they were friends. If there was one thing I'd learned from high school, it was that pretty people congregated together.

Ria was going to cry with laughter when I told her about this. Usually, these kinds of things happened to her. I grabbed my phone off the nightstand to message her, even though she probably wouldn't see it. Ria's place was so remote that she only got reception on her boyfriend Noah's satellite phone, which was how I usually contacted her. It felt kind of weird to message him to chat about boys, though. Surely, she'd get regular service eventually and see a normal message? Cell service should exist everywhere. It was just a basic human right.

Me:

I just had the most bizarro date ever, somehow with three men but not actually with three men? It's complicated and we must discuss it ASAP. Also, Frank showed up in Fairbanks. Boo.

A date with three men, ha. I wasn't meant to be dating anybody! A traitorous voice in the back of my mind reminded me that Ria was now in a full-blown relationship with three men, but I pushed that thought down deep. I didn't want a relationship anyway, and Nate was on my never-again list, but even aside from those minor details, what Ria had was not the norm. I still didn't quite know how she'd pulled it off.

My phone remained silent, as I expected, and I tossed it to the side, hitting 'play' on my laptop to fill the silence. I could close my eyes and listen to Rachel and Monica banter, and pretend I had friends. Or I could listen to Ross whine incessantly and remember all the reasons I was better off single.

Now that I was alone, with nothing to distract me, my anxiety about Frank's appearance in Fairbanks became a little more pressing. Anxiety and embarrassment. I hadn't thought I'd ever see him again after I left New York, and now I felt a little naïve for not expecting him to use his extensive resources to track me down.

Would it even matter if I got on a plane tomorrow and flew to Phuket? He'd followed me here. What was stopping him from following me somewhere else when I left?

I was probably buying into Nate's paranoia, but I looked up the requirements for a Protective Order against a stalker just in case, scanning the official court document apprehensively. My mom had been in trouble with the police *constantly* when I was growing up—mostly for theft— and I didn't have many positive experiences with cops to draw from.

Besides, I couldn't fill out the section on why Frank's behavior made me afraid of physical injury or death, which was apparently a requirement for stalking. All Frank had really said was that he wanted to bring me back to New York and give me a generous monthly allowance. If I went down to the police station and told them that, they'd laugh in my face.

Even so, I couldn't shake the questions about Nate and why he'd been so adamant that I go with him. I hadn't given it a second thought when I'd told Frank that Nate was my boyfriend, it had just seemed like a convenient way to get him off my back. I had hoped he'd play along, but I definitely hadn't expected him to get *so* tangled up in it that he thought I'd move in with him, even temporarily.

It was like he'd seen something sinister in Frank that had freaked him out, something I couldn't see. So the guy was smarmy and confident in the way that rich, powerful men were. That was hardly the end of the world.

Had Nate always been so growly? His voice had a naturally rough quality, but it bordered on animalistic when he'd been trying to convince me I was in some kind of mysterious grave danger. Actually, he sounded pretty growly in bed too. Especially when he'd panicked and run away. Maybe that was just his panicky voice.

"Secrets are poison to a relationship, you know."

Why had Frank said that? His reaction had been incredibly weird too, and the whole interaction between the three of us had left me unsettled. Nate had sworn they didn't know each other, but they hadn't acted like strangers meeting for the first time.

Stop it, I chastised, closing the stupid court document. Why was I even contemplating getting law enforcement involved? Frank was just a rich asshole who was throwing his weight around. He could have any woman he wanted! He probably found women through camming sites all the time. I doubted I was anyone special.

That realization was not great for my ego.

I shook my head to clear it, forcing myself to concentrate on the show. Tomorrow, I was going to take a bunch of clothes to Goodwill, list the furniture I didn't still need online, and paint the entryway. I didn't have time for stupid men talking in riddles in my driveway, making me second guess my sanity.

My agitated thoughts blended together with the laugh track from *Friends*, and I fell into a restless sleep filled with dreams of running through the forest, pursued by men with wolfish grins, not knowing which one was the one I needed to be afraid of.

NATE

Chapter 12

Brooks' ice blue wolf eyes met mine from a few feet away where his big furry head was resting on his front paws, his gaze full of judgment.

He didn't understand why we were here, not really. I'd tried to explain it on the car-ride over here, but I'd been stuck between lingering horniness from Lou's enthusiastic performance back at the bar and animalistic rage at Frank for showing up there.

Somehow, Brooks and Gabriel hadn't been able to interpret my grunts and broken sentences, but they'd come with me to patrol Lou's house anyway because they were good friends. Good friends who were a little *too* interested in her, but good friends regardless.

They probably thought I was being overcautious, guarding Lou's house like this, but I knew I wasn't. I'd seen that flare of excitement in Frank's eyes when he'd left the bar. He'd looked at Lou like he was thinking *let the games begin*, then called her by the wrong name like he was dropping a bomb at the table.

It had taken everything in me not to dive across the fucking booth and go for his throat right there and then. Only having Gabriel and Brooks' calming—or rather confused—presence had kept me grounded. Well, that and Lou's dainty hands fisting my shirt, the taste of her still on my tongue. So much for protecting her from a distance.

"You do realize I hate you as well, right? You're not the good guy in this scenario."

Lou's words kept playing in my mind on repeat, never letting me forget that this was all for show. I deserved her hatred, I'd wear the scar from that self-inflicted wound. I wouldn't abandon her to Frank's games though, even if she resented me every step of the way. I'd prove to him that as far as Lou was concerned, there was nothing here for him.

But I couldn't let myself get lost in the lie, either. Even if it wasn't for show, I had to keep my distance so the mating urge didn't rise again.

"You're not the good guy in this scenario."

Fuck, that hurt. I'd always thought of myself as a good guy. I was a little unsettled, sure, but I always tried to do the right thing. I called my parents twice a week, no matter where I was in the world. I remembered all of my nieces' and nephews' birthdays—all 21 of them—and I always sent gifts. I helped old ladies cross the street, and I was very upfront and respectful with the young ladies I took to my bed.

Was I really *not* a good guy after all? It wasn't a great time for an identity crisis, but now that it was in progress, I couldn't seem to rein it in.

I glanced up to check on Gabriel, who was draped over a tree branch nearby in his jaguar form, his sleek black fur blending into the night. We'd agreed to take turns sleeping so we all got a couple of hours' rest, but I didn't think he was really asleep. He had the best vantage point and was likely keeping an eye on the surrounding woods for intruders. It wasn't sustainable for all three of us to camp out here every night. Maybe I shouldn't have interrupted Lou and Gabriel's date. Maybe she'd have gone home with him if I hadn't gotten in the way.

Then I would have interrupted.

Why the hell did Lou live out here? It wasn't *that* far from town, but her little house was surrounded by trees on three sides, with a quiet road running along the front of her place.

God, humans were so fragile. I didn't think I'd ever reflected on that fact so much.

Gabriel lifted his head and I saw the glint of brutally sharp canines shining in the moonlight as he let out a low, guttural growl. A growl that clearly said *fuck off, you are not welcome.*

Brooks and I rose silently to our feet, hackles raised as foreign scents reached us. They weren't even trying to sneak around us to get into Lou's backyard. They had already deemed us weak, and thought they'd be able to take us out easily.

Three wolves emerged from the trees, growling in response, and Gabriel leaped down to join us. Frank was front and center, an enormous wolf with fur as black as Gabriel's jaguar, who radiated alpha power, and the grayish wolves on either side of him weren't weak. We had our work cut out for us.

I refused to let any hint of fear or doubt show though, refused to let them see a sliver of vulnerability. Brooks was a well trained fighting machine, I was motivated as hell to keep Lou safe, and Gabriel was a fucking *jaguar*. He was 250 pounds of solid muscle, with a bite that could pierce crocodile skin. If provoked, he'd happily sink those canines into the back of his opponent's skull.

Frank gave a warning growl that was thick with Alpha authority, but he wasn't my Alpha so he could go fuck himself. His growls grew louder and more insistent, easily carrying over the yard to Lou's house, and I sent her a silent apology in my head as I screamed back, knowing that if the sound of a wolf growling hadn't terrified her, the earsplitting shriek of an angry cougar definitely would.

Frank's wolves growled steadily while Gabriel's jaguar made his saw-like roar and Brooks responded with a wolf growl of his own, letting them know we weren't backing down. Frank went abruptly quiet, before his bones started cracking and popping, his packmates watching his back as he shifted back into his human form, standing in the snow stark naked.

It was dismissive as hell for him to shift into his more vulnerable human form right in front of us. A not so subtle 'fuck you' to let us know he wasn't worried about us. Asshole.

"Persistent little things aren't you," Frank chuckled. He tilted his head to the side as he examined Brooks. "I must admit, you're a curious case. Where is your pack?"

Brooks' answering growl was almost feral. If Frank wanted to rile him up, mentioning wolf packs was the fastest way to do it.

"This doesn't need to be your problem, you know," Frank continued conversationally. "Scarlet and I have unfinished business. Step aside, and we'll finish it, it's that simple. Stay, and you'll make life worse for her. She won't come to any harm under my... ownership."

Fuck that. Lou wasn't meant to be owned, she was meant to be free. She wanted to see the world and discover herself and explore. She didn't need this shit.

I crouched low to the ground, baring my teeth and hissing in warning.

"Last chance," Frank said with a relaxed smirk. "If you're going to protect her, you better be *very* sure that you can." He glanced down at the wolves on either side of him before lazily gesturing at us. "Proceed."

The three of us were ready, lunging to meet the two wolves as they attacked. I attempted to get past them to Frank as he shifted, but they were obviously well practiced at protecting their Alpha, darting from side to side to block my movements.

One of the wolves swiped at Brooks' muzzle as he got close. A pained noise escaped him, enough to snag mine and Gabriel's attention, and let Frank through our barrier.

Fucking wolves. When it came to fighting in a pack, there was no animal more efficient. They were always aware of each other's movements, seamlessly working in tandem to take down opponents twice their size. Brooks launched himself at the wolf who'd swiped at him, yipping at me in a clear instruction to stay on Frank.

He was running at full speed towards Lou's house and the noises I made were unholy as I chased after him. He slammed hard against the screen door, rattling the entire back wall, and I heard a muffled scream from inside the house that had my heart thundering in my chest. Lou must be fucking terrified, and she was all alone.

Behind me, I heard the howl of one of Frank's wolves followed by Gabriel's strange barking growl. Hopefully he'd gutted them. A jaguar was a fearsome opponent, though their fighting style was very different from a wolf's, and Gabriel would be out of his element.

Frank's claws raked down the screen door, making all of us wince at the screeching sound and probably scaring the hell out of Lou. I'd bet money that scaring her was the point of this whole exercise. A way of driving her back to him, to safety.

Well fuck that noise. I launched myself at his back, raking him with my claws until I scented blood, but he was undoubtedly bigger and stronger than I was. He twisted sharply, throwing me into the wooden porch railing.

Pain bloomed slowly in my middle, my ribs cracking to the tune of the wooden railing snapping underneath me. Fucking *ouch*, he was strong. With a vicious growl, Brooks swiped at the wolf he was fighting near the house, knocking her to the ground before rushing towards me, growling furiously at Frank who was still ravaging Lou's screen door before nudging me with his nose, whining.

I scrambled back off the porch, falling over the small drop onto the snow with a pained noise I couldn't quite suppress. The scent of my blood filled the air and I realized the pain in my middle wasn't just from broken ribs. The splintered wood had sliced into me, leaving a gash all the way down my side.

Brooks jumped down next to me, nudging me with his nose, telling me to retreat, before leaping back onto the porch with a snarl, forcing Frank away from the screen door or leave his back exposed.

I knew I had to go. I had to shift back to stop the wound from bleeding and speed up the healing process, but I didn't want to leave them.

There was an agonized howl as Gabriel took a chunk out of one of the wolves, and another muffled scream from inside followed by a terrified whimper, which made up my mind. I scrambled upright and ran as best I could with my injured side, leaving a trail of blood after me as I went, but I had to get to the SUV we'd left partially obscured just off the road, hoping like fuck it wouldn't be stuck in the snow.

The second I got back to the vehicle, I forced myself to shift, shoving my fist in my mouth to stop myself shouting as my wounded skin rapidly stitched back together, my cracked ribs screaming in protest. I allowed myself five seconds to lean against the vehicle, gasping for breath before forcing myself to open the door and drag my clothes out, dressing as fast as I could and throwing myself into the driver's seat with a pained groan.

Fortunately, I managed to get out of the snow, flooring it until I pulled up noisily in front of Lou's house with the headlights on high, making as much noise as possible. Frank would have seen me leave, but hopefully he was still cautious enough to scamper at the sound of a vehicle—I wouldn't be shocked if Lou had called 911. That would be a headache.

Hopefully, some human presence would comfort Lou right now, even if it was mine. Or perhaps Frank would get his way, and she'd call him asking for help in her moment of terror.

The howls and roars of animals retreated from the house as I climbed the front steps, and I sent some silent gratitude to Gabriel and Brooks for pushing the other wolves back.

"Lou!" I called, knocking on her door. "It's Nate."

"Nate?" she muttered to herself, probably assuming I couldn't hear her. *"Fucking stalker."*

Okay. Not the best start. I probably should have thought about what I was going to say. Except it was incredibly hard to think when my ribs were throbbing and my healing skin itched ferociously under my shirt.

"I was just driving past and heard the commotion," I lied, cringing. "I guess the car scared them off."

Lou hesitated on the other side of the door before I heard the lock click and the door swung open, revealing the barrel of a shotgun she was pointing right at me.

I raised an eyebrow at her, grateful that she was at least armed, even if she looked incredibly uncomfortable holding a weapon.

"Scared who off?" Lou asked dubiously.

A sharp pain radiated from my ribs as I adjusted my stance—acutely aware of the gun pointed at me—and I did my best to concentrate because this conversation was important, even though I just wanted to pour myself a generous glass of bourbon and lie down until my fucking bones healed.

Focus, I commanded my brain, irritated that the pain was distracting me. This was an important question. I needed Lou to understand that she was in real danger, without giving away anything about shifters.

"Frank."

Fuck, that didn't come out right.

"What?" Lou sputtered, glancing down at the gun in her hand as if she was surprised to find it pointing at me and quickly lowering it towards the ground. Thank fuck for that. I had enough going on without a bullet wound to worry about.

"No, that wasn't Frank," Lou said, shaking her head. "That was wild animals or... something."

Right. That would be a more logical explanation for all the animal sounds. *Come on, Nate.* Except if she thought it was a random wild animal encounter, there's no way she would take the Frank threat seriously.

Everything in me rebelled at manipulating Lou, especially given our history, but... I had to. I had to keep lying to her and distracting her. If she found out about shifters, I would have to mate her, or I was leaving her at the mercy of the shifter world.

Humans who knew things they shouldn't didn't get to live.

"You have a lot of trouble like that with wild animals?" I asked. Lou opened her mouth. Closed it. Shook her head.

"I didn't hear all of it," I said slowly, feeling like a calculating piece of shit. "But it sounded like your house was under attack. I assumed it was Frank, unless you have any other stalkers."

"Just you," Lou shot back, giving me a scathing look, but then she was chewing nervously on her lip, thinking about what I'd said. "It sounded like animals, but it was like they were trying to break through my screen door..."

He might have been, but I thought it was more likely that he'd been trying to make Lou more amenable to his twisted form of protection. I'd be shocked if he didn't try to contact her tomorrow, trying to tempt her back into his fold.

"I'll go and check the yard for... animals," I volunteered. "Stay inside. Pack a bag, just in case."

"Not this again," she muttered, though she didn't look as against the idea of staying with me as she did earlier in the night. "I guess you should take the gun," Lou added reluctantly, looking at it like she didn't want to part with it, which made sense since she didn't trust me either.

"Keep it," I told her firmly. "I'll be fine. Pack a bag."

"Bossy asshole," she muttered as she closed the door, and I couldn't tell if she meant for me to hear it or not.

Gabriel and Brooks were hovering just beyond the treeline, completely naked as they shifted back into their skin to heal the worst of their wounds. Fortunately, it looked like they'd gotten away with just scratches. I had definitely been the weakest link tonight. Too emotional. Too worried about Lou to focus.

"You good?" Brooks asked somberly, squinting like he could see my injury through my shirt.

"Fine," I replied, waving away his worry. "Cracked ribs, but they'll heal."

"Only if you rest," Gabriel pointed out, rolling his neck. "We'll patrol between here and our place, you look after Lou. If she'll let you."

Shit, we probably should have sent Gabriel in to talk to her, but then again, she already thought I was a stalker. May as well keep the damage isolated to me.

"She thinks it was wild animals," I said, wincing as I moved and aggravated my injury. "I said I thought it was Frank, but there's no way I can convince her of that without sounding like a lunatic."

Brooks made a noise of agreement. "You probably shouldn't have mentioned Frank at all," he pointed out unhelpfully. "She's going to think you're fucking with her."

"Weren't you going to ask her carrier friend to talk to her?" Gabriel reminded me.

"You're a genius," I told him, clapping him on the shoulder and wincing when the movement pulled at my injury. "I'll see if I can get Ria to talk to her."

"Nate?" Lou called hesitantly, the back door creaking open slightly.

"Shit," I muttered, walking back into the yard as fast as I could while the guys slunk back among the trees.

"Nate?" she called again. "Did you get eaten by a wolf?"

I snorted quietly. I'd definitely gotten too close for comfort.

"I'm here," I replied, walking to the bottom of the steps. Her porch was wrecked—the screen door had been shredded like it was made of mozzarella, and the entire railing had collapsed. Lou had turned on the kitchen light, illuminating the damage, but I doubted her human eyes would be able to see the amount of blood staining the snow.

She was standing with the light at her back, entirely too vulnerable behind the remnants of the screen door in her pajamas, the gun held loosely at her side. She looked *distraught*, and I wanted nothing more than to pull her into my arms and tell her everything would be okay, except that would only make things worse.

"Lou," I said softly, swallowing the urge to tell her off for opening the door.

"You know what, I think I'd like to leave now," she murmured, fingers tracing the shredded screen. "But I'm not sure going to your house is the best idea either though."

"Firstly, bring the gun," I told her seriously. "Point it at me the whole time if you want. It isn't safe here, you know you can't stay."

"And secondly?" she asked, sounding resigned.

"Secondly, call Ria. She knows me. Her, er, guys know me. I know you don't trust me, but you trust her, right?"

"Right..." Lou agreed tentatively, pulling out her phone. "I have the number for Noah's satellite phone, but I don't know if he'll answer in the middle of the night."

"He'll answer," I replied drily. There was no way Mr. Control Freak wouldn't notice a call coming in at any time of the day.

Lou dialled and held the phone up to her ear, squinting into the darkness as she waited for someone to pick up. It only took two rings before I heard Noah's gruff voice on the other end of the phone.

"Lou? Everything okay?"

She opened her mouth before closing it again, looking a little lost for words. "Um, no. Not really. I'm sorry, I know it's late."

"That's okay. Hold on, Ria is coming to the phone."

I catalogued Lou's every reaction, the nervousness that she was trying to hide, and the way she'd catch herself any time that mask of calm slipped. It was always subtle—straightening her shoulders, flexing her fingers to stop them drumming, regulating her breathing...

Perhaps that was what had made my cougar so enamored with her. Lou was prey from the top of her red hair to the bottom of her dainty toes, but she refused to show it.

"Lou?" Ria sounded frantic, which probably wasn't helping Lou's state of mind.

"It's okay," she soothed despite her own fear. "I'm okay. Something weird just happened at my house."

"What kind of weird?"

Lou gave me a helpless look before shaking it off again. It was kind of fascinating to watch. "There were these noises, um, like wild animals? Like wolves and stuff? I didn't see anything, I was getting my gun out, but whatever it was seemed to... attack my house," she finished lamely. "I know it sounds weird, but my screen door is shredded and the porch railing is in pieces—"

"I'm coming to get you. Eli! Wake up! How is he sleeping right now?" she snapped at someone in the background. God, Eli was such a consummate bear.

169

"No, no, it's fine," Lou said hurriedly. "Um, Nate is here, actually. He suggested I go stay at his place."

"Oh, thank god for that," Ria sighed dramatically. She may have just become my favorite person. *"Nate will keep you safe."*

Lou gave me an assessing look, like she was trying to decipher the truth in Ria's words just with her eyes.

"Is he close? Can I talk to him?" Ria pressed.

"Uh, yeah. He's here, hold on." Lou reached through the door to pass me the phone. "Ria wants to talk to you."

"Ria," I greeted.

"It wasn't wild animals," she guessed flatly. I grunted in the affirmative. *"Can you keep her safe?"*

"Without a doubt," I replied instantly. Even if I had to deal with a few more broken ribs. There was a scuffle on the other end before Noah's voice came through the phone.

"You know Chase will give you backup, just ask. Us as well. Don't take stupid risks, Nate."

I grunted in agreement, because that was basically a declaration of undying friendship from Noah, and I was a little bit moved.

"Lou will send you updates," I promised, hanging up before she got any more suspicious.

"What did Ria say to you?" Lou asked, eyes narrowed.

"She just wanted to make sure I'd take care of you," I assured her, thankful that for once I wasn't lying.

"Okay. Fine. I'll stay. Just for the night," she sighed. I felt my entire body relax and hadn't even realized I'd been holding my breath, waiting for her answer. "But I will be bringing my gun, and I will shoot you in the dick if you're fucking with me."

"Good," I told her solemnly, almost repressing my wince. "I'll meet you out front."

Lou retreated, closing and locking the back door behind her and I heard her moving around inside while I kicked snow over the bloody patches by the house as best I could before returning to the front porch to wait.

Lou emerged a few minutes later, fully dressed with a duffel bag over her arm, gun in one hand and phone in the other.

"Do you think I should call the cops?" she asked, frowning. "Or animal control? I don't want to, but the insurance company..."

"Me and the guys will fix the damage," I told her, selfishly hoping it would earn me some brownie points as I watched her lock the front door behind her. I turned my gaze back out to the road and scanned our surroundings. I could only scent Brooks and Gabriel nearby, but I wasn't going to be able to relax until I got Lou out of here. Even then, I wasn't sure my heart rate would return to normal.

"Expecting someone?" Lou asked nervously, watching my movements as we made our way to the vehicle. I could feel my nose twitching as I scented the air, struggling to keep it still. She didn't need to think I was any weirder than she already thought I was.

I heard a wolf howl in the distance and scooped Lou up, lifting her into the passenger seat while she made an outraged noise, but fortunately didn't shoot me in the face. That howl hadn't been from Brooks.

I jumped in the driver's seat and started the car up, already pulling out of the driveway before Lou even had her seatbelt on. It wasn't that the rental I was staying in was much more secure, but it was at least properly scent-marked, and we'd have a better case for defending our own territory than that of an unclaimed human's.

"If this is all a trick to get me to your house so you can murder me and have sex with my corpse, I'm going to be annoyed," Lou grumbled, glancing nervously out the window.

"Just annoyed?" I asked absently, eyes moving between the mirrors, checking every side of the vehicle.

"Well, I'll be dead," she pointed out. "But I will haunt your ass *forever* if you murder me. I'll follow you to your studio every day and distract you while you're working so all your tattoos turn out shit. And every time you have a girl over, I'll be in the room, knocking things over and opening windows and freaking you out until you can't perform."

Ha. The idea of fucking anyone else was laughable at this point. I was too twisted up over this woman I couldn't keep.

"That is very good incentive not to murder you," I agreed seriously. "For what it's worth, you're infinitely more fuckable living than dead, but I promise that's not why I'm bringing you back to my house. You can take my bed, I'll sleep on the couch."

"What a compliment," she sighed, fanning her face dramatically. "Won't Brooks and Gabriel find it weird you're dragging home a stray in the middle of the night?"

Right. Of course she would expect them to be there.

"They're... out for the night," I said in a strained voice, glancing out the window as I caught a glimpse of Brooks' tawny fur.

"No witnesses," she said sagely, nodding her head as I snorted. "Smart move, killer."

Despite the sassy retort, she was frowning like she didn't particularly like my answer. *Of course she didn't. She was on a date with Gabriel tonight.*

God, I hoped I could keep this woman safe without destroying my friendships. Or myself.

Chapter 13

This was the weirdest night of my life, without a doubt. The weirdest *day*, period.

From Frank to Nate to the spite date to... whatever was happening now. Whatever had just happened.

I'd woken up wondering if the animal kingdom was hosting an exorcism in my backyard. It wasn't just an odd wolf howl, it was *multiple* howls, plus a bunch of other noises I couldn't even identify because apparently I needed to brush up on my wildlife sounds. Except that wasn't how wild animals behaved, as Nate pointed out. Nothing about the sounds I'd heard or the *attack* on my back porch sounded like regular wild animals scavenging for food.

But what he said didn't make any sense either. He'd said it was Frank, which was ludicrous. It's not like Frank would have stood outside my house in the middle of the night, making weird noises, destroying my porch and shredding my screen door to try to frighten me.

That would be *insane*. No one would do that.

I needed to sleep. Maybe after I got some rest I wouldn't be so thoroughly questioning my own sanity.

My hands shook slightly around the gun I was still clutching, although I wasn't entirely confident I could fire it at someone, so I really hoped Nate was being honest. I'd used it for warning shots before when there was a coyote in my yard, but I'd never shot to *hurt* anything before, let alone a person.

We drove along the tree-lined stretch of highway that led back towards Fairbanks proper, and I caught a glimpse of my frowning reflection in the window as we passed under a streetlight. How had Nate got to my house the first time without a vehicle?

"So," Nate began before I could interrogate him. "Are we going to talk about Scarlet?"

"Scarlet?" I repeated dumbly. It was a distraction tactic, and I contemplated calling him out on it but after everything that happened... maybe a distraction wasn't the worst idea. And of course he'd be curious about Scarlet. I'd put on a wig and called myself a different name, and as far as I knew, that wasn't entirely normal behavior for a one night stand. I was still somehow disappointed that he wanted to know more about my stage persona rather than little ol' Lou though.

Remember, you hate him. Embrace the hatred.

"I started camming when I was 20. Some... things happened, and I needed to figure out how to make money on my own quickly. That's how Scarlet was born."

"How'd you get into it?" Nate asked. He didn't sound judgmental like I expected him to, just curious.

"I've always had a fascination with sex, and almost zero parental supervision most of my life. Basically, I watched a lot of porn," I replied flatly. Plus daddy issues and a whole host of other things I didn't want to think too hard about. "I'd seen ads, and decided to give it a shot."

I could only see Nate's profile in the dark car, but he just nodded like that was entirely reasonable, and some of the tension in my shoulders eased. I didn't have a lot of people in my real life to tell anyway, but I tended to keep my old career a secret from the few people I could share it with. Ria had lived in the same house as me and not known what my job was.

"Is that how you met *Frank*?" Nate asked, spitting out his name like it was poison.

I hummed in agreement, but didn't elaborate. I felt unexpectedly comfortable talking about the cam stuff, but the Frank stuff... if I'd just treated him and our arrangement like a job, it would be a whole different story. But I'd gone and gotten myself embarrassingly attached and the whole thing was too humiliating to talk about, honestly. Nate opened his mouth to ask a follow up question, but I cut him off.

"It's all irrelevant now. Scarlet is retired," I told him. "At least in a professional sense."

Nate was quiet for a long moment, only the rumble of the engine filling the silence. Maybe he was disappointed? If he was just into me to fuck a camgirl and score man points, it was probably a lot less prestigious to bang a retired one.

Scarlet could seduce the pants off anyone, but I had no clue what went on in a man's head. At least not the one on their shoulders.

"We're here," Nate said quietly, pulling into a tree lined driveway that hadn't been maintained over winter as well as mine, judging by the bumpiness.

We were parked next to a truck in front of a small, dark cabin—very serial killer-esque—and I kept my gun clutched tight in my freezing hands as I opened the passenger door. Before I could jump out, Nate was there, reaching towards me without actually grabbing me, which I appreciated because I was feeling a little twitchy and I didn't want to *accidentally* shoot him. Shooting a person seemed like the kind of thing you should do intentionally, or not at all. Preferably not at all.

I looped my bag over one arm and shuffled forward into Nate's waiting arms, a little amazed when he scooped me up bridal style, kicked the truck door shut behind him, and carried me and all my stuff up the front steps of the cabin. I was pretty sure he didn't get those muscles from tattooing all day.

I adjusted myself in his grip so I didn't feel like I was about to fall and I could have sworn he grunted like he was in pain, but when I glanced at his face it was completely blank.

"Uh, so this is it," Nate said, sounding a little embarrassed as he set me down on the stoop and unlocked the door, stepping aside for me to enter first. "It's a rental."

I let myself in, feeling around for the light switch and turning it on. It was small and impersonal, but well maintained, if a little chilly. The living room we were standing in was only big enough to house a three-seater couch, a coffee table, the television and a fireplace. I couldn't imagine how cramped it must feel with all three guys in here.

"You can't sleep on that couch," I pointed out, raising an eyebrow at the offending piece of furniture. "Can you even lie down on it without your feet hanging over the edge?"

Nate shrugged, closing the door behind him. "I'll bunk up with Gabriel tonight."

Unless Gabriel brings a girl home, I thought bitterly, since he and Brooks were *out* tonight. Or maybe Nate didn't care about that. Maybe he was into that.

Oh my god, I needed to get some sleep. My brain was being ridiculous.

"I'll show you to my room," Nate offered, tugging my bag gently off my arm but leaving me with the gun. I couldn't decide if he was uber trusting or a little delusional. Maybe both? I followed him through a miniscule kitchen and down a hallway that he seemed almost too big for. Three bedrooms and a bathroom were all packed into the tiny space, and Nate gestured to the one at the farthest end of the hallway.

There was a double bed with a pretty wrought iron headboard that didn't look like Nate at all and a flowery white quilt, even less like him, and some built-in closets at the back. I wasn't even sure how the doors opened, there was so little space between them and the small nightstand by the bed.

"Bathroom is through there," Nate said, gesturing at a door behind him. "I'll be up for a while, so I'm going to get the fire going. Shout if you need anything."

Despite all of the assurances he'd made that this was all in the interests of my safety, I was still surprised when he walked away, actually leaving me alone.

I let myself into the room and locked the door behind me, stripping out of my outer layers and setting the gun next to the bed. Maybe I'd wake up tomorrow and freak out about, well, all of this. But for now, a few extra hours of sleep sounded like a great idea, and I had to admit, I did feel safer not being alone in the house.

I just had to hope that I'd put my faith in the right stalker.

* * *

I woke up confused, and not nearly as well rested as usual, so it took me a minute for the events of last night to come back to me. Right. Weird, not-animal, animal sounds. Nate showed up. I agreed to come back to his place for the night. Gabriel and Brooks probably having one-night stands with beautiful women who weren't me.

Just a regular... Tuesday? I didn't even know anymore.

I grabbed my phone, messaging Ria via her boyfriend's satellite phone to let her know I was okay, before scrolling idly through my social media comments.

Message Request from Frank Ashford.

I snorted, rolling my eyes. I hadn't bothered blocking him on social media, but that was about to change. Curiosity got the better of me though, and I decided to see what he had to say first.

Frank_Ashford:

Meet me for lunch at midday at the bistro on 1st Avenue.

Delusional. Absolutely delusional. *Block.*

The house was quiet as I let myself into the bathroom and got ready for the day and applied my makeup before digging through my bag in Nate's room for something presentable to wear out of the weird combination of stuff I'd shoved in my bag. I eventually settled on some lavender leggings, gray fluffy socks, and a pale turquoise sweater before undoing my bun and running my fingers through my wavy hair. I probably looked like a red-headed easter egg, but whatever. My options were limited.

I thought I'd been moving around quietly, but by the time I was ready, I could hear all three of them talking in the kitchen, and the smell of coffee drifted down the hallway.

Huh. On reflection, I realized I felt a little bit nervous as I approached the three of them in their own house. I channeled some Scarlet-style confidence, because I had no room for nerves right now. I didn't even know exactly *why.* There was a strange, almost instinctual need for me to show them that I wasn't afraid.

"Good morning," I sang as I squeezed into the overcrowded kitchen. Super chill, not intimidated in the slightest. "Is there any coffee left?"

"If there's not, we'll make more," Brooks mumbled, slumped over the dining table, not looking surprised in the slightest to see me. "I'm going to live off it today."

Gabriel passed me a cup of black coffee with a tight smile, looking as exhausted as Brooks did. *I guess whichever girls they hooked up with last night wore them out,* I thought bitterly.

"Did you sleep okay?" Nate asked raspily. Had he slept? There were dark shadows under his eyes that I didn't remember seeing yesterday.

"Fine, thank you," I replied carefully, sipping my black coffee. "So, uh, we should probably discuss what happened last night. I'm sure your roommates want to know why I'm here."

Brooks gave me a puzzled look, like he didn't understand the question. Maybe Nate had filled them in while I was sleeping.

"They already know. I drove past your house because I had a bad feeling, pulled into the driveway, and whoever was there ran," Nate said in a monotonous voice, staring at the floor.

I frowned at him, irritated he wouldn't make eye contact.

"You said last night you thought it was Frank," I pointed out.

"I'm confident it was," Nate replied, finally meeting my gaze.

"Did you *see* him?" I pressed. I couldn't imagine him terrorizing my house then inviting me out for lunch the next day. "Because it didn't sound like a person. It sounded like animals. Which is weird, yes, but not exactly a reason to hide out at your house."

All three of them exchanged a panicked look that had warning bells ringing in the back of my mind.

"Why not just stay a few days, querida?" Gabriel suggested gently, rubbing his stubbled jaw, looking delightfully rumpled in the early morning light. "Until you know for sure that it wasn't a deliberate attack on your property."

I opened my mouth to argue, but Nate beat me to it. "You're painting your house anyway, right? Surely you'd be more comfortable staying here while you're working on it."

I would be. And as much as I believed that last night was just animals, I was still a little nervous about going back. Being alone in the house while the walls shook and growls filtered through from outside... I'd never felt so afraid in my life.

"I'm keeping the gun," I warned Nate.

"I would expect nothing less," he agreed, while Brooks and Gabriel nodded like that was completely rational.

"And I need to go back to my house to check the damage, and get my stuff."

"I'll come with you, whenever you're ready," Nate replied easily. I had to give the guy credit. I'd told him multiple times I hated him, but he wasn't deterred in the slightest.

"Pack a swimsuit," Brooks said with a lazy wink, grinning when I gave him a *seriously*? look. "There's a hot tub out back."

181

"Fine. And maybe in the car, Nate can fill me in on whatever it is that you're all lying about," I announced primly, spinning on my heel to go find my coat while Brooks choked noisily on his coffee behind me.

* * *

By the time I emerged in my winter layers, Gabriel was waiting for me at the door, swinging a keychain around his finger. "Sorry, querida. Nate had to go into the studio to meet a client."

"Sure he did," I said drily, walking past Gabriel out into the snow. *Coward.* The SUV from last night sat in the driveway, but the truck was missing.

"Did you have a nice night?" I asked, shooing away Gabriel's hand when he offered to help me into the vehicle. I was annoyed. For reasons I didn't quite understand.

"I wouldn't say *nice*," Gabriel chuckled, moving around the car and climbing into the driver's side.

It was probably more than nice. It was probably sweaty and passionate and screamy, featuring a woman who didn't wear a wig and asked a guy to call her by a different name.

"Are you feeling okay?" Gabriel asked gently, pulling out of the driveway. "It sounds like last night was frightening."

"The noises were a little creepy," I conceded. "Whatever they were."

Gabriel stared determinedly ahead, fiddling mindlessly with the radio until quiet country music came through the speakers, not engaging in that line of conversation. Did he believe Nate's theory that it was Frank?

We'd been driving on the highway heading out of town for a few minutes when I realized I'd never told Gabriel my address. I guessed Nate could have told him and it could have been a totally harmless thing, but I was adding it to my pile of evidence that these guys were keeping secrets and all men were liars.

He pulled up in front of my house, leaping out of the vehicle before I had a chance to move—shit, he was fast—and stomping around like he was looking for threats, jaw tense, nose... twitching? I needed more coffee.

Leaving him to whatever it was he was doing, I let myself out of the car and climbed the front steps, looking for any more unwanted deliveries on the porch and finding nothing. Maybe Frank was listening to me after all.

"You okay over there?" I called, craning my neck to look at Gabriel behind the pillar.

"Fine," he growled, his voice rougher than I'd ever heard it. "The smell is a little overwhelming."

Rude. My house didn't *smell*.

I unlocked the door and let myself into the house, relieved to find that it all looked as it should. Of course it did. Frank wasn't going to *break into my house*. I really needed to stop letting Nate's paranoid ramblings get to me.

Gabriel followed me inside, but I ignored him in favor of heading to my bedroom and pulling out the rolling cute floral print suitcase I'd bought specifically for my trip to New York to meet Frank. I hated looking at it now, it just reminded me what an idiot I'd been.

I moved around my room quickly to distract myself, going through my drawers and pulling out a few days' worth of clothes. If they happened to be extra tight yoga pants that made my ass look phenomenal, well that was just an added bonus, wasn't it?

Since Brooks had mentioned the hot tub, I packed a skimpy one-piece.

For absolutely no reason, I packed some cute lingerie.

Work. I told myself. I'd still need to take some photos. I didn't know how I was going to manage to do that staying with the guys, but I still needed *some* content. Carefully, I packed my ring light, tripod and wig on top.

Satisfied I had enough stuff to last me a few days, I rolled my suitcase into the living room—which looked *so* much better now it was all painted—and took a deep breath before heading towards the kitchen. The door was already open, exposing the decimated screen door behind it, and I followed the sound of creaking wood to find Gabriel already outside. He'd pushed his sleeves up and was yanking the broken balustrade rails off with his bare hands, tossing them in a pile on the snow.

"I took photos of the damage," Gabriel said, not sounding out of breath in the slightest. "I'll send them to you. But we'll fix this, you don't need to get insurance involved."

"You're really strong," I said, watching him work in awe, barely registering what he'd said.

Gabriel looked a little panicked for a moment before laughing awkwardly. "I lift."

"I can see that." He could probably lift *me* with one arm. Or whoever he'd been doing last night. "I had planned on painting the entryway today so, uh, I'll just meet you at your place later."

Gabriel raised one dark eyebrow at me, and I must be a little bit fucked in the head because his judgmental expression really did things for me.

"I'm not leaving you alone, querida. Did you forget what happened last night?" He gestured at the decimated porch.

"I didn't forget," I replied carefully. *I'm just not sure I believe the story you're trying to sell me.*

"I was going to finish with this and take the screen door off anyway. Then I'll come in and help you paint."

"That's not necessary," I assured him. "I wasn't fishing for extra help. I'll be fine here, I'm sure you have work to do."

"I've never painted walls before. You can teach me." His expression softened a little from the tense look he'd been rocking since we'd arrived at my place, and it melted my resolve to argue with him.

It would get the job done faster and he'd probably get all this damage cleaned up faster than I could.

I got my toolbox for Gabriel to remove the door then set everything up in the entryway, too vain to change into my ugly painting clothes and hoping I didn't ruin these ones because I liked these leggings. Gabriel joined me inside, stripping off his sweater to reveal a fitted t-shirt underneath and tanned, muscular arms that I wanted to lick.

"Did Nate do those?" I asked, nodding at his tattoos.

"He did," Gabriel said with a small smile, pushing his sleeve up so I could see. He had one of the old-fashioned maps—the kind with two circles that showed the two hemispheres side-by-side—split across both arms. The continents were shaded around the edges in a way that made them look almost three dimensional, and surrounded by incredibly thin latitude and longitude lines, wrapping around each arm.

It was a masterpiece.

"You know, I was kind of on the fence about having my tattoo filled in, but not after seeing this," I murmured, tracing one of the lines with my finger, slightly in awe. Except spending hours in Nate's company was a terrible idea, so maybe not.

"Can I see it?" Gabriel asked, hot breath fanning across my face. When had I gotten so close? "Your tattoo, I mean."

"You'd have to get me naked for that," I retorted, a little bit of my flirty Scarlet confidence popping up at the worst possible moment. As already demonstrated by last night's disaster of a date, nothing could ever happen between me and Gabriel. Not now that I knew Nate was his friend, and I was fake dating Nate. And had *history* with Nate. And Gabriel had probably gone out and screwed another girl last night.

There were a lot of extenuating factors at play.

I took a step back, pasting a friendly smile on my face and pretending I hadn't just issued him a not so subtle invitation. "So, paint. Um, we're going to start by cutting in the edges. You've never done this before?"

"Where I grew up, in Brazil, it was a community and we all lived in cabanas that had been there for generations. We couldn't really make changes because they belonged to everyone," Gabriel explained.

"Like a commune?" I asked dubiously, letting Gabriel move the ladder for me when I went to drag it into the corner.

"I suppose a commune is one way to look at it," he replied thoughtfully. I couldn't think of any other way to look at it, but maybe I was being narrow minded. I guess the trailer park I grew up in had a pretty communal vibe too.

"How did you meet Nate and Brooks?" I asked, ignoring the mildly alarmed noise Gabriel made when I climbed the ladder. Worrywart.

"We met in our early twenties. Many years ago now," Gabriel added with a chuckle like they were *so* old when I was pretty sure they were all in their mid-thirties, tops. "It was in Mexico. Drunk on a beach in Sayulita."

There was a wistful quality to his voice that I found kind of adorable.

"And it was love at first sight?" I teased.

Gabriel barked a laugh. "Not at all. Nate and I got along right away, but Brooks was a real little shit back then."

"I don't believe it," I deadpanned, making Gabriel grin.

I was pretty sure Brooks could be a real little shit *now*, but he was so charming that he got away with it. I'd already mentally given myself a gold star for resisting his charms when I'd met him at the coffee shop. Well, mostly resisting. But I had told him I wasn't interested, so the gold star was still well earned. If stupid Nate hadn't ripped my heart out through my vagina, I would have *definitely* been interested. But I was also dealing with the whole Scarlet/Lou conundrum, because while Nate asked me to take the wig off, it wasn't lost on me that he wouldn't have actually fucked me if I hadn't gone full Scarlet on his ass. My insecurities had been throwing a week-long fiesta in my head.

Gabriel seemed interested in me as I was last night, though. Before everything went wrong.

"After a few weeks, Brooks settled down," Gabriel continued and I forced myself to concentrate. "Stopped getting drunk and trying to fight everyone. We realized he wasn't a bad dude after that."

"Brooks doesn't seem like a brawler," I replied as I squinted up at the ceiling, attempting to not get *too* much paint on the crown molding.

"He's not really, not now," Gabriel admitted, working slowly on the corners. "But he left home very young and was a little lost for a few years. I'll let him tell you that story though."

I glanced down at Gabriel in surprise, but he was entirely focused on what he was doing. I doubted he'd meant it the way it sounded. I was staying for a few days at their insistence, we were hardly going to start ripping open our emotional wounds for each other.

Though maybe we could be friends after all of this. Not me and Nate, obviously. But Brooks and Gabriel seemed really cool, and their jobs were super interesting, and they'd traveled all over the place. I definitely wouldn't mind getting to know them better.

We got into the groove of painting, and eventually Gabriel got my speaker out of the kitchen and connected his phone to it. My expectations were low, but his taste veered towards sing-along style golden oldies, and I could definitely roll with that. He wasn't even a terrible singer.

"Nate is the talented one," Gabriel laughed when I pointed that out, heaving the roller up the wall. "In places where he isn't licensed to do tattoos, he bartends, sings, whatever odd jobs he can find."

"Don't tell me if he plays guitar," I told Gabriel, shooting him a warning look. "I don't want to know."

He'd look so hot with a guitar.

Gabriel was silent for a moment, lost in thought with a faint smile on his face as he worked on the wall adjacent to mine, and I was more curious than I had any right to be about what was going on in his head.

We finished the entryway in record time and I was blown away at how much better it looked. I was going to be able to sell this place in no time.

"For a newbie, you did an amazing job," I told Gabriel, bumping him with my shoulder as we worked together to clean everything up.

"You're a good teacher," Gabriel replied affectionately. "Though I might faint if I don't get away from this smell soon."

"It's really not that bad," I scoffed. The windows had been open the entire time, airing the place out. "Want to have a coffee on the front porch? Actually, you don't have a jacket," I added, frowning at him. I wanted to leave the windows open a little longer and I doubted Gabriel was going to leave me here on my own.

"I'll be fine," he assured me, grabbing his sweater and pulling it back on.

"You really must run hot," I commented, grabbing my bulky layers and heading to the kitchen to put coffee on. "Doesn't that get uncomfortable when you're in a warmer climate?"

"I'm very adaptable," Gabriel replied, leaning back against the counter and watching me work. "Querida, I'd like to talk to you about something."

I snorted. "I gathered that after all the long contemplative silences. What's up?"

Gabriel looked pensive, and I did my best to suppress my natural urge to be snarky at every opportunity—a very *Lou* response, Scarlet was sweeter—to listen to him. I didn't know Gabriel at all, but I got the impression he considered words carefully before he spoke them. Besides, after the ordeal I put him through on our "date" last night, listening to him was really the least I could do.

"I understand that you are in this... pretend relationship with Nate, and I am not objecting. Having seen Frank last night, I think that's a sensible course of action," Gabriel began.

Uh, why? It had been a spur of the moment excuse I'd spouted that had spiralled *wildly* out of control. What's done was done, but in no universe was it a "sensible course of action." It was possibly the least sensible course of action I could have taken.

"I was wondering if you'd be open to getting to know me, regardless of your arrangement with Nate?" Gabriel asked, the politeness of the request taking me off-guard. "You called me last night, and I hope that means you have some interest in me. Of course, that was before you discovered Nate and I knew each other, but I'm hoping that you'll consider spending time with me anyway."

"I'm spending time with you now," I pointed out.

189

"Dating me," Gabriel clarified, his lips tipping up in amusement.

"Usually, when a guy sees a girl he's interested in shoving her tongue in his friend's mouth, that's kind of a dealbreaker."

I needed a filter. The words just spilled out like they had a mind of their own.

Gabriel laughed, not at all perturbed. I was perturbed. I'd perturbed myself.

"If it was anyone else, sure. Nate and Brooks are... it's hard to explain. Family, I suppose. Whatever you do with them, it doesn't bother me. Well, perhaps if I'm left out," he said ruefully. "But I don't say that to pressure you. If you aren't interested, you aren't interested. I just sort of *hoped* that you were."

"I don't know if I should be dating right now," I said slowly, because had he just told me he was fine with me fucking his friends? It kind of sounded like that was what he said.

"You're here until the end of winter, no?" Gabriel shrugged. "So are we. Brooks and I, at least. Nate is being difficult. Why not enjoy ourselves while we're here?"

That... that did sound kind of perfect actually. Maybe Gabriel was a giver? I really wanted another round of oral sex, just to verify that it was, in fact, as glorious as I remembered it.

"Do you think Nate will be okay with that?" I asked slowly, my resolve crumbling into dust. "Not that I care," I added hastily. Fuck that guy.

"He might surprise you," Gabriel said, all sexy and mysterious, and not really answering my question.

"You are talking about me potentially hooking up with any of you, right?" I clarified, my cheeks heating instantly. "This will be awkward if you're not."

"Hooking up sounds a little cheap," Gabriel replied with a small frown. "I'm talking about you dating any combination of us for a fixed set of time. If a fixed set of time is what you want."

I disregarded his last comment, not willing or able to process that right now. The winter was a nice finite stretch of time that I could comfortably focus on.

It would be nice to just agree to this and jump Gabriel's bones here and now—he'd asked *me* out. Me! Not Scarlet. No fake identity or elaborate internet seduction required. Still, it would probably be a good idea to discuss this with the other people involved first. Nate was a no-go, I'd been thoroughly burned by his fire already, but Brooks...

He'd been flirty as hell, but he'd also gone out last night. So had Gabriel for that matter.

My eyes narrowed on him and his eyebrows lifted. "What exactly were you doing last night?" I asked, aiming for a relaxed tone and missing the mark entirely.

Way to be cool, I groaned internally. All he'd suggested was casually dating over the winter—you know, with his two besties, as you do—and I was going full jealous girlfriend on him already.

Gabriel looked momentarily surprised, like my question had taken him off guard, before his mouth spread into a smug grin that shouldn't have been as attractive as it was.

Be infuriated, I instructed my idiot brain with no success.

"You're jealous," he announced. I could have sworn his chest puffed up a bit, like an arrogant peacock strutting about.

"I am not," I protested instantly. "I'm doing recon."

Gabriel snorted. "What an unusually hostile approach to beginning a casual relationship."

"Just keeping you on your toes," I sassed back, rejecting the R-word completely. "Are you going to answer my question?"

"Brooks and I were hanging out together. There were no women involved, I assure you," Gabriel said sincerely.

Soooo.... were they hooking up with each other? I almost opened my mouth to ask, but that seemed a little personal. Did it really matter if they were? This was just a temporary thing anyway. It'd probably be hypocritical for me to ask, given Gabriel had just given me the go-ahead to pursue Brooks if I wanted to.

"There is no one else we are interested in, querida," Gabriel continued, misinterpreting my silence. "You managed to separately snare all of our attention in the short time we've been here."

"This is a lot to process," I admitted.

"Then just think about it," Gabriel replied easily, accepting the cup of coffee I handed him. "Now let's go outside before the smell of paint knocks me out."

Chapter 14

It was another hour before we returned to the guys' cabin in separate cars. I parked on the other side of Nate's truck, mentally preparing myself to go another verbal round with him to figure out what it was he was being so secretive about, though it was difficult to verbally spar with someone who locked themselves up like a safe the second he was faced with any kind of confrontation. It didn't help that he seemed so genuinely remorseful. His shame tugged at my stupid empathy.

Gabriel somehow appeared behind my car before I even had a chance to open my door, pulling my bag out of the trunk. Either I moved at a particularly leisurely pace, or these guys were seriously fast.

I shook my head at my weird musings as I climbed out of the car. My mind was playing tricks on me recently.

"Querida," Gabriel said suddenly, turning back to look at me as he led me towards the house, a look of absolute horror on his face. "Fuck, we haven't fed you today."

I snorted. "I'm not a pet. I can feed and water myself, thank you very much. Besides, you haven't eaten either."

"I ate before we came back this morning," Gabriel replied absently. "And of course you are not a pet, you are our *guest*."

I stepped past him into the cabin that looked even smaller in the light of day, but the fire was roaring in the living room and the whole space was lovely and cozy.

Nate was pacing in front of the television while Brooks lounged on the couch, legs spread wide with one arm draped over the back, entirely dominating his space.

"Hey, Red," he said cheerfully as Gabriel closed the door behind me and I began stripping out of my coat and snow boots.

"Brooks and I were just talking about Frank," Nate volunteered, giving me that slightly kicked puppy look he'd been wearing since yesterday.

"Gabriel and I were just talking about how I should have sex with all of you," I replied airily, because apparently seeing Nate's face made me angry, and being angry brought out my inner petty.

"Oh?" It was an artform the way Brooks packed so much intrigue, amusement, and disbelief into two letters. I was low key envious.

"Actually, we were talking about how Lou hasn't eaten all day," Gabriel said, a mild chastisement in his tone.

"And..." I replied pointedly.

"And whether or not Lou would be open to dating any or all of us while we're here," Gabriel said with an easy shrug. "But the food thing is a higher priority at the moment."

"The *Frank* thing is a higher priority," Nate grumbled, taking far longer to speak up than I had expected him to.

"You stress too much. It's bad for your health," I told him, patting him on the arm as I wound my way between the coffee table, Nate, and the fireplace to get to the kitchen. This place made my house feel like a palatial mansion, though maybe it was just the oversized men making it feel so cramped.

I hummed under my breath as I made a beeline for the fridge, stopping abruptly when I saw what was in there.

Creamer, string cheese, and two full shelves of Lunchables.

What the hell? How were they all so buff and ripped like they lived off grilled chicken and protein powder pancakes when *this* is what their fridge looked like?

"Oh yeah, we don't really cook," Brooks admitted, sounding a little sheepish as he sidled into the kitchen, leaning on the bench. "There are Hot Pockets in the freezer. I'm trying to catch up on all the American food I miss when we're out of the country, but tonight I was thinking of ordering pizza. Or we could get cheesesteaks—"

"Not cheesesteaks again," Gabriel groaned, taking a seat at the dining table while Nate leaned against the doorframe. "Tacos?"

"I guess I could go for tacos," Brooks sighed dramatically.

"Hold on." I held up a hand to stop them, barely believing what I was hearing. "You three grown men in your thirties don't know how to cook?"

"It takes ages," Brooks replied with a shrug. "And then someone has to clean up afterwards. And everything we make tastes like shit. I mean, if we were making a pros and cons list..."

"Heathens," I snorted. "I'll cook while I'm staying here, as a thank you for all of this unnecessary protection you're insisting on."

"You might poison us," Nate muttered. I shot him a dirty look, wondering why I'd ever been so cut up over him. He was kind of a dick. Maybe I dodged a bullet.

"Just you," I replied with a sugary sweet smile, making Brooks laugh.

"Ótimo, we'll go to the store later," Gabriel said, sounding amused. "Sleeping arrangements? It would make sense for you to swap with Brooks," he said, looking at Nate.

"Gabriel and I don't mind sharing a bed," Brooks explained to me. "Nate isn't a cuddler."

"I'm well aware," I replied drily. Nate winced slightly, and honestly, it had been kind of a cheap shot, but whatever. He hadn't given me a real reason for why he'd run out into the snow in the middle of the night, so I was going to assume it was for ridiculous reasons until he bothered to correct me.

"This boring as fuck winter just got a whole lot more interesting," Brooks declared, flashing me a dimpled grin.

✳ ✳ ✳

In the end, I wrote a grocery list for Nate who had to go into the studio for a while anyway. Gabriel had disappeared into the shower muttering about the paint stench, so I dug out my laptop and made myself comfortable at one end of the couch while Brooks occupied the other, flicking aimlessly through a list of movies while I checked my emails and ate a nacho Lunchable.

It was delicious, but didn't really fit in with my whole 'my body is a temple' mindset.

I bit down on an excited squeal when I opened an email from a woman-owned lingerie store with a real focus on female sexual empowerment. I'd reached out to them without any real expectation of it going anywhere because, while I had a lot of followers, higher end companies didn't want brand ambassadors with my kind of history.

Dear Scarlet,

We would love to work with you! We've been looking through your posts, and your relaxed, confident, positive approach to sexuality is exactly in keeping with our values.

I waited for the 'but', which I'd already got in a few responses so far. The 'we like you but the sex work history is a deal breaker even though we sell sexy lingerie/toys/lube, sorry.' Obviously they weren't all like that—I'd partnered with brands before and used their products in live shows when I was camming, but I expected this company to choose reps who had a cleaner online presence.

We appreciate you letting us know about your work history, and would like to assure you that is not a dealbreaker for us. We are firm believers that sex work is work, and not something to be stigmatized for.

If you could let us know your address and sizes, we'll send you some products to get started with. It'd be great to get a feel for the kind of content you'd like to produce.

"Someone got good news," Brooks teased while I grinned like a lunatic at my screen and quickly shot back a reply with my PO box and sizes.

"Just being the boss lady I am," I replied, flipping my hair because I was feeling some *big* Scarlet energy at the moment. If I could build a good relationship with this brand, it could turn into a pretty lucrative revenue stream.

I had no idea what I was going to *do* with all this stuff I was sent once I was on the road. Maybe I'd keep a storage unit somewhere just for my sex toy and fancy lingerie collection. Then when I died, I'd go down in *Storage Wars* history. They would call me *The Girl With The Dragon Dildos* and I would live on in infamy.

"What is it that you do?" Brooks asked, furrowing his brow like he was trying to remember if I'd told him or not as he cracked into his second— maybe third?—Lunchable.

I hesitated for a moment, not wanting to risk his judgment by telling him, but then Nate hadn't been necessarily judgmental. He'd fallen prey to Scarlet's charm, if anything he liked her more than plain old Lou.

Sex work is work.

I pulled up one of my social media profiles on my laptop and spun it around to face Brooks, bracing myself for his response.

He tilted his head to the side, eyes skimming the page before reaching out and scrolling down, the silence of the room a little stifling. Actually, I was pretty sure I could hear my own heartbeat slamming against my chest, so there was that.

"You're so photogenic," Brooks murmured, taking me off-guard. "These pictures would look amazing with your natural hair though."

I had that thought myself. My "stage" clothes were in more neutral colors, and I took selfies against an oatmeal colored sheet with a pale blonde wig on. My darker hair would add great contrast.

"I don't know if my followers would like that," I admitted, turning my laptop back to face me.

"Ask them to vote," Brooks suggested with a shrug, picking up the remote again and returning to his movie search. Easy as that.

Logically, I knew that at first glance, it wasn't obvious from my social profiles that I'd ever done camgirl stuff too, but even so, his reaction to me taking racy photos as a job had been more relaxed than I'd anticipated.

"Want to get more Lunchables and binge watch all the *Fast & Furious* movies?" Brooks asked, looking genuinely thrilled at the idea. His pale blue eyes lit up with excitement, and his grin made him look more like a 19-year-old than a man in his thirties.

How could he be sexy and kind of adorable, all at once?

"You really don't know me at all," I laughed. "But sure. Put on the car movies."

"Not this again," Gabriel sighed, glancing at the screen as he entered the living room. His dark hair was wet from the shower, his usual curls straight and clinging to his skin. I was meant to be editing together a video of me modeling a lingerie haul I'd received last week—my screen turned awkwardly away from Brooks—but my fingers froze as I admired Gabriel standing in the doorway, our conversation from this morning repeating in my brain on a loop.

His gaze shifted from the television to me, and he gave me a smile that bordered on *sinful*, like he knew exactly what I was thinking about. The sensible part of my brain reminded me that I'd already had a one-night stand with one of these guys, and it had ended spectacularly badly. The other part of my brain that was actually my vagina said *screw it! Fuck the rest of them! Collect 'em all!*

Both sides made very intelligent points. I had a lot to think about.

"Gabriel doesn't appreciate films of quality," Brooks told me conspiratorially.

Gabriel snorted. "I'm thinking of Lou, not myself. What kind of films do you like to watch, querida?"

"Ones where Colin Firth emerges from a lake in a soaking wet blouse," I sighed.

"That's... oddly specific," Brooks chuckled. "If you've got a thing for men going swimming fully clothed, I'd be more than happy to fulfil those desires for you, Red."

"Save it, Fabio," Gabriel laughed. "Let's help Nate unload the groceries. Not you, querida. Stay inside where it's warm," Gabriel added as he and Brooks moved towards the door. I frowned in confusion as they let themselves outside before hearing the faint sound of Nate's truck bumping down the driveway.

Yikes, maybe I should get my ears checked? I hadn't heard the truck at all.

The three of them came back inside a few minutes later with arms full of grocery bags, not looking like they were exerting any energy at all.

"How long was your list?" Brooks asked in awe as I led them into the kitchen so I could put everything away where I wanted it. Maybe I was being a little presumptuous, but it wasn't like they were using the kitchen anyway.

"Long," Nate muttered, setting his bags on the counter. "I had to look up a bunch of stuff. Green onions don't look anything like onions."

I was trying to hold onto my Nate Rage, but a small giggle slipped out at that admission. He got all moon eyed at the sound, and I forced myself to put my unimpressed mask back in place because I was *mad*, damn it.

"Can you two *please* just tell us what happened between you?" Brooks all but begged, watching the two of us like we were never-before-seen, exclusive *Fast & Furious* footage.

"Nope," I replied, shooting Gabriel a grateful smile as he put the canned tomatoes on the top shelf I was struggling to reach on tiptoes.

"I'll get it out of you," Brooks shot confidently. "In the meantime, I have a very important question for you, Red."

"Is that so?" I asked wryly, setting aside the ingredients I needed for the grilled fish and vegetable dinner.

"Very important," Brooks agreed seriously, pausing for dramatic effect. "Are you a cat person or a dog person?"

I expected Nate or Gabriel to groan at the question, but they were surprisingly silent, like this was actually an essential piece of information they needed from me.

"Er, cat person," I replied, looking around the quiet room.

"What? *Why?*" Brooks asked in a tone that bordered on a whine. I felt my eyebrows rising slowly in disbelief.

"Because cats are smarter, sleeker, and more superior in every way, *irmão*," Gabriel chuckled, looking delighted. "Brooks here is a *dog* person," he added for my benefit, shaking his head like that was a travesty.

"Pity. I guess no one's perfect," I told Brooks with a sweet smile, batting my eyelashes at him. I didn't feel particularly strongly either way to be honest, but I respected the fuck-you vibe that cats put out. I'd always found that quite relatable. Then I remembered how easily I'd turned into an eager little puppy when Nate had told me I was a good girl, and wondered if I needed to think on this question a little further.

Brooks grinned at me like I'd just laid down a challenge. "So, shall we help you make dinner and you can tell us about your conversation with Gabriel this morning? I would *love* to hear more about this dating-all-of-us idea."

Nate made a strangled noise, aggressively shoving produce into the bottom of the fridge like it personally offended him.

"I think we should talk about Frank instead," he suggested in a strained voice. "You said he's been sending you things—"

"Oh my god, not this again," I groaned. "What is there to say? Frank and I had an *arrangement* for a few weeks, but that turned sour because it turns out he's married and I was reading too much into things anyway. I left New York, he sent some messages, sent me money, but I never responded. He sent a gift to my house, which shouldn't have been possible because he theoretically didn't know my real name, and then he showed up."

"So, what part of this makes you think you *don't* need to be worried?" Brooks asked, sounding genuinely baffled.

I mean, it did sound worse when I laid it all out like that.

"Because," I sputtered. "I was with him in New York a whole bunch of times one-on-one. If he wanted to *hurt* me, he had plenty of opportunities."

"That was before you rejected him, querida," Gabriel pointed out gently. "Some, er, *guys* struggle with that."

"So, let him struggle," I replied with a shrug. Fuck him. He could learn the meaning of 'no'. Babies and dogs figured it out just fine.

It was polite of them not to ask me to elaborate on 'arrangement', I'd give them each a point for that. Unless Nate had given them a heads up on *Scarlet*, but Brooks had seemed genuinely curious earlier when he asked about my career.

"Frank is... not like other guys," Nate said, that frustrated tone coming back into his voice that made me feel like he was hiding things. "He's a powerful guy. Very, er, influential. I can't understand why he'd be so interested in you."

Why had I ever missed interacting with real life men? They were the *worst*.

"That came out wrong," Gabriel said quickly, jumping to his friend's rescue while Brooks made siren noises and repeated "danger" over and over again in a robotic voice.

"Did it now?" I drawled, raising an eyebrow at Nate and giving him two seconds to scramble out of the hole he'd just launched himself into.

"Uh, I just mean... we've heard of Frank Ashford, you know? He's a well-known guy. Coming all the way here... I mean, he must really like you." Nate rubbed the back of his neck awkwardly, and if I wasn't still mad at him for the tap and gap, I might feel sorry for him. Maybe.

"Wait, you've *all* heard of Frank?" I asked, frowning. Frank was a successful guy, but he was hardly famous. I definitely wouldn't have expected a travel writer, a photographer and a tattoo artist to have heard of him. "Why didn't you mention that when you saw him at the bar?"

"We don't know much about him, just remember hearing the name, you know? We travel a lot," Gabriel replied quickly. *Very* quickly. "We've heard of all kinds of people."

"O-kay..." I said slowly. That was definitely a lie. Maybe they'd specifically looked into Frank because of me? I wouldn't have held it against them if they had, but I couldn't understand why they'd lie about it.

"We've been to New York," Nate added in what he probably thought was an encouraging, convincing voice.

"I haven't," Brooks supplied, looking a little put out about it. "I think my sister knows Frank though. I've been trying to get a hold of her, but we're not that close, so it's tricky."

"Mm, I still feel pretty strongly like you're all not telling me an important piece of information."

All three of them suddenly found the floor very interesting as I replayed their interactions with him in my head. "When you met Frank, it really seemed like he knew stuff about you," I said, glaring at Nate, who was still refusing to make eye contact. "And he's full of shit, yada yada yada, but some of the stuff he said to you was *weird*. Not like, stir-the-pot, make-a-scene kind of weird, just straight up unusual. *Unless* you two already know each other."

"We don't," Nate insisted, finally meeting my gaze with a pleading look in his eye. "I promise you, Lou."

I wanted to believe him. His face was open and honest, and he was looking at me like he was begging me to see the truth in his words. But I'd been burned by Nate once before. Maybe he hadn't *lied* when he'd abruptly ran out after sex, but he'd definitely disrespected me, and I wasn't about to take anything at face value when it came to him.

"Can we go back to the dating all of us thing?" Brooks asked hopefully.

I shot him a scathing look, because I was pretty content to not date anyone who was obviously lying to me.

What Would Scarlet Do?

Probably something really confident and sassy that left these three idiots on their knees, panting after me, but I just… didn't have it in me. The less Scarlet-ing I did, the harder it was to slip the mask on when I needed it.

"I don't think it's a good idea," Nate muttered, finally answering Brooks' question that had been hanging awkwardly in the air. "I can't stop you, but I feel that getting involved is too… risky. With her."

What. The. Hell.

What had I ever done for Nate to talk to me like that? Sure, I'd played up the seduction stuff a little because of all the garbage he spewed about me being too fragile to handle him or whatever, but he made it sound like I'd *tricked* him into something.

"The fuck is your problem?" I snapped, whirling around to face him. "Seriously. You're the one who—"

I slammed my mouth shut, remembering we had an audience, both of whom were looking wide eyed at the *rage* in my voice. Maybe I'd done a good job of shoving it down over the past twenty-four hours and pretending like I could be civil with Nate, but now it was boiling up to the surface and I was ready to drown in it and take Nate with me.

Forcing myself to calm down before I said something I would regret, I closed my eyes and took a deep breath, reminding myself of all the exciting things I had ahead of me. I had plans. I was going places—quite literally. All these men with their pretty eyes and even prettier lies were just a stupid distraction that I'd leave behind me one day.

This time next year, I'd be lying on a beach in Mexico drinking a cocktail, snuggled up to my latest fling—who would have more abs and a bigger dick than Nate—and I would barely remember any of this.

"Forget it. Doesn't matter. Tell me what it is you're hiding from me," I demanded hoarsely, staring Nate down. *Redeem yourself, at least one percent. Show me you're not an entirely terrible person.*

Nate's lips thinned as he held my stare, the tension evident in the lines of his face, even as those brilliant green eyes begged me to just drop the subject. Breaking eye contact, I cast my gaze over to Brooks and Gabriel, who were both unnervingly silent, looking at anywhere but my face.

"I'm going to lie down," I announced, impressed with how even I kept my voice. I swung by the living room to grab my laptop before disappearing past the guys into my borrowed bedroom. The sound of absolute silence followed me.

BROOKS

Chapter 15

"Nate," Gabriel sighed as Lou's door shut with a resounding click. "You need to tell us, what is going on with the beautiful woman staying in our house who you are both intrigued by and terrified of?"

"The one who fucking despises you," I added, just in case there was any confusion.

"*My* house," Nate grumbled, subtly reiterating to Gabriel that we weren't a pack before he started having those delusional ideas again. "Nothing is going on. I'm not terrified of her," he added, giving Gabriel a surly look, but not bothering to contradict me since we all knew I was right.

"Why is she staying here?" Gabriel asked patiently.

"You know why," Nate shot back, giving him an affronted look. "You were there last night. You heard that guy. You fought him."

"He's a powerful as fuck Alpha," I agreed. My muscles had been aching all day, and I'd bet Nate's ribs were still smarting. "No one is disputing that. But pretending to be in a relationship with her? That's pretty extreme."

Nate scrubbed a hand over his face, his usually clean shaven jaw dotted with dark stubble. We were all exhausted after running patrols between here and Lou's place all night. Nate had stayed at the house with her, but I knew he hadn't slept. When Gabriel and I finally came home around six am after hunting our breakfast, we found Nate pacing back and forth in front of the cabin, clutching his aching side, looking slightly deranged.

Frank had left right away, but his packmates had hung around just to antagonize us. Mostly by pissing all over Lou's property. I had no idea how Gabriel had survived there this morning, it reeked.

"I wasn't going to contradict her when she told Frank that I was her boyfriend," Nate replied wearily, repeating the same line he'd given us in the car after we'd left the bar last night. He hesitated for a moment, but finally elaborated. "It would have been a dick move, and covering for her was the least I could do after... anyway... I just thought if I could convince him that she'd chosen me, he'd take it as an insult and leave."

"Because you're weaker than him?" I asked. Nate snarled reflexively, his eyes glowing as his cougar rose to the insult.

"Stop irritating him, Brooks," Gabriel muttered, massaging his eyes with his thumb and middle finger. "I see your logic, Nate, but there were easier ways, you know that. Frank won't believe she's chosen you unless there's a mating mark. Anything short of that is practically an invitation."

Nate grunted, digging out a beer from the fridge before slamming it shut and slumping back against it.

"You like her. You feel protective over her," Gabriel pressed. I started feeling a little sorry for Nate—I'd been on the receiving end of one of Gabriel's *talks* where he pushed me to talk about my *feelings*, and it was the absolute worst. "I feel protective over her too."

Nate full on *growled*, muscles rippling like his shift was imminent, and I darted towards the hallway to make sure Lou didn't come out to investigate the fucking lawnmower sound that had started up in our kitchen.

It totally wasn't as impressive as my growl. How could Lou possibly say she was a cat person? I bet she'd be a dog person if she heard *my* growl.

"Shush," I chided Nate, looking between him and the still closed door at the end of the hallway. "They were literally on a date last night. He suggested she date all of us. Don't act surprised that Gabriel is into her."

It probably wasn't the best time to mention that I liked Lou as well. She'd agreed to be friends and I totally respected that, but if she was open to Gabriel's idea, then I wasn't going to object. We were only here for a few more weeks anyway, it couldn't *go* anywhere.

Even knowing that, I was surprised at how protective I felt about Lou, and how willing I'd been to jump into the fray last night. It was probably just because I hated wolf packs. I didn't need to read any further into it than that.

"I can't stop you, and I wouldn't ever let it come between our friendship, but it's not a good idea for you to get involved with her," Nate gritted out, his voice a little too rough to be completely human.

"For mysterious reasons you're not going to explain to us?" I deadpanned.

"Lou said she didn't want to talk about it," Nate snapped. "All you need to know is that there's something about her that tests my control. I'm worried she'll test your control too."

"And you're jealous," I snorted. Nate downed his beer in one go, giving me a death glare the whole time. "That sounded like approval to me though," I added with a shrug.

Not that it really mattered. It was *Lou's* approval we needed.

"Tests your control..." Gabriel mused, mulling over the words.

"I'm done here. I need to run," Nate grunted. "My brother is going to meet me at Lou's house so he can catch their scents."

He slipped out of the kitchen as silent as a shadow and I had no doubt we wouldn't see him again for hours. Maybe even a couple of days. For all his 'it's a bad idea to date her' talk, he trusted us to look after Lou while he self-flagellated and undoubtedly chased Frank around town on his own.

Gabriel moved around the kitchen, gathering up the ingredients Lou had pulled out for dinner like he was going to pick up where she left off.

"You're going to give us all food poisoning," I chuckled, grabbing us beers from the fridge since Nate rudely hadn't offered us any.

"Shut up," Gabriel murmured, examining the fish. "How hard can it be? Though maybe... maybe not fish. I don't know how to cook fish."

"You don't know how to cook anything," I countered. He *could* grill, but this rental didn't have a grill and I'd never seen him cook anything in a pan.

No, that wasn't true. He'd attempted eggs once, but we had to throw the pan away afterwards.

Gabriel hunted through the fridge, shoving the fish back in and emerging triumphantly with a pack of steaks in his hand. "Steak, I can do. Maybe if I make them smell good enough, I can entice Lou out of the bedroom, because I'm not sure she'll be coming out otherwise."

I grimaced in agreement. She'd been furious when she walked out, and it was a testament to her inner strength that Nate's cougar hadn't risen up when she'd snapped at him like he was a naughty kid. Unless Nate had done something that both the man and the animal were ashamed of...

"What do you think Nate meant about testing his control?" I asked Gabriel, sitting down at the dining table. I wasn't even going to pretend to help him. If it couldn't be microwaved, I wasn't interested.

Gabriel glanced back at me, a thoughtful expression on his face. "My guess is that his cougar made himself known somehow, or tried to. Which is... unusual, since Nate has excellent control."

"Do you think it's something we need to worry about?"

Gabriel shrugged, but the movement wasn't as relaxed as he thought it was. "My jaguar is aggravated that there is a threat to her, but I'm not concerned that I'll shift in front of her or anything. Are you?"

I gave the question some serious thought, because my wolf and I weren't as in sync as Nate was with his cougar or Gabriel with his jaguar. I'd spent years resenting my wolf side because it was why I'd grown up in a pack, and the pack was the cause of all my worst memories. As a kid, I'd wanted nothing more than to be human.

My wolf didn't seem to get agitated when I was around Lou though. Just curious, if anything. It was more of a reaction than he gave most human women, but nothing to get alarmed about.

"No, I don't think it's an issue," I said eventually.

"Then I vote we get to know Lou if she's open to it and see what happens," Gabriel replied easily before wincing. "If we can convince her to speak to us ever again."

While Gabriel was inside, trying to sweet talk Lou into joining us for dinner to no avail—probably because his steaks smelled like crisp-yet-rubbery garbage—I decided to take a walk around the outskirts of the cabin to check for any unusual scents and try to call my sister again.

I wasn't surprised that Bea hadn't been picking up. She was a decade younger than me—just a kid when I'd left the pack—and was a Gold Star Pack Member who valued all the things that I despised. We couldn't be more opposite.

She'd for sure know who Frank Ashford was. She'd probably already looked into him as potential mate material.

Brooks:

Call me back, baby sis.

I knew I'd get a response from her after that. Bea couldn't stand any implication that she was *lesser* in any way, even if just in years we'd both been on the planet. It was a little absurd, but that kind of thinking was a hallmark of pack life and exactly why I'd left.

My phone rang and I immediately answered it with a grin, even though she couldn't see my face. "Bea!"

"Brooks," she replied flatly. "I assume you want something."

"Couldn't I just be checking in with my favorite little sister?" I teased.

"You never have before." *Ouch.* I always called on her birthday and holidays. It was more contact than I had with anyone else in my family.

"Harsh. Okay, fine. I did have a question for you. Does the name 'Frank Ashford' mean anything to you?"

Bea scoffed. "Obviously. Everyone knows who he is. Even you, apparently. Why?"

"A, uh, friend of mine has caught his attention. Just a regular girl, you know?"

I did not take chances talking about shifters on the phone. What if the Government was listening? I traveled too much to be on a watchlist.

"Big yikes," Bea breathed, sounding more animated than I'd ever heard her. "That's not great, Brooks. Not unusual for Frank, but not great for your friend."

"Why?" I demanded, stopping my pacing. "What do you mean by not unusual?"

"Frank keeps a bunch of *regular* girls. A harem of sorts, except I'm not sure they all know about each other. It's a strongman thing, you know? He thinks it impresses people." Bea made a noise of disgust. "One of his own was kicked out of New York and joined us in Colorado. He was more than happy to spill the beans on his old... *boss*."

"So, Frank what, *takes* these women?" I asked, my brain running through a hundred human trafficking scenarios, imagining Red with terrified eyes and duct tape over her mouth.

"No," Bea replied slowly. "He doesn't need to, you know? He's a rich guy and he finds plenty of willing participants, though he often looks for women who are already vulnerable. It's all part of the power trip for him."

"But?"

There was a long pause, and I forced myself to be patient, waiting for Bea's response.

"Look, he may collect them or whatever, but he in no way thinks of *regular girls* as equal to himself. He's not great at taking no for an answer, because he doesn't believe they're worthy of saying no to him, if that makes sense. Everything has to happen on his terms, in his timing."

Not good. Definitely not good.

"Even his wife is a *regular* girl—some wealthy heiress he's sucked the life out of over the years—but he won't have kids with her because, you know."

Because the kids might not be able to shift. The perks of being a dude, I guess. He could just go mate with and knock up some 20-year-old wolf shifter when he was 70, with wrinkly but still functional balls.

"You're not involved with this, are you?" Bea asked, sounding unusually worried about me.

"Define *involved*."

"Brooks, seriously. Frank Ashford is no joke. Especially with others like him. Like *us*. Don't get on his bad side, okay? Is some girl really worth it?"

I thought of Lou cooped up in some fancy glass cage in the city, her wings clipped so she could be just another pretty toy in that psycho's collection, and had to physically stop myself from shifting.

My wolf wouldn't stand for it. I wouldn't stand for it.

"She's worth it," I said firmly. Here was me, thinking that I was the Big Bad Wolf to her Little Red Riding Hood, but it turned out there was a *real* Big Bad Wolf on her trail, and there was nothing cute or funny about it.

"Idiot," Bea replied affectionately. "Let me know if you're going to make a move. Maybe I'll make a play to be the new Wolf of Wall Street."

She hung up and I chuckled to myself, half wondering if my sister was actually crazy enough to try to become Alpha of the New York pack.

Probably.

I pulled out my phone, messaging the group chat with Nate and Gabriel so they knew more about Frank's motives. Nate was my brother from another mother, and I'd have his back through anything, but faking a relationship with Lou to get Frank off her back had been like throwing chum at a shark.

And we couldn't even tell her why.

I woke up snuggled up to Gabriel, which wasn't all that surprising because he was warm and comfortable, if not a little more muscular and hairy than I preferred my bed partners.

"Get off, *irmão*," he grunted, shoving me into the wall that the double bed was pushed up against.

"You need to work on your pillow talk," I laughed, sitting up and climbing out the end of the bed, deliberately pulling all the blankets off with me.

"Brooks," Gabriel snapped, hauling them back up before rolling onto his side again. "Fuck off and let me sleep."

Gabriel seemed all suave and cool on the outside, but on the inside he was a surly teenager when the sun came up each morning. I grabbed some clean clothes, not making much of an attempt to be quiet, before heading out of the room to go shower. I'd been so busy annoying Gabriel that I hadn't heard Lou moving around, and we both startled when she emerged from the bathroom in dark pink yoga pants and an oversized gray sweater, her damp red hair sticking to her face.

I'd barely seen her in *days*. Well, two days. She moved through the house like a ghost. Though after Gabriel's sad attempt at steak and vegetables, she'd snuck into the kitchen yesterday while Gabriel and I were running in our fur outside and made turkey chilli for all of us, which made me feel extra shitty.

If it weren't for the fact that she'd posted maybe the sexiest pic I'd ever seen—because I'd obviously followed her account straight away—I'd be seriously worried. As it was, I'd been fighting the urge to hunt Nate down, wherever he was, and show him the boudoir-style photos Lou was taking on his bed, just to see what his reaction would be.

"Hey Red," I said cheerfully, leaning against the wall at the end of the hallway so I didn't crowd her.

"Brooks," she drawled, mimicking my posture.

"Have you been avoiding us?" I teased, already knowing the answer. Since when did beautiful women *not* want to hang out with me? Never! I was kryptonite to beautiful women.

"I have absolutely been avoiding you," Lou replied, raising an eyebrow at me.

Argh. Besides the fact that I wanted to get in her pants more than I'd ever wanted to get into anyone else's, she was cool as hell, and *funny* on the rare occasions she'd deigned to speak to me.

"Cool, no hard feelings. What are we doing today?" I asked.

I was determined. I was going to hang out with her today. I'd taken roughly a million photos recently and edited the ones Gabriel liked the best to accompany the articles that he was working on. The photos he wasn't using I would edit and sell, but I could take a few hours off for a beautiful, intriguing woman. If she'd have me.

"We?" she asked drily.

"We," I agreed. "See, there's this ridiculously beautiful woman who kicked me out of my room—"

"I did not!" she gasped.

"—and now I have to snuggle *Gabriel* all night. And this woman is funny and sarcastic and interesting, and totally impervious to my charms, which is honestly unheard of—"

"Mm, poor you," Lou said with mock sympathy.

"—and today is the day all of that changes, and I prove to her what an exceptionally *excellent* person I am," I finished with a bow. "After all, we're friends, are we not?"

"Friends," Lou deadpanned, trying to hide her smile. "I'm sure that's all you want."

"Red, you wound me," I accused, clasping my chest. "All the greatest love stories start from friendships."

"First of all," Lou began, holding up a finger and giving me an appraising look. "This is not a love story. Second of all," she continued, holding up another finger. "That's not even true. Romeo and Juliet weren't friends. Elizabeth and Mr. Darcy weren't friends. Antony and Cleopatra weren't friends."

She paused for a moment, frowning to herself. "Actually, all the greatest love stories started out as enemies."

"Damn it, you're going to fall in love with Nate then, aren't you?" I teased, enjoying the way she flushed as red as her hair.

"Absolutely not," she replied, shaking her head. "Like... never. No, just no."

Curious. I was assuming whatever had gone wrong between them had involved sex, and usually Nate's partners had no complaints. He'd said she tested his control, but that could mean *anything*. Did he get a little too excited? Didn't get her over the finish line? Butt stuff on the first date? Options. So many options.

"The more you protest, the less I believe you," I laughed. "So, anyway. What are we doing today?"

Lou sighed. "I had all these ambitious plans for remodeling my house, but all the weirdness with Frank has put me off. Now I just kind of want to get it sold. I was going to head over there today and clear out the kitchen cupboards, get rid of shit and be done with it. You know?"

Not specifically, home ownership had never been something that particularly interested me. But I definitely understood the desire to just pack up and leave.

"Hell yes, Red. Let's go."

✱ ✱ ✱

We grabbed coffee on the way to Lou's place and I kept an easy smile on my face even as we approached her house and my wolf started getting agitated from the lingering smell of foreign wolf piss. Even now that had faded, I could scent the other shifters who'd been stopping by to keep an eye on things, and their scents so close to Lou's home bothered me too.

"Nothing weird has happened since the other night," Lou announced, parking in her garage and climbing out of the driver's side. "I really think I should just stay at my house now. It's kind of weird to crash with you guys, you know?"

"I strongly disagree," I told her, hoping the grin would throw her off, because I *really* didn't like that idea. "Besides, you've fed us now. *Chilli*. It was glorious. We can never let you leave."

"I'm going to teach you to cook," Lou scoffed, leading me into the house. "You should really be ashamed of yourself."

"Not even a little," I chuckled. "In fairness, a lot of the time we're not staying in places with decent cooking facilities. And when the local food is so good, it seems ridiculous to stay in and make ramen."

Also, when we were lazy we just shifted into our fur and dined al fresco.

I followed her through the house, impressed at the work she'd put in already in painting the entryway and living room. Had she seriously planned on staying here throughout? My sensitive nose burned from the smell of drying paint, and I almost sighed in gratitude when she opened some windows to air the place out.

"Where was your favorite place to visit for the food?" Lou asked, leading me into the galley kitchen and standing with her hands on her hips, looking up at the cupboards like she could just will the job to be done with her eyes.

I frowned to myself, considering my answer. I liked *all* food. That would be like asking someone to choose which of their children they liked best. I assumed. I didn't know shit about kids, but maybe people had favorites.

Actually, my parents *definitely* had a favorite. Bad metaphor.

"You look like I just asked you to solve an impossible riddle," Lou laughed, leaving the room and returning with a dining chair to stand on so she could reach the top cupboards.

"Hey, that was a *hard* question," I replied defensively. "I love all food everywhere. I remember on my first trip to France, I got some bread and cheese at a gas station for lunch and it was the best bread and cheese I'd ever had in my life. France doesn't fuck around with good food. That was kind of a game changer."

Lou smiled a little wistfully as she began emptying the cupboards, handing me things to put on the counter. God, when she smiled it was like seeing the sun after being in the dark for too long. It was soft and radiant and I wanted more of it.

"France is definitely on my list," Lou told me, a longing note to her voice. I'd teased her about going to Phuket together when we both left Fairbanks, but I was suddenly struck by this urgent need to make that a reality. I wanted to see the look on her face when she finally got to see the places that she'd been dreaming about in person. To hear the excitement in her voice and remember what it was like to feel that rush of experiencing something *new*. That pinch yourself moment when you question if you're really here and is this real life and how the fuck did you ever get lucky enough to experience *this*?

"Anyway, Brooks. Tell me more about yourself," Lou said, breaking me out of my fantastical daydream as she stretched on her tippy toes to reach the items on the top shelf. Huh. Sometimes Lou did this *voice*—I couldn't explain it. It was a combination of phone sex operator and customer service representative. Considering her usual voice was sort of dry and vaguely unimpressed with everything, I found it a little unsettling.

"What do you want to know?" *Please ask me about my rippling muscles and not my childhood.*

"Where are you from?" she asked. *Okay. Easy enough.*

"Originally? Colorado. I left when I was a teenager, never been back."
She definitely could have asked some follow-up questions, but she just
nodded like my answer was totally normal as she handed me an ugly lime
green platter.

"And obviously you travel a lot."

"I do," I replied with a grin. "Gabriel and I are almost always together
for work. We're freelancers, but we collaborate a lot. Nate pretends he
can stay away, but he can't."

"Oh, that's cool." Lou gave me an indecipherable look, pursing her
lips like she was struggling not to say something and I grinned at her.

"Spit it out, Red."

"Okay, fine," she sighed like I was being totally unreasonable. "You
asked for it. Do you guys fuck each other?"

I choked on my own spit. Fuck me, no wonder this woman wasn't
falling for my charms. I *had* no charms around her.

"Ah, no. I mean, I get why you'd think that, but we are all strictly Team
Pussy." *Why was I so un-suave right now?* "Which brings us back to your
little revelation from the other night."

Lou went as still as a statue, pausing halfway to handing me a floral-
printed gravy boat that I would bet money she'd never used. "Did I make
any revelations about my pussy?" she asked, genuinely thoughtful.

This woman would be the death of me. I might give anything to hear
Lou talking about her pussy in a sexy way. While naked. Specifically in
relation to my cock and how awesome it was making said pussy feel.

Concentrate.

"I was referring to your admission that you're more of a cat person
than a dog person. But if you want to talk about your pussy, I'm a very
good listener." I winked and she gave me a withering look.

"I've talked about my pussy enough to last several lifetimes," she said drily, taking me off-guard. "Though I'm sure Nate told you all about that."

"No," I replied slowly, sensing I was on dangerous ground. "Nate would never kiss and tell."

"Interesting. He's marginally less of an asshole than I previously thought then."

I frowned to myself as I stacked up serving platters. Nate was one of the best guys I knew, but I wasn't about to argue with Lou—she obviously had her reasons for feeling the way she did, but it was weird that she still disliked him so much after Nate had moved her in to keep her safe from her ex. He must have *really* pissed her off.

"So, your ex hasn't messaged you at all since he's been in town?" I asked casually.

Lou scoffed. "He messaged me on Instagram, but I blocked him, and I blocked his number before he even got here. And he's not really my *ex*."

"Oh?" I asked, not at all about to explode into my fur with jealousy and rub myself all over Lou and everything she owned.

"It was an... arrangement." She waved her hand absently, like the unpleasant memory was a fly that she was swatting away.

"Like a fuck buddy arrangement?" I asked, taking a sudden interest in the formica countertop. *Why was I asking this? Did I actually want this knowledge? No. No, I did not.*

"Like a he-paid-me arrangement," Lou said, twisting to properly see me, an assessing look on her face, like she was waiting for me to be disgusted or something. She stared at me and I stared back, lips twitching.

Honestly, it was pretty impressive that she was staring me down, being a human and all. Lou was a ballsy little thing.

"I mean, I'm jealous," I said eventually. "I'd be lying if I said I wasn't. I'm also jealous about whatever you had with Nate and that you called Gabriel for a date, not me."

Lou's eyes narrowed like she didn't believe me. "Usually I just did stuff on camera, by myself. Frank I made an in-person exception for, which obviously worked out swell for me."

The idea of Lou getting herself all worked up, *pleasuring* herself, and knowing exactly what got her motor running, was a massive fucking turn on. Fortunately I was wearing a loose hoodie that was long enough to disguise any evidence of my feelings, because I didn't want her to think I was a total fucking creep.

"I was a sex worker," Lou reiterated, like I hadn't understood. There was a defensiveness to her tone that I hated. I didn't want her to feel like I was going to be an asshole about it.

"Alright." I shrugged. "I follow Gabriel around, taking photos of stuff. It's just my job, not who I am. Same for you, right?"

I mean, photography was a little harder than that, but I was aiming for a pep talk.

Shit, I *really* hoped her beef with Nate wasn't to do with this. Had he found out and said something dickish about it? That didn't seem like him, he was generally pretty good at not pissing people off. Out of the three of us, he was the only one who actually required a decent amount of social skills for work.

"You're alright, Brooks. Did you know that?" Lou said with a small smile, eyes softening slightly. It was a rare hint of vulnerability, and she shut it down instantly. "Now help me clean my house."

NATE

Chapter 16

I closed up the studio as quickly as I could after finishing with my client, giving thanks to the universe that the guy had only wanted a simple geometric tattoo because I was not on form today. I was exhausted, so exhausted my ribs were still twinging from the skirmish in Lou's backyard the other day, which I'd had more than enough time to heal from under normal circumstances. *Tonight*, I promised myself. I'd ask Brooks or Gabriel to guard the property for a couple of hours instead and take a nap.

I knew they wouldn't object. Gabriel had messaged me a dozen times already insisting I rest, but I'd been trying to make Lou's stay at the house as comfortable as possible by keeping the fuck away. She'd liked Gabriel and Brooks well enough until I'd come along and ruined that too. It was almost a gift, the way I managed to get every interaction with Lou completely wrong.

I pulled out my phone as I trudged through the snow to my truck, opting to message Gabriel since he was the more reliable of my two friends when it came to replying.

Me:

Have you seen Lou today?

I really hoped they'd manage to work their charms to at least entice her out of the bedroom she'd been holed up in. Selfishly, I hoped their charms had ended there, despite Gabriel's suggestion that they get to know her as well. *Date* her.

I had no claim on her. I didn't get to be pissed about whatever Lou decided to do, except that it was undercutting the lie we were telling Frank. Either he'd think I was lying, or that she was dating all of us. Polyamory wasn't unheard of among shifters—Chase shared his mate, as did the bears—but that wasn't what we'd told Frank. He'd probably take it as another sign of my inability to keep her.

I had no idea how anyone shared a mate. Why would anyone put themselves through all this agonizing jealousy? Brooks and Gabriel were my best friends, but the idea of Lou with one of them, away from *me*, made me want to shift and claw their stupid faces off.

Gabriel:

Brooks has gone with Lou to her house. She sounded pretty happy this morning.

Probably because I wasn't there. Oh well, at least she wasn't hiding from all of us anymore. *That was a good thing*, I told myself as jealousy viciously twisted my gut. I climbed into the truck, starting it up and letting the windows defrost before I responded.

Me:

I'll do a quick perimeter check at her place.

Brooks was a formidable opponent when he was alert, but he also had a tendency to get caught up in the moment and not keep an eye on his surroundings, relying on me or Gabriel to cover for him. I snorted to myself—for all Gabriel's insistent declarations that we were a pack, Brooks was probably the one who *acted* most like we were, even though he rejected the idea as much as I did.

My phone rang, Gabriel's name flashing across the screen, and I picked it up with a heavy sigh.

"*Don't go over there,*" he said by way of a greeting.

"You know Brooks won't have even done a cursory scent check," I grumbled. "I'm looking out for both of them."

"*If you look at both of them right now, you might see something you don't like,*" Gabriel pointed out, chuckling to himself.

"Her safety is more important than any of that stuff," I snapped, failing to keep the petulance out of my voice. What a nightmare. "Doesn't it bother you? You were on a date with her the other night."

"*If it were anyone else...*" Gabriel let the sentence hang, and I grunted, begrudgingly seeing his point. If Lou had another guy over at her house right now, I'd probably lose my shit and do something I couldn't take back. It wasn't quite that dire with Brooks or Gabriel.

"Just be careful," I gritted out. "*Very* careful."

Like, *keep your fucking teeth out of her neck* kind of careful. There was a beat of silence over the phone before Gabriel responded.

"*Do your unnecessary perimeter check for peace of mind, then come home. You need a nap, and then we're going to talk about what exactly happened between the two of you.*"

I made a noise that he may have interpreted as agreement—but definitely wasn't—before hanging up. Lou hadn't specifically banned me from talking about our amazing then disastrous night together, but I didn't think she'd appreciate it if I did. Especially the Scarlet stuff. That wasn't my secret to tell.

Of course, I could mention that I almost bit her without giving Gabriel the full play-by-play. The only excuse I had not to talk about that was my overwhelming shame.

Lou was probably safer with Brooks than with me. He had *relations* with human women more than I did. I doubted he'd lose control the way I had.

I parked in a wooded area in Lou's neighborhood that would lead me to her property, triple checking for humans before strolling among the trees like it was entirely comfortable to be traipsing through snow in soaked boots. Running around in my fur would attract too much attention, even if it made me feel more secure.

I'd be well and truly fucked if Lou saw me wandering around her house like this. I doubt she'd hesitate to shoot a second time.

As soon as Lou's little pink house came into view through the trees, I realized that Brooks wasn't the only wolf nearby. *Fucking Frank*. Also a little bit *Fucking Brooks* because he obviously hadn't been outside to do a cursory check. My ribs smarted as I forced my head high and rolled my shoulders back. As tempting as it was to shift and go on the offensive, I stayed where I was, trusting that Frank was arrogant enough to swagger up to me and talk a big game like he did last time.

He could actually back up his big talk, which was inconvenient, but the further I pulled him away from Lou's house, the better.

Sure enough, within a couple of minutes, an enormous wolf appeared between the trees, his black fur standing out in stark contrast to the snow. Frank was alone, which should have given me some comfort, but the feral glint in his eye undercut any advantage I might have had. He wasn't going to shift and boast today.

He wanted blood.

Briefly I contemplated shouting to alert Brooks, but Frank was *all* wolf right now, and I didn't need to draw his attention back to Lou while it was on me.

Frank snarled, lips pulled back to reveal vicious teeth, and fear momentarily stole the breath from my lungs. I could take on a normal-sized wolf and be almost certain of success, but Frank was bigger and stronger than the average wolf. The kind of pack he led was the kind forged in blood and battles. He'd pick his teeth with my bones if I slipped up.

Back yourself, I chastised silently. *Trust your animal.*

I turned and ran, letting the shift take me while I was in motion, ripping free of my clothes as I darted through the trees and back towards the road, a growling, furious wolf on my tail.

We needed to get away from humans in general, but away from Lou specifically. I didn't like to think of it as running *away*, I could admit I needed some fucking backup.

Fortunately, the highway was quiet as I sprinted across it, diving into the thick of the forest that led towards my brother's house. It was a potentially risky move—my brother and his family weren't the only shifters in these woods. The local wolf pack tolerated my presence near their territory only because of my connection to Chase. They didn't owe me any loyalty, and I doubted they'd like me after I led a foreign Alpha into their backyard.

Welp, I'd had a good run, I guess. I'd seen a lot of the world. Met some great people. Had a stab at responsible adulthood. Met a woman who I could have fallen in love with and mostly managed not to ruin her life.

That was more than a lot people got, right? I could die mostly satisfied.

Frank lunged, and I turned sharply, relying on my more agile build to dart through a narrow gap between trees and force him back. I could almost smell his bloodlust from here, and the jog through the woods hadn't cooled him off in the slightest. What the fuck was going on? He hadn't been anywhere near this out of control the other times I'd seen him.

As I got closer to my brother's house, I let out my best screech, alerting Chase to my presence. I couldn't scent any humans nearby, but if any heard me, I was confident they'd run. Even to my own ears, I sounded slightly demonic.

My ribs ached. Between the pain and slowing down slightly to call for Chase, Frank closed the gap between us. With a furious snarl, his enormous body slammed me into a tree with enough force to make the trunk crack ominously.

Shit, if I thought my ribs hurt before, it was nothing compared to now. My vision swam as Frank's open jaw loomed closer, ready to clamp down on my skull.

I rolled onto my back and his responding growl was almost gleeful, like he thought I was surrendering. I was no dog though, and Frank didn't fight cats often if he thought I was less of a threat with my belly exposed.

A wolf may have a powerful bite, but I had a powerful bite and hind claws that could gut a wolf like a fucking chainsaw if I got underneath him.

Come on. Pounce, I urged silently. Blue eyes glowing savagely, Frank leaped.

My brother's screech echoed through the forest, followed by the *terrifying* roar of a pissed off brown bear, distracting Frank. He threw his weight sideways at the last minute, and my claws sliced through his vulnerable underbelly, blood splattering over the snow. *Not deep enough*, I growled silently. Fuck! I should have trusted myself to take him on without enlisting backup.

On second thoughts, my head was spinning and 1500 pounds of bear Noah would send Frank on his way real quick. I blinked hard to focus as the sounds of fighting filtered through the fog, but it was all too much. Too hard. I should have had a nap yesterday and given my ribs a break.

Was Lou okay? Was Brooks keeping her safe?

Maybe he could put in a good word because I really hated that she hated me.

"Nate!" Chase's panicked voice sounded a million miles away. "Shift. You have to shift."

I didn't have to do anything. He couldn't make me. I could take a nap if I wanted to.

"Stop closing your damn eyes," he commanded, sounding frustrated for some reason. "You're going to find it very awkward when you wake up if Noah has to give you a bear ride back, and you know it."

A bear ride sounded heavenly.

✱ ✱ ✱

I woke up to the splash of cold water on my face, which was a pretty guaranteed way to wake anyone up.

"Haven't I suffered enough?" I grumbled, draping my arm over my eyes, too exhausted to wipe the dripping water off my face.

"You've been asleep for over an hour," Chase replied. "Lacey panicked and got the local healer, and now there are wolves in my living room and you have to drink this revolting smelling broth."

It *did* smell revolting, but I'd take all the help my sore bones could get.

"Frank?" I asked, wincing as I pushed up on my elbows and shuffled back against the pillows to accept the foul-smelling drink. I was in a purple bedroom that had once belonged to my nieces, though they were living in Anchorage now. Lacey kept her kids' rooms eternally unchanged, like shrines to them. It was a little terrifying.

"You put a decent scratch on him," Chase said approvingly, and I shot him a glare over the bowl. There was nothing decent about a *scratch*. "He was already injured and wasn't about to take on another cougar and a raging bear."

"Fuck, I need to call the guys—" I winced as I tried to sit upright, and Chase pushed me back down gently by the shoulder with a warning look.

"Rodrigo is in town checking on your girl and filling the guys in," he said, referring to one of his mate's other mates.

"She's not my girl," I sighed, pinching my nose and downing the broth in one go, getting it over with.

It tasted like boiled feet, but I could feel the warmth making its way to the worst of my injuries like a soothing balm.

"Sure," Chase agreed, not sounding like he believed me in the slightest.

"He's not going to tell them I'm injured, is he?"

Chase shook his head. "We didn't want to worry them. We knew you'd be fine if you just slowed down for a few hours to recover. Well, Lacey was more worried, but I knew you'd be fine. As much as I'd like to leave you up here to rest more, I'd rather get these wolves out of my house."

"Fair enough," I agreed, waving him away when he tried to help me up. Chase was my oldest brother, with fully grown kids of his own, and sometimes he felt more like a parent to me than a sibling. My inner kid still wanted to prove to my big brother that I could handle myself, and I was already cringing thinking about how they'd transported me back here after I'd passed out. Probably on Noah's back, like Chase had threatened. I didn't want to ask.

I grabbed the sweatpants on the end of the bed, my ribs protesting wildly as I tugged them on and left my chest bare. The scrapes I'd gotten on my back from the tree bark had healed over, but the skin was still a little itchy, and the cool air helped.

Moving at a slower pace than usual, I followed Chase down the stairs to the enormous living room. It was a bright, open space, all pale wood and cozy blankets, but it felt cramped with the number of bodies in there. Chase's mate, Lacey, and two of her other mates, Sergio and Casen, stood in front of the fireplace, looking a little tense at having foreign wolves in their home. I'd expected to find Noah still hanging around, but his youngest brother, Eli, had taken his place. He grinned broadly at me, lounging on an armchair with his ankle crossed over his knee, content as could be. Eli never let anything bother him.

On the sofa was the Alpha of the local wolf pack, Marsh Mckinney, flanked by two pack mates. The healer, Roger, stood behind the sofa with a woman I didn't recognize. Another wolf.

I could see why Chase had been uncomfortable.

I glanced sideways at Chase, waiting for him to take the lead. Was I supposed to apologize? I didn't get involved in territory disputes or pack politics. Mostly, I spent my days around humans, except for Brooks and Gabriel.

"Nate. I'm not sure we've met," the Alpha began. "I'm Marsh Mckinney, this is my mate, Rosa, and pack mate, Jeff. You've met, Roger, the healer, I believe. And this is Francisca, who is also part of our pack."

"Hello." I nodded my head stiffly in greeting, unsure where exactly this was headed. My family didn't look overly worried though, and Eli was still grinning like this was a party.

"Chase has kept us filled in on our unwelcome guest," Marsh continued with a heavy sigh. "It's a difficult situation. Frank Ashford has been careful to stick to town for the most part, which our pack has no claim over, and therefore can't get involved with. I'll be honest with you, we don't want to get involved."

Chase made a frustrated noise in the back of his throat, and Lacey sidled up next to him, pressing against his side.

Chase was Chief Ranger. Not getting involved was against his nature, and I knew he'd see it as a sign of cowardice that Marsh wasn't doing the same, but I kind of got it. Frank wasn't the kind of enemy any sane shifter would want—his pack back in New York was huge and could make for a formidable foe if they sought revenge.

"However," Marsh continued, shooting Chase a disgruntled look. "If we *have* to intervene, we'll intervene. Today was a close call. He was very near our border."

I waited for the chastisement for leading him that close, but it never came. Maybe Marsh wasn't such a bad guy after all.

He turned his attention to me, cocking his head to the side and giving me a considering look. "The human woman, what's her name again?"

I fought back a growl as my cougar surfaced, furious that even more shifters were focusing on Lou, and I questioned for the millionth time if I'd done the right thing by getting involved with this situation. Sometimes I felt like all I was doing was bringing more trouble to Lou's door. Maybe if I'd gotten out of her way, she'd contentedly be one of Frank's well kept human pets by now, living in a fancy apartment in New York, having forgotten all about me.

"Her name is Lou," I forced out.

Marsh hummed, and I noticed out of the corner of my eye that Eli had lost his playful grin. He sat forward in his chair, resting his elbows on his knees, observing the Alpha closely. Hopefully, as Ria's friend, Lou would benefit from the bears' protection by default.

"You're spending a lot of time with her," Marsh commented lightly.

"Not really. I've been following Frank around town almost constantly. She's staying with my roommates."

"Who are also shifters," he pointed out.

"Yes."

"Are you sure that's wise?" Marsh asked. "Chase mentioned that Frank has threatened to reveal things she cannot know, and while that is a risk, the more time *your* pack spends with her, the more you risk revealing those things for yourself."

"They're not my pack," I countered instantly, hackles raised. "Unlike Frank, none of us have any desire to put Lou at risk. That's why we're doing all of this. We would never jeopardize her safety, her freedom, that way." *No matter how tempting it was,* I added silently. They didn't need to know how close I'd come already.

"Be sure you don't," Marsh replied, standing and extending his hand to his mate to help her up. "A decade ago, I had to kill a hiker who accidentally saw one of my young pack members shift. She was a young woman, a Fairbanks local whose scent was familiar to us because she enjoyed walking through the woods." His gaze bored into mine, willing me to understand. "It haunts me to this day. She had her whole life ahead of her until she saw something she shouldn't. But I will never place the safety of my kind in the hands of a human who has everything to gain from sharing our secrets. Don't make me relive that experience, Nate."

I said nothing as he led his mate and his second out of the living room, the room silent as the front door clicked shut behind him. Roger, the healer, hung back, probably to check on me, as did the woman Marsh introduced as Francisca, and I was glad for the distraction at that moment. Chase had been remarkably relaxed about offering Lou protection, but I knew he would take Marsh's words as an opening to discuss her with me.

Roger insisted I lie down on the couch to check my injuries and I forced myself to stay still as he worked, muttering under his breath the entire time. He only owed his pack his loyalty and seemed to help all the other shifters who lived around here out of the goodness of his heart. Since it was nice of him to check on me, I kept my moody attitude mostly to myself.

"Anything we need to be worried about, Rog?" Chase asked, standing behind my head with his arms crossed, looming over me. If it was any of my other siblings, I'd worry they were going to call Mom. But then she'd visit, and Chase wouldn't want that either.

"He needs to rest," Roger instructed. "*Really* rest. For a few days."

I nodded like I was going to do that, already planning on shifting as soon as I had a chance and running back to Fairbanks. Gabriel would be on the lookout and hopefully he'd reminded Brooks to pay attention, but I wouldn't feel calm until I was physically closer to Lou myself.

"I'll leave a few herbs for you," Roger announced, already digging through his bag. Francisca stood back, silently observing everything, attracting the attention of both Eli and my family, and I got the distinct impression she was waiting for me. Roger must have realized the same, giving her a confused look before excusing himself to wait outside, leaving an assortment of medicinal herbs on the side table for me.

"May I have a moment alone with Nate?" Francisca asked politely as I pushed myself into a sitting position, hating how vulnerable I felt.

"Nate?" Chase asked. "Are you good with that?"

"Francisca is good people," Eli assured me as he stood. "She therapies my weird brain."

"Um, good to know," I replied, a little lost for words.

"I should head back anyway, Noah just wanted me to listen in on what Marsh had to say. This is me taking on more responsibility," he added proudly, puffing up his chest while Chase snorted loudly.

"Yeah, no worries," I said absently, waving him off. "Wait—Eli, do you think Ria would come and visit Lou?"

Eli raised his eyebrows in surprise. "She'd probably love that. Seth has to head into town tomorrow anyway, Ria could go with him. Ooh, I could build her a sleigh and he could pull her through the snow. Bear power!"

"Please don't do that," Chase sighed, rubbing his temple. "I don't need to deal with humans asking questions about seemingly trained, sleigh-pulling bears. Come on, let's give Francisca and Nate some privacy."

They all filed out of the front door, and I heard Eli's boisterous laugh as Chase continued to grumble about bear sleighs on the porch. If I could hear them, they could hear us, but they were all making a show of being loud to give me some peace of mind.

"How can I help?" I asked politely, mystified as to what this woman could want with me.

Francisca gave me a long, thoughtful look. "I was born with clairsentient abilities, which have served me well in my career as a psychologist for human clients. Now I do more therapeutic-type work with shifters, which allows me to use my abilities without limitation or fear of being found out."

"What does 'clairsentient' mean?" I asked uneasily.

"Think of it as a gut feeling," she replied kindly. "Emotional intuition, a deeper understanding, that kind of thing."

"You're definitely underselling it to make me feel better," I muttered.

"A little," Francisca admitted with a light laugh. "I am not trying to make you uncomfortable—which you are—but rather to explain how I know you lied to my Alpha earlier. You would never intentionally jeopardize the human woman who has consumed your thoughts, but your animal may not be gracious enough to give you a choice. Both the man and the beast are fascinated by her, which will make it difficult to keep your distance."

My blood rushed noisily in my ears as Francisca verbalized my worst fears with the calm, pleasant tone of a server reciting the daily specials.

"Are you going to pass all that on to your Alpha?" I asked flatly. God, I'd really done nothing but make Lou's life worse from the moment she'd walked into my studio.

Francisca hummed thoughtfully, turning to stare out the window at the darkening forest.

"Keep an open mind, Nate. Your convictions are noble and honestly held, which is admirable. But you are the one who decided a mate bond was a death sentence. Perhaps a decision of that magnitude warrants a conversation first?"

"Are you suggesting I tell her about shifters?" I asked incredulously.

Francisca shot me an amused smile as she made her way towards the door. "Humans are perfectly capable of understanding the concept of commitment without the supernatural bonding element, Nate. Start there."

I scoffed to myself as she left, flopping back on the couch and closing my eyes for a minute. I had absolute faith that Lou understood the concept of commitment, she just wouldn't be interested in pursuing it with a guy who'd had sex with her—sans protection, no less—then run out.

"All good?" Chase asked, letting himself back into the living room while the rest of his family disappeared into the house, giving us some privacy.

"Fine," I grunted.

Lacey appeared, handing us each a bottle of beer with a knowing smile before vanishing back into the house.

"I'll head off soon—"

"You need to let your broken ribs heal. *Again*," Chase said firmly, sitting in the armchair opposite me with a heavy sigh.

"I'm fine," I muttered, popping the lid off the beer and downing the bottle in one. "The broth helped."

"Roger left other things for you, but nothing is a replacement for what your body can do on its own if you just slow down enough to let it happen," Chase replied impatiently. "Casen is heading down to guard Lou's place now, but I doubt, unlike you, that Frank is stupid enough to push himself while he's injured."

"Gee thanks," I said drily.

"Anytime. Now, talk to me," Chase ordered, all alpha pushiness.

"I thought I was supposed to be resting."

"I can see your brain going a million miles a minute, Nate," Chase laughed. "Unload a little, it'll help you relax. Then you're going to sleep for a few hours."

"You already know everything I know about Frank."

"I'm not interested in that," he replied, flicking his hand absently. "Let's talk about *Lou*. You feel something for her. That's huge for you."

I grunted, regretting downing my beer in one. I could have used something to do with my hands. This was shaping up to be a Gabriel-style interrogation into my feelings.

"Tell me about the woman who dragged my famously flighty little brother's head out of the clouds."

"What do you want to know?" I asked flatly, ignoring the strange twinge in my gut that made an appearance whenever I thought about Lou. What was she doing right now?

Did she ever think of me at all? Was it better or worse if she didn't?

"There's a lot I want to know," Chase admitted. "But I guess the only thing that matters is whether or not you meant what you said to Marsh."

The Alpha's words echoed in my head and I felt like I'd still be hearing them on my deathbed. *The more time your pack spends with her, the more you risk revealing those things for yourself.*

Lou wanted adventure. She wanted to see the world, and experience all the things she'd been longing to experience, but hadn't had the opportunity to yet. Lou had plans and goals and *dreams*. Even if I wanted to keep her to myself—a selfish idea that I refused to let myself consider—I couldn't. She didn't want to be kept, she wanted to be *free*.

"I meant what I said. I would never jeopardize Lou's freedom."

Chapter 17

Brooks was a good helper. He spent hours happily taking directions as I pointed out which boxes to put stuff in, carried the heavy stuff out to my car, tidied up as he went, and was just a generally *joyful* person to be around. I got the sense that there was a bit of darkness underneath that cheerful persona—Gabriel had already alluded to it—but Brooks worked hard at not letting it show.

I thought the kitchen cupboards would take me days to empty and sort, but we'd got the whole job done at once and I'd barely broken a sweat with Brooks doing all the hard labor. Maybe I should consider painting the other rooms after all, if I had him around to help.

"We're a good team, Red," Brooks said cheerfully, returning to the kitchen after loading the final box into the Yukon. He held his hand up for a high five and I raised up on my tiptoes to reach it, making his grin widen.

"We're a great team," I agreed. "I feel like we've earned a reward. Donuts? I'll eat mindfully... later."

I could have sworn his blue eyes got a little brighter at that. Was he happy I remembered us binging donuts at the coffee shop when we'd met? Maybe Brooks had an unexpectedly sappy side.

"You know I'm always down for donuts, Red."

I shot him a shy smile because after a few hours together my resolve was as shredded as my screen door and I really *liked* Brooks, which was massively inconvenient given I was supposed to be staying away from men.

But you don't have to, the slutty Scarlet devil on my shoulder whispered. *Just take Gabriel up on his offer.*

I waited for the Lou angel to pop up on my other side in a white gown to remind me that the Nate thing had been an absolute shitshow and all three of them were keeping secrets, but she was suspiciously quiet.

I had put my water bottle up on the shelf to keep the counter clear while we were working and I reached up on my tiptoes to get it—suddenly hella thirsty—one hand planted on the counter to give me some extra reach.

"Let me, Red," Brooks rumbled in a smooth low voice, a lot less playful than usual. His firm chest pressed against my shoulder blades as he easily grabbed the bottle over my head, his arm brushing against mine.

Don't overthink it, I instructed myself. *You've already got permission. Enjoy it for what it is.*

I leaned back against Brooks, dropping back onto my heels and letting my shoulders slide down against him. Brooks' arm curled around me, setting the bottle down on the counter, but his hand lingered at my waist.

God, it sounded super needy even in my own head, but even this weak not-quite cuddle was *so* nice. I didn't realize how much I'd missed just being held until Nate had bailed before we could get to that part.

"What are we doing, Red?" Brooks murmured next to my ear. His nose brushed against my hair and I could have sworn he took a deep breath like he was trying to inhale me. It was unexpectedly erotic.

"Whatever I want with any of you, wasn't that the arrangement?" I replied, my voice dropping a little as I automatically slipped into Scarlet mode.

Brooks grabbed my hips, turning me to face him without moving back, pinning me between him and the counter. I had to lean back against it so I could tip my face up to meet his eyes, my hands resting on the counter behind me, my chest pushed up on display.

"And what is it that you want?" Brooks asked, leaning down and running his nose up the side of my face. I tipped my head back, exposing my neck in case he was feeling in a throat kissing mood. Brooks paused before making a rumbling sound deep in his chest that was definitely *all* pleasure, even if I didn't exactly understand how he was making it. It was so... *growly*.

"What was the question?" I breathed, forgetting all about how I was *supposed* to act, how I was *supposed* to seduce, and just letting myself *feel* for a moment.

Brooks pulled back to smirk at me, all hooded eyes and sharp jawline before his huge hands found my waist and lifted me up onto the counter. I pulled him in to stand between my legs, gripping his hoodie to keep him close, and he closed his eyes, inhaling again like he had just smelled the most delicious thing on earth.

"Lady's choice," he rumbled. "What does the lady want?"

A large part of my brain was flashing 'SEX' in neon lights, but there was another part of my brain that was more reluctant. That remembered how rejected I'd felt when Nate had run out on me, and she wasn't in a rush to repeat that experience.

"I want to taste you," I murmured, leaning forward to brush my lips against his. "Everywhere."

I felt Brooks' lips curl into a smile against mine before he deepened the kiss, sucking my lower lip into his mouth and letting his teeth drag against my sensitive skin as he released it. I felt refreshingly out of control. Maybe I'd started this thinking I was running this seduction, but it was pretty clear that Brooks could give as good as he got.

"That's a very generous offer, Red," Brooks murmured between kisses. "But I would *much* rather taste you."

"Really?" I breathed with way too much excitement, completely losing my chill in the face of oral sex. Oral sex with Brooks' face. Whatever.

"Fuck yes." Brooks slid his hands under my butt, lifting me off the counter like I didn't weigh anything as I wrapped my legs around his waist, clinging to his shoulders. I seriously didn't understand how they were all so strong when they lived off junk food and I'd never even heard them mention a gym. "Direct me to your boudoir, my lady."

I laughed, pointing him towards my bedroom. It was only as he pushed open the door that I realized I hadn't even contemplated heading down to the sex cave. Having him in my room felt infinitely more personal.

Brooks tossed me down on the bed before crawling over me, his tongue sweeping my mouth like he couldn't get enough of my taste. I writhed impatiently underneath him, tugging at his stupid hoodie—why was he wearing so many clothes?—before giving up and concentrating on myself, shimmying my leggings awkwardly down my legs.

Brooks moved down my body, pushing my jumper aside to rest his nose against my neck, holding himself impossibly still for a moment, before moving down my body with another one of those deep rumbly noises that seemed to connect straight to my clit.

"You smell fucking *delicious*," Brooks growled, helping me get my leggings over my feet before rather unceremoniously tugging my panties off me.

"I *smell* delicious?" I repeated doubtfully, pressing my thighs together self consciously. I mean, I didn't think I smelled *gross* or anything, but delicious seemed a little generous.

"Like melted chocolate," Brooks murmured, his hand tracing the wing of the phoenix tattoo on my thigh for a brief moment, making my breath catch before he pushed my thighs apart and stared at my pussy like it was a portal to heaven.

Eh, maybe I wasn't self conscious after all. When he looked at me like that, I sort of felt like a goddess. Or a succubus.

Brooks settled himself between my legs, shooting me a devastating smile, his blue eyes so bright they almost glowed. And then his thumbs were brushing the inside of my thighs, his tongue running teasingly over my slit, and my brain was short circuiting.

Brooks had always struck me as kind of impatient, but apparently when it came to *this*, he was more than happy to take his time. There were moments where I thought my pleasure may have just been incidental to Brooks' exploring as he thoroughly mapped the contours of my pussy like he was an adventurer discovering new lands.

He was infuriatingly slow to explore my clit, and there was nothing accidental about it. Maybe he was more a mountaineer than adventurer, and my clitoris was the summit.

"You're killing me," I gasped, trying to wriggle down the bed to get his mouth where I wanted it.

"What a way to go though," Brooks drawled, shooting me a salacious grin before returning to his all consuming work.

Finally, his tongue grazed my clit, the most featherlight of touches, and my back arched entirely off the bed. Brooks pulled away again, the fucking tease, and I contemplated draping a leg over his back and kicking him a few times like a horse to see if it would spur him into action.

"Are you always this impatient?" Brooks tutted, sounding amused, his thumbs spreading me wide. The cool air on my folds only added to my frustration. I needed *more*.

"This is only the second time someone has done this to me," I groused. "So I don't have a good sample size to choose from. I'm leaning towards yes though."

Brooks stopped completely, head popping up comically fast. Or it would have been comical if my throbbing nerves hadn't been throwing a tantrum from lack of attention.

"This is only the second time someone's gone down on you?" Brooks repeated, sounding mildly horrified. "Oh no, that is not okay, Red. Hold on tight. I'm staying down here until my tongue cramps."

I spluttered a noise that might have been outrage or excitement, impossible to tell, because Brooks rolled up his metaphorical sleeves and went to *work*. He catalogued every little reaction and worked fucking *magic* with his tongue from every angle, settling into a rhythm when he found what made me squeal. I assumed I'd need penetration as well to come, but apparently not because when he sucked my clit lightly into his mouth, an orgasm jumped up on me and dragged me into its depth when I least expected it, ripping me apart from the inside so thoroughly I wasn't sure I'd ever be able to put myself back together again.

"That was *glorious*," Brooks finally said, staring at me like he was in awe before licking his shiny lips. I couldn't find it in me to be self conscious now. If anything, I was a little smug. That was *me* on his lips. If I kept this up, I was going to start sniffing and growling the way they seemed to.

"Don't tell me your tongue is cramping already," I teased, though it didn't sound as sassy as it was meant to since I was panting like I'd just run a marathon.

"Not even close," Brooks replied with a grin. "But I think it's time for the next step in your oral sex journey."

"Oh?" I asked, definitely curious. "And what would that be?"

Brooks flopped down on his back next to me, shooting me another grin that lit up his entire face before tapping his mouth with his finger. "Hop on, baby girl."

It was like all my years as a cool-as-fuck seductress never existed. I scrambled up the bed like my ass was on fire, swinging a leg over Brooks' head to straddle his face. It wasn't like I hadn't given people close ups of the downstairs before, though this definitely felt a lot more intimate than angling my lady bits towards a webcam. I could feel Brooks' hot breath on my skin, and even that bordered on too much stimulation for my still tingling nerves.

Brooks smiled up at me through my spread thighs and I couldn't quite suppress my giggle in time. His hands smoothed up my legs, helping me come down from my high before working me back up again.

"You have a beautiful laugh, Lou," Brooks said quietly. My heart stuttered in my chest at the sincerity in his voice, and a tiny thread of panic zipped up my chest. Sexy stuff was safe ground. Heartfelt compliments were a rickety bridge suspended over a bubbling pit of lava. Like he knew that I was flailing, Brooks' soft expression turned reassuringly arrogant again, and then there was no more talking.

I slumped forward, bracing my hands on the wall behind the bed and held on for dear life as Brooks' hands gripped my ass, holding me in place as he made good on his promise.

* * *

Two hours later, I was curled up in a boneless puddle in the middle of my bed, fighting to keep my heavy eyelids open. *So good. So many orgasms. Just a little nap.*

"Just rest," Brooks chuckled, pulling the blanket up over my naked body. I had mentally prepared myself for him to just leave when he was done, Nate-style, but he hadn't. He hadn't even orgasmed! He'd been on a single-minded mission to make up for all the years of me not receiving oral apparently.

I wasn't exactly complaining about it.

He was lying on his side next to me, still fully dressed—which made my nakedness seem all the more scandalous—stroking my hair which felt *divine*. If anything, I was the one resisting snuggles, keeping my body firmly *next* to him on the bed, rather than draped all over him like I wanted to be. Managing my expectations and all that.

"You're probably hungry," Brooks said, sounding as concerned as Gabriel had that first day I'd stayed with them.

"You all make it sound like I'll drop dead if I don't eat every few hours," I slurred, my face half buried in my blanket. I was probably drooling and I didn't even care.

Brooks chuckled. "Sorry not sorry. Should I see if there's anything in the fridge?"

I mumbled an affirmative. "If there's not, just give me two minutes and we can go out to eat. "

Maybe five minutes.

"I know what I want to eat," Brooks teased, brushing an entirely too affectionate kiss over my hair before he rolled away. My lower belly flip flopped, like my body had forgotten we'd just had at least a week's worth of orgasms in two hours and my clit needed a nap.

"I'm off the menu. For like, at least an hour."

Brooks scoffed as he paused by the door. "You have no idea how tempted I am to prove I can change your mind."

I felt around for a pillow to throw at him, but it was too far away and I was too wrecked to move. "Shoo. Too sleepy to deal with you."

I heard Brooks laugh as he disappeared into the house, hopefully to find whatever sad remnants were still in the fridge, because I hadn't ordered groceries in a few days. This was definitely a much more pleasant post-orgasmic experience than what Nate and I had shared. Everything had been much easier with Brooks, much more relaxed, much less *work*, but weirdly it hadn't erased Nate from my mind the way I'd hoped it would.

I still wanted him, now I just wanted Brooks too. And there was zero doubt in my mind that if the opportunity presented itself, I'd have my wicked way with Gabriel. I wasn't sure he realized the can of worms he'd opened when he suggested I date all of them.

Except I wasn't dating Nate because I didn't like Nate. *We don't like Nate*, I repeated sternly, making sure my hormones got the message.

Eventually, as comfortable as I was, I felt weird about Brooks pottering around my house while I laid around naked, so I forced myself to get up and put clothes on, stopping in the bathroom for a quick cleanup. My cheeks were flushed such a vivid shade of pink, I was worried they would just stay that way. Like maybe I'd had so many orgasms I'd burst some blood vessels?

I wobbled towards the kitchen on weak legs, expecting to hear Brooks in there, but the house was silent. *Oh good. It would be just my luck that he would pull a Nate and run. That was obviously the kind of man I attracted in real life. Married men and assholes.*

Maybe I should have just stayed married. Jake hadn't been an asshole, he just wasn't right for me. People stayed in miserable marriages all the time, didn't they? I could have school-aged kids and entirely given up on my hopes and dreams by now.

Before I could spiral any further into that abyss of misery, I spotted Brooks in my backyard, frowning as he paced around the treeline, staring at the ground like he was following a trail. Weird. I let myself outside and Brooks was so absorbed in what he was doing that he didn't even seem to notice my presence.

"Helloooooooooo," I called from the back porch. "Are you done doing... whatever you're doing?" I asked, arms crossed over my chest because it was fucking cold out here.

Brooks looked up in surprise, shooting me a strained smile as he walked back towards the house. "Just getting some fresh air, Red. Ready to get some food?"

My heart sank a little even though I forced myself to keep my mask in place. At the end of the day, they were still all keeping something from me, and it would do me good to remember that. For all the delightful orgasms and easy banter between us, Brooks was keeping a secret.

"Let's hit the drive thru," I replied with a tight smile. "I have a lot of stuff I need to do today."

"Lou—" Brooks sighed, sounding pained.

"See you in the car," I called breezily over my shoulder, locking him out. If he was going to lie to my face, the least he could do was traipse around the house in the snow.

250

Don't forget, I told myself. *Don't ever forget that no matter how good any of them make you feel, they're not being honest with you.*

* * *

Nate shuffled into the kitchen the next morning while I was making my coffee, careful as always to keep a few feet between us like he'd catch cooties if he got too close to me, and I suddenly realized I hadn't seen him since I'd stormed out of the kitchen three days ago. That was kind of weird, but then again I had been actively avoiding him, so I guess he could have been here the whole time.

Though had he just come in from outside? Where had he gone so early in the morning?

I stirred my coffee as I leaned back against the counter, waiting to see if he was going to speak to me or not. One of us had to be the first to break the tension after our confrontation the other day, and I voted it be him.

"Ria is stopping by today," Nate grunted, not making eye contact. He reached up to get a cup and I could have sworn his entire face contorted in pain, but it happened so fast I might have imagined it.

"She is?" I asked, surprised. "Why?"

I knew Nate was friends with Ria's boyfriends—that's how he'd met her—but I didn't realize they were close enough to make plans.

"To see you," Nate replied, shooting me a sidelong look like that was an obvious answer. "I bumped into Eli and suggested they come for a visit."

Huh. That was unexpectedly nice of him.

"When did you see Eli?" I asked. "I thought they were basically holed up in their cabin for the winter."

Nate froze for a moment as I brushed past him to grab a mug.

"I, er, ran into him in the woods," Nate said evasively before scurrying out of the kitchen even faster than he'd bailed from my bed, obviously forgetting that he'd been getting coffee.

"*O-kay*," I said to myself. I mean, maybe other people enjoyed going on walks in the woods in snow up to their eyeballs? That was... a very unrelatable experience for me.

I'd put cookie dough on Nate's grocery list so I decided to chuck in some chocolate chip cookies while I had my coffee, patting myself on the back for my excellent hostessing skills the entire time. I changed into an apricot-colored yoga pants and sweater set that Ria would probably hate because her wardrobe was mostly black like her soul, before heading back into the living room when I heard the sound of a vehicle rumbling down the driveway.

Brooks was out somewhere and I had no idea where Nate had vanished to, but I was pretty sure I'd heard Gabriel typing away when I'd walked past his room. I pulled open the front door, ushering them in from out of the cold before they could knock, not that Ria needed any encouragement. When I'd first met her, I'd thought she was obnoxiously confident, but after I'd gotten to know her I'd realized she just didn't give a fuck about things that didn't matter to her, and gave a lot of fucks about the things that did. She was kind of my hero that way.

"Oh my god, Lou!" Ria announced, striding into the guys' house with her quietest boyfriend, Seth, on her heels. "You're living with three guys? What the actual fuck?"

I gave her a disbelieving look as Seth helped her out of her winter clothes. He must run hot too—like Nate, Gabriel, and Brooks, he was way underdressed for the Alaskan winter and didn't seem bothered at all by it.

"This feels like déjà vu," I laughed. "Did you not end up living with three guys totally out of the blue?"

"That was different," Ria replied, flicking her hand dismissively before wandering into the living room, inspecting the place. "Ooh, did you make cookies? It smells like Pillsbury heaven in here."

"How was it different?" I asked, squeezing past her to get to the kitchen, pausing in the doorway.

"You probably didn't break in," Seth supplied quietly, sounding amused.

"Well, that's true," I admitted, gesturing for them to take a seat on the couch. "This whole extended visit was very much at Nate's invitation. Or insistence, rather."

"He mentioned you had an unwanted visitor," Ria said, looking furious on my behalf. "The nerve of that guy, showing up at your house in the middle of the night."

I frowned at her. "That's just Nate's theory. Frank is in town, but I'm pretty sure it was animals outside my house the night I called you. Weirdly aggressive ones, sure, but just animals."

"Right," Ria said, clearing her throat. "Of course, that's... animals. Um, you know you can come stay with us whenever you want? You don't have to stay here."

Seth nodded, his expression serious, though he always looked like that.

"That's not necessary," I assured her, letting her change the subject. "I mean, maybe it'd be less awkward, but I need to be close to my house to finish getting it ready to sell. Also you're savages who don't have internet at your house and you know I'd die without it."

"You wouldn't die," Ria scoffed. "It's actually very therapeutic being off-grid. I feel very in touch with my inner nature goddess these days."

"Mm, sure," I replied doubtfully. Ria had weird romanticized dreams about life in the wild that I could not relate to at all. I assumed it was a phase that she'd get over after actually living out there, but apparently it was still going strong.

"Are you okay here? Are they treating you well?" Seth asked seriously.

"If they're not, my guys can totally kick their asses," Ria added smugly. A sudden urge to defend Nate, Gabriel and Brooks rose, and I shook my head slightly to clear it. They weren't *my* guys to defend. Even if they were, one of Ria's boyfriends, Noah, was built like a fucking tank and probably could take them all out.

"No ass kicking necessary," I told her with a smile, though I was a little tempted to tell them to kick Nate's ass. Maybe one percent tempted. "They've been really accommodating, if not a little overprotective."

And a lot squirrely. I didn't want to talk about that with Seth here though. I didn't know him well enough, and I felt kind of awkward.

Ria's smile turned brittle. "In this situation, I don't think that *over*protective is a thing, Lou. The more protection you have, the better."

Huh. I hadn't expected Ria to react with the same intensity that the guys had to the whole Frank situation. Was I being too relaxed about it? He'd shown up, stalked me a little, but mostly left me alone. It really felt like a lot of hype over nothing.

"Seth has to go meet some people, can I hang out here?" Ria asked, perking up. "We could watch *Austenland* again? I love my guys, but they have a tragic lack of interest in Jane Austen. I guess nobody's perfect," she sighed dramatically while Seth looked indulgently at her, like nothing more adorable had ever existed.

Ugh, I was so jealous. I wanted someone to look at me like I was cute when I was acting ridiculous.

"Sounds great," I told her. "I'll get the cookies."

✳ ✳ ✳

I had to admit, the girl-time with Ria had been seriously amazing. For a few hours, I hadn't thought about stupid Frank, or the house, or the sexy liars I was staying with.

"I really think you should do a big reveal and then *bam*, red hair," Ria said, scrolling through my profile on my phone. "You're a cute blonde, but you're a smoking redhead. And do you really want to be dealing with the wig while you're traveling?"

"No," I sighed, curling up into a ball in the corner of the couch with my hot cocoa. "It's just a crutch, I guess. The wig helps me slip into character."

"My favorite character is Lou," Ria declared confidently.

"That's because you haven't seen Scarlet orgasm from nipple play alone on camera," I shot back.

"Dang girl, you're going to have to give me pointers," Ria laughed. "I think my nipples might just be decorative?"

I heard a cupboard door shut in the kitchen and exchanged a wide-eyed look with Ria because I had *completely* forgotten that Gabriel was home. She not-so-discreetly leaned over the arm of the couch, craning her neck to peer into the kitchen.

"I saw him, but he's gone back down the hallway now," she whispered dramatically. "Also, please tell me you're tapping that *muy caliente* ass."

"Except make it Portugese because he's Brazilian," I replied, bumping her leg with my foot. "And no. Not yet. I don't know."

Ria wiggled her eyebrows at me and I sighed loudly as if I hadn't been *dying* to talk about this with someone.

"I slept with Nate. And got frisky with Brooks. And Gabriel was like 'do whatever with whoever' since we're all leaving Fairbanks in a few weeks anyway. Well, except Nate, but I despise him, so you know."

Ria frowned. "No, I don't know. Why? What'd he do?"

"Tapped and gapped." I shrugged. "Whatever, I was probably reading too much into things anyway."

She opened her mouth to argue, but I kept going, not wanting to explore that emotional minefield. "Do you think I'm being a super hoe?"

Ria choked on the sip of cocoa she'd just taken. "I have three m—, er, boyfriends. No, of course I don't think that. Why?" she asked suspiciously. "Did you think I was a super hoe?"

"Hard no. You're out there having foursomes on the regular like a Queen. Zero judgment from me," I assured her. "It's not the same thing though. It's all separate. I'm not in some kind of poly relationship here—"

"Yet," Ria interjected.

"Ever," I corrected. "We're all going our own ways at the end of winter."

"So go together." Ria shrugged like it was no big deal. "These guys... they're not so different from my guys in a lot of ways. I don't think they're going to go to all this effort to keep you safe just to walk away from you at the end of it."

She was making some pretty big generalizations, considering she hadn't actually *met* Brooks or Gabriel, but I appreciated the sentiment.

"I'm going to miss you," Ria told me seriously, leaning over to squeeze my arm.

"Not as much as I'll miss you," I promised. "You'll be here popping out babies with all your lovers and you'll probably forget all about me."

There was a strange twinge in my chest that might have been jealousy. Not on the baby front, but the fact that she was surrounded by men who absolutely adored her and had a whole future ahead of her that she was excited about... I had *things* in my future that I was excited about, but I was also aware of how alone I was. How alone I would continue to be.

"Pft, I will not forget about you. And you better come back and visit. And message me all the time. I want photos of all the places you visit. Without the wig," she added pointedly. "It's time for the world to see *Lou.*"

Chapter 18

My catch up with Ria yesterday had made me feel invigorated about life. I was going to call the realtor today and set things in motion after I did my modified yoga routine hidden away in the room I was borrowing from Nate, which mostly involved standing up because there was only a sliver of space between the bed and the wall. I was ready to have my *own* space back.

It was either that or do yoga in the living room here which might give the guys ideas, and I couldn't tell if I was for that or against it.

"Querida," Gabriel called, knocking lightly on the door. "Are you awake?"

"I am. Come in," I said back, not raising my voice just to see if he could hear me. I was getting a little worried about my own hearing living with them.

Gabriel opened the door while I was reaching upwards, bending backwards to get a good stretch in my spine, and I felt his gaze track over my gray crop top, the exposed skin beneath, and down my pale blue leggings.

"Brooks and I were thinking of visiting Chena Hot Springs today to get some new content. We, er, wondered if you'd like to join us."

Ooh, he sounded adorably nervous. Like he was asking me on a date with both him and Brooks at the same time.

"Have you been before?" Gabriel asked, clearing his throat as I straightened.

"Not since..." *My honeymoon. Yikes.* "It's been awhile. I'd love to come with you."

I could definitely think of worse ways to spend my day than hanging out in my swimsuit with two hot guys, especially since one of them had made me come so hard I'd *almost* forgotten the fact that they were all lying to me. Maybe with a little help from my sexy swimsuit and some Scarlet-style interrogation tactics, I'd get some secrets out of them today.

Gabriel smiled, the faint lines around his eyes wrinkling and lordy, that did it for me. "Meet us outside in thirty minutes."

✳ ✳ ✳

The drive to Chena Hot Springs took just over an hour. Gabriel had driven the three of us while Brooks played DJ in the front seat and I lounged in the back, memorizing the scenery as it went past. Who knew when I'd be back? I may not want to live here anymore, but it was still objectively beautiful and there were definitely things I'd miss.

Gabriel insisted on paying and we made our way through the complex, trudging through bright white snow towards the pool area. Brooks followed behind us, snapping photos the entire time while I tried to stay out of frame.

"You gonna let me take some photos of you, Red?" Brooks asked, waggling his eyebrows at me. "These would make some awesome shots for your social channels," he added absently, returning his gaze to his camera while he looked through his test shots. "Your hair looks amazing against the snow."

God, was there anything sexier than a man who hyped you up? Brooks seemed like a big time player, but I bet if some lady was lucky enough to lock him down, he'd be her biggest cheerleader for life.

I chewed on my lower lip, remembering what Ria had said about introducing Lou to the world.

"You don't have to post them," Brooks added with a shrug. "But you look fucking phenomenal right now—like a fiery winter goddess—and I am dying to photograph you."

"Thanks." *Oh my god, was I blushing a little? How embarrassing.* "I've been thinking I'd prefer to have a more natural look on my page for a while, but I guess I don't know how anymore."

"Just do it, *querida*," Gabriel answered, rejoining us after taking some notes on his phone. "You do look very striking against the snow. It would be the perfect way to debut it."

"You have really good hearing," I told him, blinking slowly. He'd been super far away when Brooks had said that. Hadn't he? Maybe I was imagining things.

Brooks coughed. "He does. Anyway, let's get a few shots and we'll see what you think."

I didn't have my blue contacts in and I was barely wearing makeup since my gaiter covered my face and I'd sweat it off in the springs anyway, so I turned away from the camera, fluffing out my hair underneath my beanie and spreading my arms wide as I faced the snowy trees in the distance.

"Work it, girl," Brooks teased.

I poked my tongue out at him over my shoulder before facing away again, doing a few more natural poses as well so we had options.

"Good?" I asked, spinning around to face Brooks with my gaiter pulled down.

"Stunning," he replied from behind the camera, still snapping away.

"Enough," I laughed, covering my face again and darting out of frame.

"Fine, fine," Brooks sighed. "Let me get some video footage for your article," he said to Gabriel, fiddling with the camera.

I watched as Brooks panned around, getting a bunch of scenic shots that would probably look amazing on screen while Gabriel stood patiently in the background, waiting.

He looked incredibly sexy in his gray coat and black beanie, curls of dark hair visible where the fabric ended, black stubble lining his jaw—like a rugged, sexy model, waiting for his moment in front of the camera in a dramatic, windswept location.

Why wasn't he in front of the camera?

"I think I'm good," Brooks mumbled, looking at the display.

"So, you guys don't ever film yourselves?" I asked.

Brooks gave me a knowing grin, undoubtedly thinking about the ways I filmed myself, and I was tempted to throw a snowball at his very expensive camera.

"Like a vlog," I clarified with a pointed look.

Gabriel shook his head. "No, we've never done anything like that. Brooks shoots video footage which I sometimes include in articles, but we don't ever appear on camera."

"That... seems like a wasted opportunity, honestly," I told him, frowning. "You're going to these amazing places anyway, you've got the equipment to take great quality footage, and you're both, you know." I gestured at them.

"We're both what?" Brooks teased.

"Not entirely hideous," I shot back, batting my eyelashes at him. "You'd get a ton of views."

Brooks and Gabriel exchanged a look, both contemplative.

"It's a good idea," Brooks pointed out. "We've been talking about doing more on social media, and video content is the way to go right now. Can you make all that sexy Brazilian charisma happen on screen?"

Gabriel blinked at him. "No. Absolutely not. I'm a writer, not a... *personality.*"

"Don't overthink it," I advised him, picking my way carefully over the snow to step into the center of where Brooks had been shooting. "Here, I'll do a practice run, and you can copy me."

Gabriel gestured at Brooks, who quickly fiddled with the camera before centering on me. I pulled down my neck gaiter so I could speak clearly on camera, immediately aware of how dry my lips were in the cold. *Ugh.* I needed to get my house on the market as soon as possible—the Dominican Republic was calling my name.

"Action!" Brooks yelled with totally unnecessary dramatic flair.

I pasted a bright smile on my face, looking down the camera. "Hey guys! My name is Lou, welcome to our channel. We are here at the *gorgeous* Chena Hot Springs in Fairbanks, Alaska. How great is this?" I asked with another dazzling smile, gesturing at my snow-covered surroundings. "While I am loving this view, I am going to love those springs even *more.* Let's go!"

I held my smile for a second longer before turning to look at Gabriel. "So then you grab some footage of walking to the springs, speed it up to double time with some mood music in the background, then pick up the narrative again once you're in the springs. Easy peasy."

"Easy peasy when you do it," Brooks laughed. "Master disaster when Gabriel does it, I bet."

"That's not a thing," I shot back, trying not to smile. "And you're not being supportive. Come here, Gabriel. Try."

He looked dubiously between me and Brooks before walking to where I was standing in frame, dragging his feet. I patted his arm reassuringly before making my way over to where Brooks was standing so I was out of the way, trudging clumsily through the snow.

"Okay," Brooks called. "When you're ready."

"Er, hello? My name is Gabriel..." Okay. It was his first time on camera. I'd been super awkward when I started out too. "Welcome. Hello."

I pointed at the sign, hoping he'd take my cue to introduce the location. He frowned at me in confusion for a few seconds before his eyes lit up in understanding.

"Ah, right. We are at Chena Hot Springs in Alaska."

"This is terrible," Brooks murmured in awe. "Like, next level terrible."

"You do it then," Gabriel groused. I startled, amazed all over again that he'd heard Brooks' quiet voice from so far away.

"No, no," Brooks laughed. "My technical expertise is required behind the camera. Try again, but do it less shit this time."

"Let's try again in the springs," I said in a soothing voice, throwing Brooks a dirty look. "It can just be a test run today to see if it's something you guys are interested in."

We headed in and separated to change, which gave me ample time to question whether or not this outfit was a little over the top.

It was. There really wasn't any question about it. But I was going to flirt some information out of these two men, and I needed all the help I could get.

I had never actually worn this swimsuit outside of a home photoshoot before, and I stood in the changing rooms for a little longer than necessary trying to stuff my boobs more securely into the top before I traumatized some poor child. It was a one-piece, which should theoretically make it more modest, but there were cut outs under my breasts and it came up so high on my hip bones that I'd probably be more covered in a bikini.

Fortunately, the springs weren't super busy yet, but it was still early. I could definitely give some unsuspecting tourist an eyeful before the day was done.

I gave myself a final once over, my gaze catching on the wings of the phoenix tattoo that decorated my thigh and hip, the bird's head just hidden by my swimsuit. I really did love my tattoo, even though it reminded me of Nate every time I saw it.

That was probably a good reason to never sleep with the artist permanently marking your skin. It would have been helpful for me to have had this epiphany a few weeks ago.

I loosely knotted my hair at the base of my neck before pulling my gray beanie down, vague memories of my hair and eyelashes being coated in frost last time I came here with Jake floating through my mind, before making my way out through the heated tunnel to the springs.

It was weird that I'd barely given this place a thought over the years. Even though most of my memories from that time in my life were at the very worst, mediocre, I'd still done a pretty great job of compartmentalizing and never thinking about them again.

I hadn't really given Jake much thought either. Last I'd heard, he'd left Fairbanks to work on an oil rig. I hoped he was doing okay wherever he was, and he'd found what he was looking for.

The tunnel between the changing rooms and the springs was heated, but I still walked as fast as I could to get my half-exposed ass into the warm water.

"What in the actual fuck is that?" Brooks asked, staring at me like I was a meteor rapidly approaching the Earth. It was a delightful mixture of shock, awe, and lust, which had been exactly what I was aiming for.

"Querida," Gabriel whistled. "Are you trying to kill us?"

They were already partially submerged in the water, waiting on the rocks near the tunnel exit for me. Both shirtless. Both were absurdly buff, considering their Lunchables-and-Hot-Pockets diet. That was some fucking *sorcery* right there.

Gabriel's muscles were sleeker, his skin tanned and covered in a smattering of dark hair, while Brooks' muscles were more rugged somehow, his skin fairer. Both of them were covered in tattoos that were no doubt Nate's handiwork. Gabriel favored maps and travel iconography that I wanted to trace with my fingers. Brooks' had a dark sleeve down one arm that showed an eerily realistic wolf emerging from the trees.

I didn't know where to look.

Fortunately, they were too busy perving on me in my itty bitty swimsuit to notice that I was perving right back.

"Get in here," Brooks urged as I shivered slightly. I didn't need any extra encouragement—the water was gloriously warm and the air was *fucking freezing*. Brooks had switched to a GoPro to film in the springs, and he flicked it on as I waded into the water, grinning playfully as he focused the camera on me.

I raised an eyebrow at him before blowing a flirty kiss at the camera, spinning around in the water as I moved deeper, giving them a quick peek of my ass cheeks before the water hit my waist.

"I've died and gone to heaven," Brooks muttered. "That's the only explanation."

"Stop ruining the shot," I chastised with a smile before grabbing Gabriel's bicep—*why, hello there*—and pulling him into frame next to me. He gave me a wary look before reluctantly facing the camera, keeping me pinned to his side with an arm around my waist. I always knew he was a lot *bigger* than me, but without all the bulky winter clothes in the way, it was evident just how much bigger he was.

"Practice run, remember?" I said with a soft smile, looking up at him. Gabriel's hand rested low on my hip, his fingers brushing the exposed skin through the cutouts of my suit.

What were we doing again?

"Focus," Brooks laughed. "Guys, where are we?"

Gabriel beamed at me, clearly buttering me up so I'd do the talking.

"Ugh, fine. I'll do a demonstration, then you copy. Deal?"

"Deal," Gabriel replied somberly, the liar.

"Okay." I cleared my throat, fiddling with my beanie and wishing I had a mirror to check my face in.

"You look great," Brooks assured me, looking at me over the GoPro. "Like, ridiculously great. *Unnaturally* great. Like I think I might be dreaming this moment."

"Hush," I laughed, shoving some water at him. Though he had succeeded in making me forget my vanity. "Okay. Hi everyone, Lou again, we're here at Chena Hot Springs and as you can see, we've just gotten into the water. It feels *ah-mazing*, right Gabriel?"

"Right," he grunted, all of his natural charisma dissipating into the steam that rose off the water's surface.

"Gabriel is enjoying the water so much, he's lost for words," I said to the camera, winking like the viewer and I were both in on the joke. "Brooks is behind the camera, say hi, Brooks!"

He glowered at me for a moment before holding out the GoPro and flipping it to point at himself. He did his best fuckboy 'sup' nod and smirk which I had to admit, with him shirtless in the water, was probably going to look *excellent* on screen.

"I'm ready to head a little deeper in, what do you guys think?" I asked, forgetting I was supposed to make Gabriel take the lead.

"Let's do it," Gabriel replied, relaxing slightly and letting me grab his hand and pull him further into the water, walking backwards so I could reassure him with my eyes that he was doing a great job.

We made a beeline for the far edge of the springs, which turned out to be the hottest bit and definitely why we were all alone down here, but I had no complaints about that.

I talked through what we were doing and how it felt for the camera's benefit, and Brooks took a few more sweeping shots while Gabriel stayed silent. After some underwater shots which would probably not be suitable to post considering how much of my ass was on display, Brooks switched the camera off and lounged against the rocks, finally relaxing with us.

"This could be really awesome you know," he said, looking at Gabriel. "I could even put together some videos of places we've been before, just without the narration."

"Just do a voiceover," I suggested, fixing my bun. "Or film yourself talking to the camera."

"You're really good at this," Gabriel remarked, sounding genuinely impressed. I looked at Brooks, trying to figure out what he'd told Gabriel, and he gave me a guileless look back.

"I have a lot of experience on camera," I replied carefully, watching Gabriel's expression. He opened his mouth like he was going to ask follow up questions, and I decided to just lay it all out there before the questions got uncomfortable. I didn't need him thinking I'd been a journalist or something. That would only make this conversation more awkward for everyone.

"When I was 20, I found myself in a pretty dire financial situation." Divorced. Almost homeless. "I'd seen ads for camgirl work before. I thought I'd give it a try."

Gabriel listened, remarkably good at hiding any judgment he might have, just as his friends had been. I was really regretting not getting this over with in one group conversation.

"So, that's what I did for five years. I did have a physical arrangement with Frank, but that was the one and only time I did something like that," I added. I guess I could mention that I'd done it because I thought I could have feelings for Frank, but I didn't really owe them any additional explanation, and I was kind of embarrassed about how wrong I'd been.

Then again, Frank had followed me here, so maybe his feelings ran deeper for me than I thought? Or maybe he wanted to wear my skin. I hoped I'd never find out.

There was a fountain off the rocks at this end of the springs, and between the almost uncomfortably hot water keeping everyone away, the splashing fountain, and the steam rising off the surface, we were pretty secluded pressed up against the rocks, reminding me of my goal for the day.

No time like the present, I told myself, which was maybe the weakest internal pep talk I'd ever done. *Come on. You need answers. What Would Scarlet Do?*

"I'm getting too hot," I complained with an exaggerated sigh, fanning my face. "I'm too short to get any of the cool air."

Me, damsel. You, knight in shining armor. Do your thing.

"I'll give you a boost, Red," Brooks offered, taking the bait immediately. I wasn't lying—the water was nip-height on them and neck-height on me, and my face was feeling seriously sweaty.

Brooks wrapped an arm around my waist, lifting me up against his side so my body wasn't fully submerged in the springs. I wrapped my legs around his hips, and if he turned his head to the side he'd get an eyeful of my boobs, nipples poking aggressively through the fabric of my swimsuit in the frigid air.

"Thanks, Brooks," I purred in his ear, stroking his back like I just couldn't help touching him.

I shot Gabriel a flirty look, hoping to pull him into my web, though blatantly rubbing myself all over Brooks may well have the opposite effect. Gabriel's lips curled up in amusement, though his eyes were heated.

"You don't need to hide anything from me, querida," he said smoothly. "I know you two got up to something the other day. It was *all over your face*," he said to Brooks, whose ears went a little pink.

He couldn't mean literally, right? I mean... I had definitely been all over Brooks' face, but there wasn't like... *evidence*.

"This was your idea," I reminded him lightly, nerves fluttering in my belly.

"And I'm glad to see you're embracing it," Gabriel replied with a low laugh. Okay. Okay, he seemed fine with it. Still weird.

Brooks' hand around my waist slid down, his fingers dipping inside the cutout of my swimsuit. He was testing me, seeing how far I was willing to take this. Even though this was meant to be a reconnaissance mission, I still *wanted* them. The idea of having both of their attention on me at once was... kind of hot actually. I wasn't ashamed to admit I liked attention. *Reveled* in it.

"Do you miss performing?" Brooks murmured, his lips brushing my jaw as he read my mind. "We can be your audience."

My legs tightened around his waist and that was all the encouragement Brooks needed to capture my lips, teasing with his teeth and tongue, making me chase him.

"Be good," Brooks scolded, giving my ass a cheeky squeeze under the water. "There are families here," he teased.

"You're no fun," I groused. I mean, there were families here, but they were at the other end of the spring and we were mostly concealed by the fountain. "Maybe I'll go see Gabriel."

"Maybe you should," Brooks chuckled, stepping towards his friend with me in his arms. *Was he going to? Oh, he was.* Brooks passed me into Gabriel's outstretched arms and I found myself immediately plastered against his warm, solid chest.

"How do you say 'hi' in Portugese?" I asked breathily.

Gabriel smirked. "*Oi.*"

I giggled, and it came out all vapid and airy, and it was not Scarlet at all. "*Oi.* That didn't come out as sexy as I'd hoped," I admitted.

"You don't need to say anything to be sexy, querida," Gabriel replied with a smirk. "You know, I'm getting a little jealous."

"Oh?" I asked, draping my arms over his shoulders. "Do I need to remind you again that this was your idea?"

"Not at all. I'm just feeling a little left out," Gabriel teased.

"Well, we can't have that," I murmured, pressing my forehead against his. Our breaths mingled with the steam rising off the spring, and for a moment I let myself get lost in his cloudy gray eyes, forgetting about the tension with Nate, the things they weren't telling me, and all the other unsaid words that were lying between us.

But that was a dangerous way to think, so I leaned forward and pressed my lips against Gabriel's, closing my eyes and shutting down that connection that could never go anywhere in favor of something safer.

Sexual attraction.

Gabriel groaned, his arm banding tightly around me as he deepened the kiss, one hand sliding up to cup my jaw and angle my head the way he wanted it. His tongue stroked mine, less playful than Brooks, and less ferocious than Nate. It was all Gabriel—cool, calm, and in control.

I did not feel in control. I felt like I had lost control of the situation completely.

You are supposed to be interrogating them, you shameless hussy.

I tried to dredge up some Scarlet sassiness to wrangle this chemistry to my advantage, but she had been drowned in an avalanche of hormones and I couldn't find her anywhere.

"What is it, querida?" Gabriel whispered against my lips. "You have enticed us with your seductions. Ask us your question."

I blinked, some of the fog of lust clearing. The fuck? Was I that transparent?

To his credit, Gabriel didn't look upset in the slightest. Mildly amused, if anything. I felt Brooks' presence at my back, his lips brushing over the now cool skin on my shoulder.

"Spit it out, Red," he said cheerfully. Damn it.

"You're all hiding something from me," I grumbled, extricating myself from their grip and sliding down Gabriel's body until my feet touched the bottom. I felt like an idiot being all snuggled up to them now. "I want to know what it is."

Gabriel gave me a sad smile, and I was glad he wasn't going to pretend they weren't keeping secrets at least.

"Please believe that if we could tell you, we would," Gabriel said, the plea for me to understand clear in his voice. "But not telling you is for your own protection."

"That sounds like a massive copout to me," I replied, my frustration rising as I looked between them.

Brooks looked almost as frustrated as I felt. "I hate keeping this from you, Red."

"Whatever this... this *secret* is," I began, trying to keep my voice even. "Frank knows, right? He alluded to Nate lying to me. He said he'd tell me the truth."

Both Brooks and Gabriel looked horrified at that idea, and the naive, trusting part of me softened, wanting to believe that they really did have my best interests at heart.

"Frank didn't say that to *help* you," Gabriel said urgently, eyes wide. "He said that to *threaten* Nate. Please believe us, querida. Frank is not on your side."

I sighed heavily, looking out over the rest of the springs because I couldn't concentrate when I was staring at their pretty faces and the muscular tattooed chests I hadn't seen before today.

"I don't think Frank has my best interests at heart," I agreed, still looking into the distance. "But all this secret keeping is driving me crazy, for my own good or not."

I glanced at them out of the corner of my eye, finding both Gabriel and Brooks looking glum.

"I'm going back to my house tomorrow," I told them. For a long moment, the only sounds were the splashing of the fountain water hitting the surface and the distant murmur of voices from the other end of the pool. And maybe my own heart, which was pounding louder than usual in my chest, but not in an excited way. In a cracking-in-half kind of way.

"You're not our prisoner," Gabriel sighed eventually. "If you want to go home, we can't stop you, though we would ask you to reconsider. You remember what happened the night you came to stay with us—"

"Wild animals," I interrupted, forcing back the stupid lump in my throat. "I must have left food out or something. Frank hasn't been an issue, and I don't believe he will be."

Brooks made a sound of disagreement, but pursed his lips, letting Gabriel do the talking. Gabriel was definitely the most diplomatic of the three of them.

"I don't think Nate will be so easily put off," Gabriel said hesitantly, exchanging an almost desperate look with Brooks.

My lips twitched, though it was more from an exhausted kind of acceptance of Nate's paranoia than any kind of happiness. "I'm sure he won't, but I'm not going to change my mind."

"We're still going to make sure Frank doesn't fuck with you," Brooks muttered, more to himself than me.

"I wish things could be different," Gabriel said with a resigned smile. "Perhaps we can still enjoy this one last day together?"

He reached out his arms to give me a hug, and I didn't hesitate to walk into them, letting him engulf me in the safety he emanated, even knowing it was just an illusion.

"I'm sorry, Lou," Brooks whispered, so quietly I wondered if I'd imagined it.

One good day. We could still have one good day before we let the secrets push us apart.

I turned around and jumped onto Brooks, wrapping my legs around his waist and giving him a smile that was a little too bright to be natural. "Shall we go get some food?"

"Yeah, Red. Let's go feed you."

* * *

We stopped at a diner on the way back for lunch, all pretending like nothing had changed when everything had. I watched wide-eyed as the guys demolished two chicken sandwiches each, followed by mac n' cheese, potato salad, *and fries*, while I slowly worked through my salad wrap and cup of tomato soup. *Where did they put all that food?* I'd seen them shirtless now. It wasn't like they were hiding extra fluff under their winter layers, they were ripped as hell.

Maybe they were on steroids?

"You want some mac n' cheese?" Brooks asked, blinking at me like he was confused by my staring as he pushed the almost empty tub across the table towards me.

"Kind of," I admitted, because while I tried to be diligent about eating healthy, I *loved* pasta and cheese. "I just... don't understand how you're both so buff. I've never seen either of you work out."

Brooks and Gabriel both looked like kids who'd been caught with their hands in the candy jar, forks halfway to their open mouths, eyes wide.

"We work out," Brooks replied, swallowing thickly. "We run."

"I'm still not sure how running gives you a six-pack. I've never seen any of you run," I pointed out. *Steroids. Had to be steroids.*

"Just lucky, I guess," Gabriel replied with an awkward laugh. "Thanks for coming with us today. I hope you enjoyed it."

"Of course, I did," I replied, like it should be obvious. "I haven't done something like that in ages. And your company isn't terrible."

Gabriel smiled at me like I was a liar, and my chest cracked all over again. Their company was *awesome*, and the time I'd spent with these guys had been the most fun I'd had in years, even when I'd been pissed at them. But I didn't like to think I was an idiot, and the longer I spent with them knowing they were keeping things from me, the more idiotic I felt.

One last good day. Don't waste it.

BROOKS

Chapter 19

This is not how I intended today to go. It wasn't how Gabriel had intended this day to go either. We approached the rental house with a heavy sense of finality in the air, because while the day wasn't over, the clock was running down on our time with Lou.

Nate was going to flip his fucking lid, but I didn't know what he could have expected us to do. We weren't in the business of holding women hostage, and the only thing that would convince Lou to stay is to explain *everything* to her, but we couldn't do that either. Humans couldn't know about shifters unless they were mated to one. It was always going to be a relationship built on lies, and we should have known she'd be smart enough to see right through our bullshit.

Besides, it wasn't like Nate had actually been *around* to do his bit to convince Lou. I'd been a little resentful about him spending all of his time either at his studio or in his fur, and basically avoiding the house at all costs. But then he'd come through and lured Frank away from Lou's house when I wasn't paying attention, so I couldn't be mad anymore.

He'd claimed he was fine, but I wasn't even sure Nate had healed from his last set of injuries because he'd been running himself so ragged.

At least between Nate, his brother's pack, and the bear shifters, there were a decent number of eyes on Frank. I liked to think the guy wouldn't go for her home a *third* time, but Frank was a wild card. For all of Lou's confidence that Frank wasn't a threat, he hadn't gone away.

The three of us would just have to work a little harder to keep her safe from afar if Lou refused to stay with us.

We pulled up in front of the cabin and the three of us climbed out in silence, despite all of our weak attempts at pretending this was going to be a final day of *fun* or whatever bullshit Gabriel had spouted.

I glanced at him as he unlocked the door, trying to gauge his mood. Gabriel was more stoic than I was in general, but did he not feel his animal riding him, urging him to keep Lou in our territory? Safe? I felt like I was turning into Nate. Maybe there was something to be said for his theory that Lou tested our control.

I watched as Lou hung her coat on a hook by the door and neatly lined up her boots underneath, a pang going through my chest that absolutely didn't belong there. I wasn't interested in something serious anyway. Was I? I never had been before.

She just looked like she belonged here. Not *here*, in Alaska. Just here, with us, wherever that was.

Gabriel gave me a searching look, his eyes never missing anything, even when I would have preferred that they did.

"Ah, shit," he said suddenly, not nearly as subtle as he thought he was. "I just remembered that I need to pick something up from the post office. I'll be back in a little while."

He had disappeared out of the front door before Lou had a chance to open her mouth, and she stared after him, eyebrows raised.

"What was that?" she asked, turning to me.

"A thin excuse for giving us alone time," I replied drily, flopping down on the couch.

"Oh." Lou frowned as she came to sit next to me. She curled up with her feet tucked underneath her, and I was relieved that she at least wasn't plastered to the other corner of the couch, as far away from me as possible. "I kind of thought he was into me too?"

I coughed a little, not entirely sure where she was going with this. If she thought we were going to have a threesome then send her on her merry way, she was *definitely* mistaken. I could control myself just on my own, but seeing her with my best friend?

I'd get possessive. Or jealous. Or be weirdly into it. I didn't even know.

I was so lost in my thoughts, I barely registered Lou moving until she landed on my lap, straddling me with a stern look on her face.

"You are thinking *very* hard. I don't know how I feel about Serious Brooks," Lou teased, her hands resting on my shoulders. "Give me back Playful Brooks, who told me that if I needed to fuck the last guy out of my system, he'd politely consider my request."

"Is... is that a request?" I asked, my hands sliding up to rest on her hips.

"It is."

"That was before I knew who the last guy was," I pointed out, feeling a little guilty when I thought of Nate.

"You don't know now. You're just making an educated guess," Lou replied with a cocky shrug, her confident flirty side back in full force. Now that I knew her a little better and knew more about her past, I got the feeling that a lot of this was 'Scarlet'. I didn't hate it, but I preferred her natural dry sense of humor, and the way she totally lost herself in desire when she wasn't trying to impress anyone.

"You are trouble," I told her, sitting up to nip her bottom lip. "Tempting." I nipped her again, my wolf rumbling silently in approval, and soothed away the sting with my tongue. "Delicious."

Lou hummed, her nails digging into my skin through my shirt. *Mark me, baby girl.*

"You can keep the compliments coming, but first tell me if you agree to my request," she said breathily.

Was I interested in Lou? Abso-fucking-lutely. Did I want to fuck her? More than almost anything.

Was Nate going to lose his shit about it? Probably.

But he had given his blessing, albeit reluctantly, and I'd already crossed several lines with Lou anyway. Frankly, she was a grown woman and if she wanted to work out some tension on my body, I was more than happy to oblige. I was a gentleman like that.

Or that's how I usually felt when it came to women. While I wanted to do this for Lou, and I wanted to have this memory with her more than anything, being her palette cleanse fuck didn't feel as good as I thought it would when I initially suggested it.

She doesn't want you for your feelings, Brooks.

"What would you like, Red?" I purred, cupping her jaw and admiring the way her breath hitched in response every time I touched her. So damn responsive.

If she just wanted to ride my tongue like it was a mechanical bull for a couple of hours again, I'd be completely fine with that, but I kind of hoped she wanted more. Everything.

"I would like you to fuck all the guys I've been with out of my head," she said breathily, a touch of vulnerability in her eyes that I knew she wouldn't want me to see.

"I can do that," I replied in a low voice, my grip on her jaw tightening a fraction.

"That sounds like I'm using you," Lou murmured, her hands sliding under my shirt, stroking reverently over my abs.

I shot her what I hoped was a reassuring smile. "Use me, Little Red. I'm a big boy, I can handle it."

My hands went to her waist and before she could doubt herself again I stood up, giving her a moment to wrap her legs around my hips. Honestly, her squeal of fright was a little offensive. I was definitely strong enough to carry her. I'd carried Nate over my shoulder the whole length of the beach in Punta Cana when he'd gotten too drunk to walk.

I made a beeline for the room Lou had been staying in, grateful that it smelled purely of her now and tossed her lightly on the bed, kicking the door shut behind me.

"You sure about this, Red?" I asked, standing at the edge of the bed.

"Very sure," Lou replied, no hint of hesitation in her voice. She was all vulnerable and open, no hint of Sultry Scarlet to be found.

I definitely put a little bit of fuckboy swagger into it as I reached behind my head and tugged my shirt off, flexing my abs and biceps for maximum impact just like she expected me to. Fortunately, my pants were hanging pretty low, showcasing the V that had definitely gotten me laid in the past.

As potent as the scent of her arousal was, her expression was impressively aloof as she ran her eyes down my body, pausing at the top of my pants.

"Well?" she asked, all dry sass. "On with it. Or off with it, I should say," she added thoughtfully, gesturing at my pants.

"You sure? It might scare you off," I teased, gripping my hard on through the fabric.

Lou rolled her eyes. "Try me."

Maybe she thought I'd been exaggerating, but her eyes definitely widened when I dropped my pants. I was packing some decent equipment, and I had no shame about that.

My Big Dick Energy came from Big Dick Ownership.

"Gimme," Lou breathed, crawling to the edge of the bed, not looking intimidated in the least. I was so surprised by her reaction that her tongue had flicked out before I even registered it, licking a long stroke up my length like my dick was a limited edition flavor of her favorite popsicle.

She smiled up at me before wrapping her hand around the base of my shaft and taking me as far into her throat as she could, and I think I might have swooned a little bit. Goddamn, this *girl*. She was so... contradictory. Unpredictable. Fucking awesome with her mouth.

I'd never really thought of myself as boyfriend material before, but maybe I could figure it out for Lou. I wasn't done with her yet by a long shot.

She's done with you. This is just to get your best friend out of her system.

My hands ran through her thick red hair, pulling it up out of her way as she worked her magic, relaxing her throat and taking far more of me than I'd anticipated. It wasn't just that it felt good, it was that it was *her*.

Fuck. Danger. Do not come.

I tugged her back gently, pushing her back onto the bed and pulling down her patterned leggings.

"What are these fucking things?" I muttered, wrestling them down her legs. Why did she always wear such difficult pants to get off? Lou lifted her hips, giggling as I eventually managed to get her legs free and toss the torture device across the room, starting on her panties next.

She sat up and quickly stripped her top and bra off for me, then it was game over. I was going to get my tongue on every inch of her skin I could manage. Surely if I *thoroughly* licked her, she would be mine? I wasn't going to take any chances. Knees, elbows, armpits, the works.

"If you lick my armpits, I will dismember you," Lou said breathily as I stopped my muttering long enough to scrape my teeth over her nipple.

She made a mewling noise as I sucked the hardened bud into my mouth, swirling my tongue around it until she squirmed.

Mark her. Must mark her.

God, what the fuck was *wrong* with me? I growled at my own illogical thoughts, moving down Lou's body towards her delicious center, pausing to press a kiss against the phoenix winding up over her hip. There was no shy hesitation or surprise from Lou this time. Her legs fell open and she all but invited me to help myself as I kissed and licked her inner thighs, attempting to tease her but rapidly running out of patience.

"Don't tease, Brooks," Lou moaned, on the same page as me. "I am fucking *ready*."

She said that now. She would not be saying that when my dick split her in half because I hadn't taken the time to really get her ready and relaxed.

"Come for me first," I demanded, my voice rougher than usual as my animal instincts rode me hard.

I pinned Lou's hips down and buried my tongue in her pussy, a satisfied rumble rising in my chest at the sweet taste of her.

"Fuck, never mind," Lou sighed, writhing against me as much as she could with my arm keeping her down. "Keep doing that. That is great. You are a very smart man."

Her lighthearted words helped counter the possessive instincts that kept rudely intruding when I was trying to fucking concentrate. I didn't need this bitey, 'mark her' shit popping into my mind right now. What the hell was wrong with my brain?

It hadn't been this bad the other day, but she hadn't been planning on leaving us then.

I pushed one finger into her entrance as I lightly sucked her clit into my mouth, just the way she liked, and Lou clenched around me almost instantly, gasping my name as she came. Wanting to relax her as much as possible, I kept going, adding a second finger and massaging her clit with my tongue to prolong her pleasure.

"Fuck me," Lou half sobbed as the second wave eased. "I need to feel you."

I was right there with her. I didn't think I'd ever needed anything *more*. I crawled up the bed, leaving closed mouth kisses on her skin as I went, forcing myself to keep my canines covered.

I needed to see Lou ride me. *Needed it*. Partly because she was so small and human, that I felt like this was the safest position for her, and partly because I wanted to see her body moving on mine, see every expression on her face as I filled her up.

And I needed to keep my teeth away from her.

I laid on my back, gently pulling Lou on top of me, encouraging her to straddle me.

"Condom," Lou breathed a little deliriously as she leaned over to the nightstand and grabbed a foil from Nate's top drawer, throwing it a dirty look like she was annoyed they were even there.

Fucking hell. I'd never in my life forgotten protection, but if Lou hadn't brought it up, I wasn't sure I'd have remembered. How had this tiny human woven such an effective spell around me? It was like nothing else existed when Lou was around.

I wrapped up as quickly as I physically could before dragging Lou back over my body, her legs straddling my hips. She planted her hands on my chest and rolled her body confidently, grinding her clit against me. She was a sexually confident woman who knew *exactly* how to make herself feel good, and damn if that wasn't incredibly arousing.

"You good, baby girl?" I asked, reminding myself that I was a gentleman when I wanted to act like an animal.

"So good," Lou said dreamily, lining my dick up at her entrance and slowly sinking down, one inch at a time. If my size was off putting, she didn't let on at all, relaxing and rocking, toying with her nipples until her ass hit my thighs.

My balls already felt tight, pleasure tingling at the base of my spine. She felt so goddamn good, and for the first time in my life, I *cursed* having a stupid condom on. I wanted to feel all of her, no barrier between us.

"So full," Lou choked out, only lifting herself a little at a time before sinking down again. "How do you just walk around with this anaconda in your pants all day? Isn't it heavy?"

It is now. All the blood in my body is currently residing in my dick.

"If you keep talking about how big my dick is, I'm going to come," I grumbled. Size compliments were probably a stupid thing to get all excited about—honestly, there were times when it had been a fucking pain to deal with—but whatever. Lou turned me into a dick swinging caveman.

"You're taking me so well, baby girl. Riding me so fucking good," I murmured absently, lost in sensation as she found her rhythm, head thrown back in ecstasy.

"Brooks," she gasped, dropping her chin to stare at me with wide eyes, her walls clenching around me. "More. Talk more."

Fuck, that was sexy. Both that she wanted me to talk dirty to her, and that she was assertive enough to ask for what she wanted. I grasped Lou's hips, holding her in place and fucking up into her, reminding myself to be gentle even as Lou let out a long, exquisite moan that let me know just how much she liked me when I *wasn't* being so gentle.

"You like hearing me tell you how pretty you look on my dick? Of course you do," I rumbled, my fingers digging into her hips as I bounced her on my cock. "You look like you were made just for me. Keep taking me, like that. Good girl."

Just. Like. That.

It was like the magical keyword to Lou's vagina, because she went *off*, slumping over me with her forearms resting on my chest, an orgasm wrecking her body. I ran my hands up and down her back, stroked her hair, praised everything I could think of until words became too hard because my jaw ached with the need to mark her.

God, I wanted nothing more than for this to last forever, but I got the feeling I was playing with fire.

Fighting to maintain my self control, I rolled us both over, bracing myself above Lou and driving into her harder, my vision going a little hazy at the edges as a blinding orgasm built. She pulled her legs up, hooking them either side of my forearms in an impressive flexibility that made each thrust go even deeper, and I fucking lost it.

Pleasure like I'd never experienced in my life ripped through my body, destroying me and remaking me all at once. I was in fucking *knots* over this girl, and she was only fucking me to erase the memories she didn't want.

As soon as my soul returned to my body, I was going to put up some healthy walls between us because I could not keep going the way I was going. We were keeping secrets from her. She was leaving. I did not need to fall in love with someone who was completely unavailable to me.

Unwilling to pull out just yet, I slumped over Lou's body, guiding her legs into a more comfortable position while carefully keeping my weight off her body, trying to memorize her drowsy smile and hooded eyes. God, she looked so beautiful like this. Flushed, boneless, and happy.

I kind of wanted to ask if I had successfully fucked the other guys out of her system, but with the way I was feeling, the question would probably come across wrong. Or right, because I was jealous. But bringing up my jealousy would definitely be a dick thing to do right now.

"Holy shit," Lou mumbled. "You put my vagina into a coma."

"Yeah?"

"Uh, yeah. Just knocked it right out with that baseball bat in your pants. You hit a home run."

I dropped my forehead to hers, smiling to myself. Maybe I could stop being a jealous moron for a few minutes if she kept saying stuff like that. Reluctantly, I pulled out and took a few minutes to dispose of the condom before rejoining Lou in bed where she had rolled onto her front and buried her face in the pillow, apparently *very* chill with being naked. I was chill with her being naked too.

I tugged Lou towards me and draped her over my chest, running my hand up and down her spine, admiring the silky smooth skin of her back. Her chocolatey scent was tart with her desire, and the combination of our scents together was already making my dick stir, ready for round two. Ideally without the revolting lingering latex smell ruining it.

"Did I fuck you to sleep?" I teased, forcing myself to keep the conversation in safe territory.

"No," Lou groaned. "Not yet, anyway. I have to go pee. Safety first."

Smiling to myself, I scooped her into my arms and lifted her off the bed, earning myself a muffled shriek from Lou.

"Put me down! You are not watching me pee. That is *not* my kink."

"Fine," I chuckled. I set her down on her feet, laughing as I flopped back on the bed to wait for her.

"Come back and snuggle me after, Red. I'm feeling needy," I teased, mostly joking, but also not quite.

"Yeah, yeah," she replied drily, rolling her eyes before darting out of the room stark naked, which was a pretty ballsy move. Fortunately, Gabriel hadn't returned yet, and Nate was still in the wind, though he'd promised to come back here to sleep at some point so I should probably tell Lou to get dressed. I mean, if she wanted to walk around the house naked all day, I'd be fine with that, but Nate and Gabriel... they'd probably be fine with it too, actually.

That fact should bother me more. Even with Gabriel's talk about us all dating her over winter, the idea of sharing a woman that I was *this into* should bother me.

Her spending all this time with us should have made Nate crazy. Why didn't it?

I shook my head, trying to clear it before Lou got back. My jealousy, or lack thereof, was irrelevant anyway. Lou was leaving because we couldn't give her the honesty she deserved. What I needed to concentrate on was keeping her safe from the asshole Alpha who wasn't taking no for an answer, and then figuring out how to let her go.

GABRIEL

Chapter 20

I skulked around the edge of the cabin like a pervert, thankful that what I'm sure was the best sex of Brooks' life was now over. God, the *noises* Lou made when she came… they weren't particularly loud, but they were filled with so much unadulterated lust that I knew those sounds would live in my brain for the rest of my life.

I wished she'd made those noises for me, but she hadn't, and I had to accept that it might never happen.

No, it *would never happen*. No caveats.

As much as I wanted to spend this last afternoon with her, Brooks had been struggling with Lou's decision to leave, and he was so out of touch with his emotions that he probably didn't even realize he was struggling. He needed this alone time with her, though I doubted it was going to give him any closure. Lou had gotten under our skin in the short time we'd known her, and I was getting the feeling that even if we'd spent the entire winter together like I'd initially suggested, it wouldn't have been enough.

Perhaps Lou was smart to call it quits. If the secrets were bothering her now, they'd only get worse and harder to hide as our animals grew attached. It was the reason I was hovering out here in my fur like a creep. Nate's warning about losing control had stuck with me, so I'd stayed close in case Brooks needed to be calmed down.

It would have been helpful if Nate had been more specific about *how* Lou tested his control, but he didn't do anything for no reason. I hadn't heard anything coming from the bedroom that made me worry for Lou's safety.

I'd heard a lot of things that made me want to throw the door open and join them.

I hid as best I could in the trees, looking ridiculous with my black fur against the white ground, not even the coverage of leaves to hide me. Shifting during the day wasn't a risk I liked to take—black jaguars weren't exactly native to Alaska. Even Nate had to be careful about where he shifted, because a cougar here would absolutely attract attention. He hadn't been careful though. His desperation to be everywhere at once, to protect Lou from a threat she didn't understand had made him reckless.

Nate was going to be a fucking liability when he found out Lou was leaving. We'd just have to convince him that we could stick close to Lou without getting in her face. If nothing else, we still hadn't fixed her busted porch. That was a reason to spend a few hours with her. Maybe a couple of days if we could drag it out.

In the distance, I heard the distinctive rumble of Nate's truck approaching the property, and with rising dread I shifted back and ran across the yard naked, hoping Lou wasn't looking out the window.

I could hear both her and Brooks' even breathing from the end bedroom—Nate's bedroom, theoretically—and it seemed like they'd worn each other out. *I am not jealous*, I told myself as I dressed as quickly as possible in my room before returning to the living room to intercept Nate.

I was jealous. Not because I *didn't* want Lou to be intimate with my packmates if she wanted them. I just wanted her to be with me as well, and so far I was lagging behind. And unless we found a way to open up to Lou in a way that kept her safe, I would always be lagging behind, because she was sick of being kept in the dark.

I busied myself with lighting the fire, both for something to do and because I was worried Lou was cold. Perhaps I should have opened all the windows to air out the place, but the scent of what the two of them had been doing saturated the place. It would probably take days to dissipate, which was not a comforting thought considering Lou was leaving.

The front door opened with a bang that reverberated through the entire house, and I winced as I straightened, turning to face my enraged friend. His eyes were wild, glowing intermittently as his muscles rippled, his shift imminent.

"*Brooks*," Nate growled as he stormed into the center of the living room, his voice too low for Lou's ears though his dramatic entrance had undoubtedly tipped her off.

"It was enthusiastically consensual," I assured him pointlessly as I moved towards him with my hands up, blocking his way before he did something ridiculous. "You said it was okay."

Reluctantly, but he did agree.

"He shouldn't have let it get this far," Nate snapped.

"Why not, *irmão*?" I asked exasperatedly. "You say she tests your control, but don't elaborate. You and her keep sniping at each other, but neither of you will say why. Neither Brooks nor I have made any secret about being attracted to Lou. This shouldn't come as a surprise to you."

If he'd spent more time with us over the past couple of days, he'd know things between Brooks and Lou weren't a brand new development, but he'd been avoiding her.

Nate growled, the alarming scream-type sound that his cougar made which would definitely terrify Lou, and I placed my hands on his chest, holding him in place before he could go and rip Brooks out of the bed. Nate winced at the contact and I eased back a bit, knowing he was struggling to heal his wounds without proper rest.

"Calm, Nate," I urged. "*Think*. Concentrate on your emotions. This isn't just *anyone*, it's Brooks."

It's *pack*, and he could be open minded about this if he chose to be, but his mind seemed pretty damn closed at the moment.

"He could have—" Nate snapped his mouth shut, but I'd caught a glimpse of the emotion he hadn't wanted me to see. *Shame.*

"He could have what?" I asked softly.

"It doesn't matter," Nate muttered, some of the fight going out of his body.

"Except it clearly does. Talk to me," I pressed.

But before he could open up, Brooks emerged, leaning against the archway between the living room and kitchen in a pair of low slung sweatpants, proudly wearing sex hair and the sweet scent of Lou's arousal like he had a fucking death wish.

One step forward, three miles back.

Ah well, it had been fun while it lasted. I'd miss our little not-a-pack pack when Nate attempted to murder Brooks in human form, and Brooks immediately shifted because his wolf was a defensive beast. I wondered idly if Nate would shift too. Wolf versus man, Nate was a goner. He was too gentle in his human form, and Brooks fought dirty. If it came down to wolf versus mountain lion, Nate had the advantage.

I didn't like my chances of Lou wanting to stay with me after they turned into animals and mauled each other to death in front of her, either way.

"What's up?" Brooks asked casually, crossing his arms over his bare chest.

"*What's up?*" Nate growled, glaring at Brooks like it was the most offensive question in the world. "Didn't you listen to anything I said? What are you doing with Lou?"

"You know exactly what they were doing," I muttered. I was positive Nate could figure it out without Brooks breaking it down in explicit detail.

Brooks grinned slowly, and I could see the wheels turning in his head as he attempted to come up with the most aggravating response in the fewest amount of words. He was a goddamn expert at pushing every single one of Nate's buttons, and he always resorted to being an asshole when he was feeling defensive.

"They had sex," I answered for him. "Loudly. Enthusiastically. Loudly. Did I mention loudly?"

Brooks grinned at me as Lou emerged behind him, tugging an oversized jumper further down her bare thighs, hair delightfully rumpled. She looked gorgeous, if not a little annoyed.

"Sorry. I'm a screamer," she said drily, which wasn't even true, but the three of us had sensitive hearing so everything was loud to us. Lou gave Nate a hard look, but there was plenty of hurt there too. "So, what are we talking about?"

"What do you think we're talking about?" Nate snapped. Shit, he really had a knack for saying the exact worst possible thing when it came to Lou. It was impressive and kind of unsettling, because Nate was usually the most diplomatic of the three of us, but she seemed to completely unravel him. I took a step back as Lou stormed into the room, past both Brooks and I, and walked directly into Nate's personal space without an ounce of hesitation.

She wouldn't have done that if she knew what he actually was, and that thought was a little depressing. Would she be afraid of us if she knew? Why wouldn't she be?

"You were the one who left that night. You're the one with the problem here," she snarled, glaring up at him. "Come on, Nate. Get it all off your chest."

Brooks and I exchanged a look—me warning him to shut up, him looking confused—before we returned our attention to the unlikely standoff happening in the living room. All five feet of Lou currently held the advantage.

Nate's jaw ticked as he looked everywhere except at Lou's face.

"Come on," she pushed. "Share with the class why you fucked me and disappeared while your cum was still running down my thighs."

"The fuck," I growled, forcing myself to remain in control of my beast. Why would he treat her that way? Why would he treat *anyone* that way?

Brooks appeared at my back, a firm hand on my shoulder keeping *me* calm rather than the other way around. Apparently, he was handling this better than I was. Or perhaps he understood, because he'd been intimate with her and I hadn't.

"You were losing *control*," Brooks muttered, sounding like he'd had a revelation. Lou turned to give him a confused look, some of her anger receding at the sound of his voice.

"Let me guess," she said drily, the disappointment in her tone clear. "More secrets you have to keep for my *protection*."

Nate's gaze dropped to the floor, his shoulders hunched as the fight went out of him. Oh my god, he'd tried to *mate mark* her. He hadn't tried to *hurt* her, he'd tried to *claim* her.

"Sorry, Red," Brooks replied with a wince. Had he tried to mark her as well?

Lou turned to look at me, a sad smile on her face. "I don't think this 'one last good day' idea is going to work out."

I nodded, unable to argue with that. We certainly couldn't pretend that everything was okay now.

"What are you talking about?" Nate asked hoarsely.

"Lou would like to go home today," Brooks said firmly, in a tone that warned Nate not to argue. "And as she is not a prisoner in our home, obviously we are fine with that."

The '*but what about Frank?!*' was written all over Nate's face, but for once, he wisely decided to keep his mouth shut. He'd been busting his ass to keep Frank away from Lou already, and now he'd continue to do so with more active help from us.

"I'm going to go pack my things," Lou said quietly, slipping through the three of us like a ghost, none of us objecting as she disappeared into the bedroom. We were silent until the door shut with a click, each of us absorbed in our own thoughts, lacking the easy camaraderie that usually made it so easy to share our minds with each other.

"Did you feel it too?" Nate asked flatly. "The urge to mark her?"

I glanced at Brooks who nodded glumly. "I pushed it down, but the urge was definitely there."

Nate shifted uncomfortably. "I almost didn't... she was asking me to bite her, my teeth were pressing against her throat..."

"And you stopped," I told him firmly. As angry as I was at the way he'd made Lou feel, I wasn't sure that I'd have had the presence of mind to pull back when I was that close to the edge. "It shouldn't have gone that far, but you did stop."

Nate looked *broken*, and however I felt about his actions, he was my packmate and my brother in every way that mattered. I couldn't watch him suffer.

I stepped into his space, pressing my forehead against his and gripping the back of his neck. It spoke to how ashamed his cougar was feeling that he'd even allow such a dominant hold.

"I could have ruined her life," he murmured.

"But you *didn't*," I insisted. "And while you could have handled everything about it better, you've kept her safe ever since. You're suffering carrying this weight alone, *irmão*. Share it with us."

We're your pack.

Nate nodded, reciprocating the grip on the back of my neck before we broke apart as the bedroom door opened. The sound of her floral suitcase rolling down the hallway sounded ominously final.

"Ready," Lou announced, fully dressed.

"I'm going to get dressed and follow behind you, just to make sure you get back safe, okay?" Brooks asked, giving her a tender look. I hated that they'd just shared something so intimate and then it had all gone so terribly wrong. Especially after the way things had ended with Nate.

"That's really not necessary—" Lou objected.

"I'm going to do it anyway," Brooks replied, attempting to paste on his usually easy grin.

"Let me carry your things to the car," I offered, grabbing her things while she moved past to put her boots on.

I was definitely going with Brooks to make sure she got back safely and her territory was secure. Nate would pretend to stay here, then follow in his fur, I was confident of that.

We couldn't keep Lou a prisoner, but we could keep her safe.

Chapter 21

I wanted to laugh at my own ridiculousness for thinking I could have one last nice day together without everything turning to shit, even though I knew they were keeping secrets. Of course there were more secrets. Of course whatever possessed Nate to run out of my house like I was a witch trying to put a curse on him was also a secret that they were suddenly all in on.

Of course to all of it. It all seemed so inevitable.

I could see Brooks and Gabriel following behind me in their SUV through my rearview mirror, but I was doing my best not to focus on that.

I wasn't going to let Nate's paranoia about Frank that the other guys seemed to have bought into get to me. There was nothing to worry about.

My phone was shoved somewhere in the bottom of my bag on the passenger seat next to me and it was buzzing constantly, which was weird, but maybe I'd scheduled a social media post and forgotten about it. Or maybe it was Ria checking in on me. I wouldn't be surprised if Nate had immediately tattled to Ria and her boyfriends that I was leaving. I didn't really understand why she was on Team Nate when it came to all the Frank stuff, but she'd dealt with a persistent ex of her own, so maybe she was just projecting a little.

I had no idea what had gone down between Ria and her ex—she never wanted to talk about it—but Frank wasn't anything like that guy. Well, maybe a little, since they were both liars. But that was definitely where the similarities ended.

Frank wasn't even my ex! He was a jilted lover at best.

God, had it only been this morning I was flirting with Brooks and Gabriel in the hot spring, thinking I was a total badass? It felt like years ago.

I pulled into the driveway, pausing until I found the remote for the garage door and clicked it open. It didn't feel as good as I thought it would coming back here. My phone buzzed so incessantly, I began to worry that there was some kind of emergency happening, and felt around in my purse for it, pulling it out as it continued to vibrate. *Weird*. No calls coming through. Just so many notifications that the display was starting to glitch. I switched it off just to silence the buzzing and threw it back into my purse to deal with later. I was probably due for an upgraded model.

I could almost feel how quiet and lonely the inside of the house was from out here. It was even worse now I'd been getting rid of all the stuff inside. Bigger and emptier.

"Lou!" Gabriel yelled as I drove into the garage. I glanced at the rearview and noticed he'd gotten out of the vehicle and was sprinting after me, a panicked look on his face. Weird. I parked in the garage, and he was there the moment I opened the driver's door, trying to urge me back in.

"Go, Lou. Go! You can't be here."

"What are you talking about?" I asked with a nervous laugh. I slid out of the seat, pressed right up against Gabriel's front since he wouldn't take a step back. "If this is some ploy—"

A low, vicious growl cut me off, making me freeze in place, the hair on the back of my neck standing on end.

"Fucker," Gabriel muttered, sounding a lot less terrified than I was. "Get out of here!" he snarled, looking somewhere behind my vehicle at the still open garage door. I turned my head slowly, trying and failing to remember everything I knew about dealing with wild animals, but nothing could have prepared me for the sight of an enormous dark gray wolf standing on the threshold of my property. Its teeth were bared, ears pinned back, body low to the ground like it was ready to rush us.

This was not a happy animal.

It took a step towards us and Gabriel immediately shoved me behind his back, moving with impressive speed. "Fuck off back to where you came from. There is nothing for you here!"

I was obviously hallucinating, because it almost looked like the wolf *nodded* at me. Like it was communicating with Gabriel that it was here for me.

Oh my god. I was seeing things. *This would be a great time to faint,* I decided. I welcomed the sweet nothingness of oblivion.

Faint!

Apparently, I couldn't faint on demand.

The animal took another step and I glanced at the side door that led into the house, just a few feet away. Gabriel seemed to notice it at the same time, sighing heavily.

"We're being herded, querida," he grumbled. "But I won't risk you being attacked."

"Herded?" I repeated hoarsely.

"Into the house. Where *Frank* is waiting." Gabriel spat his name in disgust and the wolf growled ferociously again.

Frank had... pet wolves?

I could hear more snarling from outside the house, and Gabriel released an impressive string of Portugese that I'm sure was all curse words. "There's another one herding Brooks inside too. He won't risk... he'll go inside quietly."

"Then let's go inside," I breathed, clasping my hands together to stop them from trembling. I wanted us all together. The idea that Brooks was out there, facing down one of Frank's trained wolves made bile rise in my stomach.

The wolf in front of me made a strange chuffing sound that almost sounded like approval. Thoroughly unnerved at the reactions it seemed to be having to my very human words, I gripped the back of Gabriel's shirt, tugging it lightly to get him to move.

He made a frustrated noise in the back of his throat as he walked sideways towards the internal door, keeping me behind him the whole time.

"Fucking *Frank*," he muttered under his breath. Hadn't they only briefly met once at the bar?

"Manners," Frank chided, his voice filtering through from the living room. Surely he wasn't talking to us? "Come and join me and your friend here."

Fear made my feet heavy, and I desperately wanted to just stay where I was, hiding in the mudroom off the entryway, but that fucking wolf appeared again, snarling and encouraging us forward.

I mentally sent an apology to Nate for every time I'd dismissed his warnings about Frank. That was my bad. I'd definitely own that.

As we got further into the house, I finally spotted what I'd been slow to see originally.

Everything was broken. Smashed up like the shelf in the entryway, or shredded to ribbons like my coats that hung off the now broken hooks. Even the walls, the beautiful freshly painted walls that I'd worked so hard on, were decimated. How had my *walls* been ripped up? The windows were smashed, no piece of furniture was intact. It was all... destroyed.

And it absolutely *reeked* of... piss? Disgusting.

This wasn't normal revenge. It looked and smelled like wild animals had gotten in here. The same wild animals who had attacked my home a few nights ago.

These wolves weren't wild though. The one snapping its teeth at Gabriel and I seemed unnaturally aware of what was going on, and it was fucking terrifying.

Maybe they had AI chips in them or something? Frank was rich. Rich people did weird things.

The back door slammed open as Gabriel and I got to the living room, making me jump. "It's Nate," Gabriel murmured quietly, and I was scared to speak to question how he could possibly know that.

Brooks was already in the living room, glaring at a second wolf without a shred of fear in his eyes, and he immediately moved behind me, wrapping his arms around my waist and sandwiching me between him and Gabriel. I couldn't even see Frank standing there, but I didn't particularly care when there were fucking wolves either side of me with teeth that could rip the skin off my bones.

One growled at Brooks, and I swear he *growled* right back.

Nate stormed in from the kitchen with all the grace of a vengeful bull, wearing just a loose pair of sweatpants.

"Not just *your* girlfriend, apparently," Frank said as Nate spat curses at him.

God, how had I never noticed how slimy Frank's voice was before? It was like oil going down my spine.

"Scarlet, my pet," Frank called. "Come here."

"Scarlet is not your anything," I replied coolly, encouraging Gabriel to move aside just enough so I could at least see who I was speaking to. "Did you do this?"

He smiled, but there was no warmth in it.

"I've been busy. You should have listened to me, Scarlet. I thought it was... *sweet* when you claimed to be playing house with the cougar," Frank rambled. "But I watched you the other day, bring another *wolf* into your domain, and I have to say, I did not like that. Not at all. I felt the need to leave my own mark on your home, though I had to recover from injury first."

"I'll give you a real injury this time," Nate growled, making me jump.

"Perhaps I could have been patient with you today," Frank continued. "But you reek of him, and him of you. It displeases me greatly."

"What the hell are you talking about?" I asked exasperatedly. Cougar? Wolf? Injury? "Also, could you fuck off? I have stuff to do. A house to fix up because *someone* destroyed it."

Brooks pressed himself closer to my back, shoring me up. I was grateful for his presence because despite what I was saying, I was fucking *terrified*, but I needed my fake confidence right now or I'd collapse.

The ripped as fuck bodyguards boxing me in were making me a little mouthier than I probably should have been.

"I did warn you," Frank sighed heavily, but he wasn't looking at me. He was looking at *Nate*.

"Don't do it," Nate snarled before flicking a look at Brooks. "Get her out of here," he hissed.

The wolves on either side went down on their haunches, their steady growls increasing in volume.

"My friends don't much like that idea," Frank drawled. His eyes focused on me and a shiver of fear ran down my spine because it seriously looked like they were *glowing*. He grinned, and... had his teeth always looked like that? They were so *sharp*.

"Fuck!" Nate yelled, moving to shield me, but it was too late. Before my eyes, polished, put-together *human* Frank exploded out of his clothes in a blur of black fur and vicious teeth, and there was a FUCKING WOLF flying through the air towards me.

Wolf. A fucking wolf.

An actual fucking wolf.

Before the snarling, snapping, *actual wolf* could rip my face off, Nate stepped forward and punched it in the face. In its wolf face. Punched the wolf in its goddamn wolf face.

Wolf Frank crashed into the wall with an infuriated growl, before darting out of the open door, howling. Like a wolf.

"Shit, is that a camera?" someone asked, but the voice sounded a million miles away because Nate spun to look at me, his emerald green eyes glowing, skin rippling slightly like the muscles underneath were contorting.

"Do you have big scary teeth too?" I heard myself asking before someone grabbed hold of the planet and spun it faster than usual. A lot faster. And turned all the lights out. Maybe turned the sun off.

And then there was blissful nothingness.

THANK YOU

Oh my god, who left that cliffhanger there?

cackles while bathing in the tears of my readers

Don't worry, part two of Lou's story won't be too far away. I've had too much fun revisiting the crew in Fairbanks to leave them hanging for long—especially with Lou's whole world being turned upside down. Plus, we haven't had any sexy Gabriel action yet, which I know is entirely unacceptable. All will be resolved in part two!

You can preorder Seeing Red here: books2read.com/littlered2

Thank you so much for picking up this book—it blows my mind that people read the random things that come out of my head, and I'm so incredibly grateful for every single reader <3

I also need to thank my husband and daughter putting up with my grumpiness during the editing process, my wonderful PA, Julia, all of my beta readers (special shoutout to Kari who powered through this like a champ when I set myself punishing deadlines), Red Line Editing, and all the supportive souls in my reader group who give me motivation. A huge thank you to TS for listening to me complain on an almost daily basis and providing Gabriel's Portugese words—I couldn't have done it without you, Stitch! Lucy, thank you for letting me use your name as inspo and for always being my sounding board.

For book discussion threads and the latest news, join the Reader Group on Facebook, or subscribe to my newsletter at coletterhodes.com.

Colette x

Books by this author:

Empath Found series:

The Terrible Gift

The Unwanted Challenge

The Reluctant Keeper

Deadly Dragons duet:

The (Not) Cursed Dragon

The (Not) Satisfied Dragon

Cheeky Fairy Tales:

Gilded Mess (Three Bears #1)

Golden Chaos (Three Bears #2)

Scarlet Disaster (Little Red #1)

Seeing Red (Little Red #2)

State of Grace:

Run Riot

Silver Bullet

Standalones:

Fire & Gasoline

Blood Nor Money

www.ingramcontent.com/pod-product-compliance
Lightning Source LLC
Chambersburg PA
CBHW060851250626

47159CB00008B/2683